A Dragon by Any Other Name

Books by S.D. Grimm

Children of the Blood Moon
Book 1: *Scarlet Moon*
Book 2: *Amber Eyes*
Book 3: *Black Blood*

Summoner

Phoenix Fire

A Dragon by Any Other Name

A DRAGON BY ANY OTHER NAME

S.D. GRIMM

FAYETTE
PRESS

A Dragon by Any Other Name

Copyright © 2021 by S.D. Grimm

FAYETTE
══ PRESS ══

Published by Fayette Press
Bastrop, Texas, USA.
www.fayettepress.com

This is a work of fiction. Names, characters, places, and incidents are products of the author's imagination or are used fictitiously. Any similarity to actual people, organizations, and/or events is purely coincidental.

ISBN: 978-1-953419-48-4 (printed hardback)
ISBN: 978-1-953419-47-7 (printed softcover)
ISBN: 978-1-953419-51-4 (ebook)

Cover design by Jamie Foley
Editing by Lindsay A. Franklin, Avily Jerome, & Catherine Jones Payne
Typesetting by Jamie Foley

Printed in the United States of America.

To my foxy sister-in-love
and her husband, my "little" bro,
for your amazing encouragement

ONE

Hunting dragons isn't the easiest job, but it is the most fun. Isabel's words, not mine.

But I repeated the mantra to myself as I stood, heart pounding, with my back against the still-warm, charred brick of what used to be the storefront of Zane's Country Market. All that was left of the smoldering sign read "ne's try Mar."

Not the easiest. But the most fun.

My pulse thrummed, betraying my doubts. This dragon horde of five was proving difficult to take out, even for our quintet of hunters. My sweaty fingers tightened around the hilt of my boomerang dragon-claw knife. It felt different in my palm than my old blade, but if it was as state-of-the-art as Guardian Tech claimed, I could deal.

Sure. Fun. The only thing that could make this situation *fun* was a hot spike of adrenaline.

I peered around the edge of the building and looked both ways down the deserted main street. Flaming remnants of buildings littered the cracked road. No one in sight. But my rescue tech told me there were still human heat signatures—that meant people were trapped here.

The dragons had to know too. That's why they hadn't left.

My gaze fell on a tattered stuffed cat, dropped outside one of the storefronts that used to have a housing unit above it. Something clutched in my chest. Where was this family now? Had they made it out? Maybe boarded one of our rescue trucks? Were they among the lucky ones?

I pushed the thoughts away to keep my focus here, in the present. This was the third local town to suffer a dragon attack this week. Blood blazed hotter through my veins. These terrorizing lizards may have evaded other hunters, but not today. My brother and I and our team would see to that.

Today these monsters were going down.

Despite repeating Isabel's old mantra, I couldn't help but feel like the prey in this situation. We'd only taken out two dragons and had already sent two injured hunters back to base on rescue trucks.

I rounded the corner of the building, one dragon-claw dagger in each hand. There might have been movement down here, and I had to check it out before one of the beasts did. My tech pinged heat signatures behind this market. I picked my way over the debris, trying not to attract any unwanted attention.

Because that would *definitely* not be fun.

"Keira? You copy?" Dane's voice sounded a little scratchy through my earpiece. Spotty connection. "Where are you?"

"Possible civilians on the east side of the wreckage," I whispered back to my brother as I stepped carefully over a blackened head of lettuce and shards of glass from a busted-out window. "Send a rescue truck."

"On it."

"How many hunters are still in commission?"

Dane paused. "Just you and me."

I gasped, my stomach flipping. "Did—"

"She's alive. I got her out in time."

The tension in my heart eased, but it still wasn't good news. I clung tightly to hope and determination. "We got this."

"As always." Dane's tone betrayed his cocky smirk. I couldn't stop my growing grin—or my growing worry. I couldn't let anything happen to him.

A small whimper. I slowed my steps.

"I'm headed that way. I just took one out." Dane's whisper was coming through clearer now.

"Which one? Did you get a make on the others?"

"Grease-fire dragon. The two left are a desert dragon—"

"All the way out here?" I mentally catalogued the situation. Desert dragons: small, fast, with fire that could call up a windstorm. Their poison was peaches—of all things. And I had freeze-dried peaches in powder form on my utility belt. I dipped one dagger into the compartment.

"And a forest dragon," Dane said.

At that, my blood froze. Then a slow burn began simmering in my veins. I hated nothing—*nothing*—more than forest dragons. And I had zero forest-dragon poison in my belt. Isabel hadn't been able to figure out what their poison was before she was killed—murdered by a forest dragon. I had two missions now: rescue these people and kill that beast.

New fuel filled my bones. Adrenaline.

Yeah. Now we were talking *fun*.

"Keira, you still there?" Dane rasped. "Desert dragon locked on to the marketplace section. Please tell me that's not where you are."

Oh great. A shiver raced through me, cold then hot. "Wish I could."

Dane swore. "Okay. I'm coming in. Do you have eyes on survivors? Rescue vehicle is en route."

I sheathed a dagger and pushed aside a door that half-hung on its one remaining hinge. Three soot-stained faces stared back at me with wide eyes. A mom and her two kids: a little boy with a bruise on his cheek and a younger girl with pigtails coming undone. Tear streaks tracked through the dust on the girl's face. My heart cracked. They couldn't have been older than six and nine.

I crouched in front of them, banishing all the worry from my expression and offering a smile.

"It's okay," I whispered. "I'm going to get you out of here. Understand? There's a rescue truck on its way."

They all nodded. I stood and made eye contact with the mother, who grabbed my hand and murmured, "Thank you."

I patted her arm, then straightened. "Can you carry your daughter? Because we have to run."

"Yes."

I held out my free hand to the little boy. "Follow me. And whatever you do, don't scream."

He looked up at me, his brown eyes huge.

"You've been brave so far, right? Just a little longer, then this will be over."

He nodded, a choppy, bobbling movement. But I squeezed his hand to reassure him. He squeezed back and didn't let go.

"Run!" I commanded. The four of us darted to the cover of the next building and halted. But I'd seen something. Air whooshed out of my lungs, and I turned to the boy. "Take your mom's hand."

Silently, he obeyed.

Then I made eye contact with his mom. "Stay quiet. *Silencio.*"

I pulled out my other knife and made sure peach powder dusted both blades. Then I stepped toward the edge of the building and peered around the side. Kill or be killed, that was the game now. And I wasn't about to die today. Or let my little brother get hurt.

There! To my right, I caught sight of rose-gold scales slithering through the smoke between two buildings. My pulse sped, and I ducked behind the structure. More sweat clung to the hilt of my poison-coated dragon-claw knives. My breathing seemed louder in my ears.

"I smell you."

The gravelly voice sent jitters through my being, and I pressed my body against the sooty wall.

Held my breath.

The light, grating click of scales gliding over debris came closer. Closer. As I leaned out of my hiding place, the soft leather of my jacket scraped against the brick. I froze, a shiver racing through my veins. I swallowed hard and turned my head slightly to see if the dragon had heard.

The beast lay stock-still at the entrance to the alley between this building and the market. I could see its side. The small pulse, nudging against the rose-gold scales, told me where the heart beat beneath the armored skin. And it wasn't pumping fast like mine. It beat slowly. Too slowly. The thick, shiny claws on its left-front foot shifted minutely, digging in deeper to the cracked concrete. That movement told me one thing: the dragon knew exactly where I was.

Goosebumps sprouted on my arms and the back of my neck. I glanced over my shoulder at the mother and her kids. The boy was shaking.

I clutched my weapons tighter. This beast was not taking down another victim tonight. I'd get these people out of here if it killed me.

The soft hum of an electric motor drew my attention to the right—there in the woods, behind the building that sheltered us, a truck rolled slowly through the trees. I made eye contact with the mother, pointed to the vehicle, and mouthed, "Run."

A slow chuckle punctuated my silent warning, and I turned to see a towering neck rise above me, a shining, golden light against the smoke-darkened sky. Gray billows puffed from its nostrils. "Leaving so soon?"

A scream erupted behind me, whether the boy or the girl, I couldn't tell. Not that it mattered. As the dragon jerked its attention toward their movement, it revealed a clear mark to its jugular. Idiot.

Adrenaline pulsed through me as I sized up the opening. I could make this toss. If I failed, it could cost that family their lives. I had to make it.

Hunting dragons isn't easy. Understatement of the century.

The dragon opened its mouth, lowering its neck, and I gripped my daggers, waiting.

"Mama!" A cry sounded behind me.

No! I had to focus! *Concentrado.* The dragon dropped its neck a fraction more—now it loomed about ten feet above me—aiming its flame, but the idiot forgot about me standing below it. Just as the scales started to redden, announcing the blast waiting in its gullet, I let my weapon fly.

It sailed true, right toward the dragon's fire trigger. The dragon-claw blade penetrated the scaly armor. And the peach on the knife would seep into the dragon's blood. But that didn't mean the family was out of danger. They hadn't made it to the armored truck yet. And the monster still had teeth and claws.

I raced for the fleeing family. The truck was barreling toward them, ready to carry them to safety. But the boy had fallen.

My stomach dropped. Would I make it to him? I pushed myself to run faster.

Behind me, the dragon roared, and I smirked, knowing that it was mourning the loss of its fire trigger. My shot had hit where it counted. But the creature's teeth could still kill us. Feet first, I dove into a home-plate slide that would have made my granddad proud. The hot scent of smoke drew closer as I wrapped my arms around the boy, shielding him with my body. I finished the slide and popped up.

Teeth snapped behind us. Screams filled my ears. Blood thundered in my skull. I pushed the boy along and whirled to face the dragon.

Dane was already standing there, his small crossbow loaded and pointed.

I flicked my wrist, activating the button in the bracelet that recalled my knife to me. It sailed in a straight line, hilt first, to my open hand—snapping to the recaller magnets on the bracelet in the perfect position for me to grab and throw.

But I held, waiting. State-of-the-art, indeed.

The dragon roared again, lumbering closer, but Dane fired his crossbow— the dragon-tooth arrowhead sank in right between the creature's eyes.

Then my brother dropped the weapon and pulled out his knife from a compartment on his belt—one I could only assume was filled with peach powder. He threw it at the falling beast. It thwacked right into its chest.

Its jaws hit the dirt paces from us. Then it turned to ash.

Dane recalled his knife and faced me. "Nice save." He motioned with his head at the truck that the mom and her kids were boarding.

I nodded toward where the dragon had toppled. "Nice shot. A little overkill, though."

"You're welcome." He smirked.

"I had it handled."

He let out a snort and retrieved his arrow. Then he started running toward the woods. "Come on. This forest dragon is making a getaway, and it's just taken cover in its natural habitat."

As Dane shouted orders for the rescue truck to take the victims and get the heck outta Dodge, I wiped my blades clean and followed him.

Now to hunt a forest dragon. My lips stretched into a smile, fueled by the fireball of hate in my chest.

Yeah. Time for some real fun.

TWO

Decaying bark crumbled as I pressed my back against a tree, tightening my grip on the knife. Any sound, any movement would alert the dragon to my hiding place. I hadn't seen it yet. Just smelled its burning-wood scent. My whole body quivered. This could be my dragon. *The* one that had turned me into a hunter.

I could almost taste victory.

The beast was near, all right. Biding its time. Waiting for me to screw up so it could pounce. So far, it had lured Dane and me deeper into the forest. Farther from our means of quick escape: our motorcycles. But also farther from our rescue vehicles, which should already be headed to our mobile base. I hoped they'd all be okay.

Tiny crumbs of tree bark rolled down my sleeve. Knocked against the hollow trunk. Bounced off exposed, hardened roots. An echo pinballing through the woods right to the dragon's ears. I held my breath as my insides squeezed tight. Trembling.

It would pinpoint my location now.

Breathe. Think. *Concentrado.* I gripped harder on the hilt of my dragon-claw knife and glanced left, where Dane hid behind a healthier tree, crossbow ready. His gaze met mine, and he tipped his head left.

Good. At least he could hear the beast. If he was as nervous as I felt, he didn't show it. His movements remained steady and calculating. Nothing like the quivering mess I was.

I strained to listen over my pounding heart. This deep in the woods, even a forest dragon would have to stay grounded. Just how I wanted it. Easier to kill that way.

Except that I didn't have any forest-dragon poison in my utility belt—because we didn't know what their poison was.

Dane's stare intensified. He nodded once. Then he held up three fingers.

A countdown. I tipped my head to acknowledge my readiness. This monster had harmed its last victim. Tracked its last hunter. My debt would be paid.

Two.

The scent of burning leaves consumed me. It was close. My muscles were like coiled springs.

One.

Dane and I leaped out at the same time.

A dinosaur-like creature faced us through a cloud of smoke. Its thick, anaconda-long neck towered above us. Spikes encircled its head and lined its back like a row of razor-sharp teeth. Hard, lime-green scales, each like a separate shield, covered the underside of its neck and chest. Darker scales armored its legs—the perfect camouflage under the trees.

Providing extra protection for the precious fire starter, golden-green scales—denser and stronger than the others—plated the very top of its throat.

A strike with my dragon-claw knife would have to do. It wouldn't do nearly as much damage without the poison, though.

The spikes fanned out, spreading wide from its head, indicating that its other armored protrusions were sticking out like spears across its body. Yep. This beast was definitely angry.

More smoke poured from its nostrils in a rush of fog, cloaking the dragon from my line of sight. Just like that, I lost visual. And I hadn't seen its stomach—hadn't seen if it was the one I'd vowed to kill.

I charged through the smoke. I might not be able to get a clear visual on where to throw my knife, but if I kept moving forward, I'd find a dragon eventually.

"Keira, hang back." Dane's warning pulled me to a stop. "I have a long-distance shot."

I raced out of the smoke, back to where I'd been hiding. My boot caught on something hard, and I fell. One knee slammed into dirt, the other bashed into a tree root. Holy crap, that hurt.

I scrambled to my feet. "I'm clear."

A familiar *whoosh* told me Dane had fired the crossbow. The dragon-tooth arrowhead would pierce through scales if he made his shot. Hopefully he'd strike something critical—otherwise the forest dragon's fast healing ability would make the hit useless.

The red light on the end of the arrow lit up. The shaft cut through the smoke like a flashlight in the dark. A roar shattered the stillness.

Target hit.

I had a general idea of where to toss my knife now, but without knowing exactly where Dane was, I wouldn't dare.

"Where are you?" I asked.

"Moving in."

"Don't."

"Keira, this one's smart."

He thought I didn't know that?

Leaves kicked up around me, and a massive form shot upward. Its enormous wings spread away from its sides, catching wind and billowing like dark blankets. It had taken to the sky from the trees. Show off. Forest dragons seemed to like that signature move. And I'd thought this too deep of cover.

The flashing red light dropped away from its body and fell back through the smoke—Dane's arrow. Dragon must have pulled it out.

"Lost visual," Dane said.

"Me too. I—wait, I see it. Ten o'clock in the sky."

A scaly torpedo shot at us from above, closing in fast. I readied my knife. I'd have to make one of two possible shots for this to do enough damage.

With it coming in at this speed, that didn't seem likely.

I braced myself.

The dragon zoomed closer.

I'd be open to deliver a heart shot if I moved over a foot.

My pulse pounded. Adrenaline heated me from the inside out.

Now.

I threw my knife. It sank in. The dragon roared, and fire spurted from its mouth. I ducked. Rolled. Jumped to my feet to watch the beast crash into a blazing tree and then slump to the ground. Branches fell on top of it, splintering as they hit its spiny head.

I stared at its stomach. At the bright-green scales. No *x's* or *o's* marred its flesh—not the dragon I'd vowed to kill. Not the one that had murdered my dad and stepmom.

"Keira." Dane skidded to a halt behind me, and I flicked my wrist to recall my knife. The bracelet on my arm activated, returning my weapon to me.

Dane was still talking. "Nice takedown. Let's muzzle this one and—Keira?"

I whirled to face him. "Muzzle? We take no survivors."

"Whoa. We need to bring this one back."

I *hated* when he got defensive like this. "For what?"

He looked at me like he wanted to say something, and by the flexing in his jaw, I could tell it was going to be one of his "control your temper" lectures. But he refrained, schooled his expression, and instead said, "We need to harvest claws and—"

"It's a murderer. Need I remind you of what that village looks like?" I motioned toward the town we'd just rescued people from. People who now had nothing. No homes. No belongings. No food. All because these dragons had decided to go on a killing spree.

Dane held out his hands to try and calm me, which never worked, but the sympathetic edge in his gaze tugged at my heartstrings a little. Not that I would show it.

"Stand down, Keira."

"You're not my superior." I whipped my arm back for another throw.

"No." He gripped my wrist. "I'm your brother, and I'm asking you to calm down and listen to me for a second." His eyes tracked my expression, and he released my arm. "Please?"

The fire in my gut was burning. Consuming. Why would he even consider sparing such a monster? What if it got away? Killed again? I would never understand my brother's ability to be so . . . conflicted about killing these monsters or my uncle's command to bring in so many live dragons. We didn't need to harvest that many teeth, claws, or scales or that much smoke. And taking the most hostile in was a bad idea. Always. They should all be killed, like my stepmom Isabel had said. So they couldn't slaughter more innocent people.

Just as I was about to blast these thoughts at him, Dane's eyes widened. "Get down." He pushed against my shoulders, and heat raged above us as we dove to the ground.

My elbows crashed into the soil.

See? Proved right before I could even make my case. The thought of screaming "I told you so" thundered in my skull, fueled by my rage. But then I realized Dane was protecting me from the flames headed right toward us.

Fire-retardant clothes or not, my heart stuttered. I would not let this beast hurt my brother. I activated the fire shield on my bracelet and climbed up enough to buffer Dane from the rest of the flames.

The moment the dragon took in a breath to refuel, I retracted the shield and calculated a knife shot. There . . . a slight release in the forward thrust of its neck, exposing the fire trigger just enough that I could hit it from my spot on the ground.

I had to make the shot exactly as it thrust its neck forward and low again. Before the fire scalded my now-exposed arm. The dragon leaned forward, and flame surged right at us. Round two. I aimed and threw.

My knife sailed toward the dragon's neck. Right for the fire trigger beneath those armored scales.

The blade pierced deep.

The stream of flame stopped.

I touched Dane's shoulder. "You okay?"

He didn't answer right away, and something in my chest seized.

"Dane?" My voice trembled.

"I'm okay." He sat up slowly and pressed his hand to his head, one eye closed. "Smacked a rock or something." He opened his eye and smiled. "Quick thinking."

"Always." I stood and offered him a hand up. He took it, and we both faced the downed dragon.

Amid the clearing smoke, a woman sat slumped against the tree, blood pouring from the knife wound in her neck. I looked away. I hated it when they took on human form right before death. It meant my strike hadn't been enough to kill her outright, but she could no longer hold her dragon form; she wasn't going to make it without medical attention.

Her dark hair and eyes—so like mine—seared my mind. Had she made herself look like a *puertorriqueña* like me on purpose?

Dane approached the tree, so I followed. When I peered over his shoulder, the young woman was gone, a pile of ash and my knife all that remained. I retrieved my weapon and strapped it on. With my adrenaline waning, my burned arm screamed. But the ball of fire in my gut wasn't quenched, and Dane—why had he tried to stop me from killing the dragon in the first place? Why couldn't he understand that they were all here to kill us?

"You're welcome." My words came out clipped.

He stared at me a moment, and then his eyebrows ruffled as if I'd offended and confused him all at once.

It really wasn't that hard to understand. "For saving your life."

"Whoa. My life? You're the one who broke position and headed off after the dragon. We're a team, Keira. When you break position, you put both our lives in danger."

"Yeah? And you have to stop hesitating with your kill shots. That dragon was a criminal. It had a death sentence. And it almost barbecued us because you wanted to save it!"

"She." His voice was quiet.

"It." I tightened my hands into fists but found nothing soft enough to punch. Dane's shoulder almost felt my wrath.

He stopped and reached for my injured arm. "Oh. Whoa. Which one got you?" He pulled an aerosol can from his belt. "Let's get that taken care of."

I conceded, and he sprayed a thick gray cloud of dragon smoke over my burn. The pain eased as the skin healed. No scar. As if they were connected, my anger started to abate too.

Truth was, I hated that I'd snapped at Dane. He was trying to protect me. And he had.

I clutched his arm. "Thank you." I hoped he knew I also meant that for when he'd acted as my human shield. "You get hit?"

He shook his head. "Got lucky."

"Yeah, you did." My throat tightened. "Don't . . ."

I'd seen Dane nearly killed before. Trying to save me. I shook the thought away. He was okay now. No use dwelling on that.

But he was my little brother. I'd always take the shot to keep him safe, even if it meant defying Max's order. Anyone's order. And he was just doing the same for me. "Must you take such risks?"

One corner of his mouth tugged down. Then he chuckled. His levity faded as he shook the aerosol can. "It's almost empty. We have a smoke shortage. Uncle Max told us to bring one in alive. We can't heal burns without dragon smoke."

Not this again. "We can't feel burns if we're dead. Get it together, Dane." I headed back to the edge of the woods, where we'd abandoned our motorcycles so the noise wouldn't attract the dragons in town.

He followed me. Lagging. "You'll need a new jacket."

"Yeah. Maybe a new partner too."

As soon as I said it, my insides clenched. I shouldn't be so hard on him. I needed to learn to control my stupid temper.

"You're stuck with me, you know, Keira. No one else wants you as their partner." The teasing smile was evident in his voice.

I laughed. "No one else can keep up with me, either."

"Is that supposed to be a compliment?"

I grinned even though he couldn't see it. "Is your ego that bruised?"

"Ouch." He caught up to me and shot me a smirk. "Do you have to be so cold?"

I chuckled darkly. "Out here? Yes. Dragons prey on your humanity. When you're fighting them, it's a weakness. As soon as you learn that, you'll be a better killer."

His green eyes regarded me for a moment, then lit with his usual good humor. "You're the better killer, but I'm the better hunter."

I shoved his shoulder. "You wish."

But he was right.

We reached the bikes, and I pulled my phone from the flame-retardant case. Three missed messages. Of course Uncle Max wanted to know if we were all right, but the third text wasn't about his normal worry.

"Did you get a message from Uncle Max?" Dane asked.

"Yeah. All available hunters on deck." I glanced at him.

"That's never good."

"*No. Es muy malo.*"

THREE

Early next morning, Uncle Max called a secret meeting with all present staff members save Dane and me. Since he'd called the emergency meeting yesterday and dispatched most of the hunters on the mission to take down a horde of town-destroying frost dragons we'd gotten a lead on near Old Chicago, I figured this meeting was about something else entirely. So naturally, I hid in the broom closet with my wall microphone. Cobwebs clung to my skin as I reached between bottles of pine-scented cleaner and pressed the device against the adjoining wall.

I turned up the volume until Uncle Max's voice rang through my earpiece.

"There's activity from a concentrated grouping in Missoula."

I covered my mouth to stifle a gasp. Dragons in Missoula this close to the anniversary? Not a coincidence. And definitely not something Uncle Max should be hiding from me or Dane. I had a mind to march over there and demand answers.

But I stayed, because I didn't want to miss the next words out of his mouth.

"They're confirmed misfits."

Of course they were. Misfits—hordes of dragons of multiple subspecies, which made them hardest for hunters to fight. Heat ignited in my core. How could he keep this quiet?

"You have to tell Keira and Dane." Maddie's voice carried through the earpiece.

Yes. *Gracias*, Maddie.

"No." My uncle's reply fanned the inferno in my chest. Oh, he'd tell us, or he'd watch me take the fight to those *monstrous* on my own.

Light spilled into the broom closet, and Dane's silhouette filled the doorway. His blond hair spiked out in every direction as if he'd rolled out of bed and headed straight here. Apparently he knew me better than I'd given him credit for.

He turned on the light and raised his eyebrows. "When Uncle Max calls a secret meeting, you're supposed to bring a wall mic for me too."

Squinting, I pulled out my earpiece and stood. "It just got less secret. Come on." I brushed past him into the well-lit hallway.

He followed me as I marched to the computer lab next door. I stopped in front of the double doors and faced him. He deserved to know before we walked in there. The anniversary of Dad's and Isabel's deaths affected him too. Especially if it involved a band of mongrels like the ones that had left him orphaned and half-dead before Dad found him. "Misfits in Missoula."

His eyes hardened, and he clenched his jaw. "Same ones?"

"Not confirmed. But they're not playing nice."

"Then they're going down." He opened the door with more force than necessary, and I followed him into the lab.

A row of computer screens surrounded a crescent-shaped desk in the center of the room. Maddie sat at the mainframe computer, keeping track of all the scouts and hunters, while other screens showed data related to suspicious dragon activity.

Everyone watched with wide eyes as Dane and I strode in. A huge screen, front and center, mapped out the current locations of all of our hunters. All the ones with their trackers on, anyway.

I stopped in front of my uncle and crossed my arms. "Missoula?"

"Keira." Uncle Max swiveled his wheelchair around, and his piercing blue eyes met mine from behind his thick-rimmed glasses.

I thrust out a hip and made sure my glare was cold enough to ward off dragon fire. "Where?"

He sighed. "At the college. Three attacks on bordering towns this week. Small. Easily contained by the hunters stationed there. And the memory wipes on the citizens are already taken care of."

My mind fixated on one piece of that information. The college? That was mere miles from our old base. Something in my chest tightened, threatening to suffocate me, but I pushed those emotions away and grasped onto anger instead. "When were you going to tell me?"

"Us," Dane corrected.

Chairs creaked and mouses clicked as everyone else shifted their attention back to their computers. Uncle Max wheeled away from them and beckoned the two of us to follow. "You know this is a sensitive process."

I stepped in front of him. "Tomorrow is exactly five years since Isabel and Dad were killed. This is a direct attempt to draw out Dane and me."

"Which is why you two need to stay as far away from there as possible."

Oh no, he didn't. "If I wanted to be safe, I'd be a scout, not a hunter."

Dane leaned against a desk and fiddled with a dragon-tooth paperweight, rolling it between his fingers. He didn't even look up as he said, "She's right."

His calm demeanor leached some of my anger away, and I struggled to let go of the rest of it. Uncle Max wouldn't let me go on a mission if I seemed too . . . passionate.

My uncle massaged his forehead with his thumb and index finger, a classic sign that he was (*a*) hiding something, and (*b*) really frustrated at how close I was to finding the answer. "It's a band of misfits."

I crossed my arms, willing him to see that I wasn't going to back down. "Even more reason for us to go in."

"She's right again." Dane tossed up the paperweight and caught it.

"The whole thing is looking less coincidence-like every minute." He set down the dragon tooth and scrutinized Uncle Max's face with the intensity of a dragon hunter searching for a lie. His ability to go from seemingly uninterested to completely focused unnerved everyone he interrogated.

I wished I had that kind of outward control over my emotions. Instead, I clenched my fists as if that would calm my thudding heart. Might as well ask the question burning in my chest. "Does this misfit horde have any forest dragons?"

Uncle Max shook his head. When he looked at me, a soft sadness filled his eyes.

It chilled my insides. What wasn't he telling me?

He breathed in. "Nothing definitive on subspecies in this particular misfit band yet, but it's possible there are at least four different types." Again, that sad look pierced me. "If these *are* the same dragons, they could recognize you."

Didn't matter. Dragons that close to my former home—our former base—meant I needed to put the beasts away for good. "I'm not thirteen anymore."

"Your scent is the same."

"I can take care of myself." My voice got hotter than I'd intended, and I mentally chastised myself. But this was my biggest lead in four years as a hunter. I was not going to lose it, permission or no.

He leaned forward in the wheelchair. "I may not be a field operative anymore, but I haven't forgotten how to fight dragons. Frankly, it surprises me that you'd put your brother in that kind of danger."

"Who are you calling helpless?" Dane straightened and motioned toward me with his thumb. "It's her thirst for vengeance I'm worried about."

I shot him a glare and pinched the sleeve of his wrinkled T-shirt. "You can take care of yourself, huh? Did you remember your medicine this morning?"

He frowned. "I forgot my medicine once. Let it go already. Either I come with you, or I tie you down."

My eyes deadlocked with my little brother's. Not so little anymore, but I still had to protect him. *Remember that time I watched you almost die because a dragon sliced you nearly in half?* That memory shook me.

The problem was I didn't trust anyone else to be my partner, and this was far from a solo mission.

"Max, Lance is on the screen." Maddie motioned to the big screen in the center of the room where Lance's face appeared.

He looked pretty haggard. Soot stained his torn shirt. Dragon attack for sure. He and Pete had been sent after a really big ice dragon that'd been terrorizing a small harbor town.

"Did you get him?" My uncle wheeled closer to the screen.

Lance shook his head. "That ice dragon threw its scent." His words were clipped, as if he were in pain. "I can't tell how. I thought I had him, but I brought down a forest dragon instead."

"Forest dragon?" My heart jolted, and I rushed closer to the screen so Lance could see me.

Dane gently squeezed my shoulder. He'd followed me like a silent shadow. His calming touch did help, though.

"The ice dragon didn't throw his scent," Uncle Max said. "The forest dragon incurred a life debt, which made him smell like the dragon he was indebted to—apparently the ice dragon you thought you were tracking. I haven't seen this for years."

A life debt? Why didn't I know anything about that? It wasn't in any of Isabel's journals.

"Well, this one left me a little trinket." Lance held up his blistered arm. A thick gash split his skin.

I winced.

"That wound isn't from a tail spike, is it?" Uncle Max leaned forward. "You have enough antivenom, right?"

"Running low."

"Well, get back here and stock up. If you or Pete get cut and have nothing . . . I can't lose any more hunters."

Lance nodded, his mouth set in a grim line. None of us needed to be reminded of Mikey's mistake. He'd started convulsing on a check-in and died on camera. Uncle Max's rule—no fighting without a supply of antivenom—had been taken pretty seriously since. We could never be sure how fast venom would get into the bloodstream. And some dragons could pulse more from their tail spikes than others.

"Do you have any live dragons?" Max asked.

Lance shook his head.

Uncle Max swung his chair. "Maddie, send a blast out to the active hunters. They need to try and bring in a live dragon. We can't heal burns if we don't have enough dragon smoke." His voice was strained. How low on smoke were we?

"One more thing." Lance looked directly at me. "The forest dragon . . . I thought you should see this, Keira. I took a photo before it turned to ash."

The picture on the screen jiggled as Lance moved the camera. He showed a photo on his phone of a scaly green dragon hide. The picture was fuzzy, but the *x*'s and *o*'s were clearly distinguishable.

My dragon.

The one *I* had sworn to kill.

The dragon that had murdered Dad and Isabel.

As my breath left my lungs, a deep void seemed to take its place. My knees grew weak. "You killed it?" I whispered.

I was supposed to be thrilled, but a hole started expanding in my stomach. I felt hollow. Empty. I tried to stand straight, but I wasn't sure whether or not I was even standing.

All I felt was Dane's grip around me, keeping me steady. I leaned against the nearest desk.

Lance's voice broke through my haze. "I thought it was an ice dragon until I made the shot and it came tumbling down. I had no choice but to kill it, Keira."

I managed to straighten my back and free myself of Dane's support. Then I looked right at the screen and nodded. "Good work. One less monster."

Everyone stared at me. I didn't have to look—I could feel their eyes boring into me like lasers on my skin.

"Thanks for the report, Lance. Come back to base." Though I registered Uncle Max's words, everything still seemed cloudy.

"Roger that." Lance clicked off, and the screen showed what Maddie had been working on last: dragon activity near Missoula.

Immediately, everything grew sharper. I balled my hands into fists, that familiar fire of revenge singeing my gut. My dragon might be dead, but the rest of his band of misfits were still trying to draw Dane and me out. I still had an enemy to hunt, and these wouldn't get away from me.

"As it just so happens, we've found a band of dragons perfect for capturing." I glanced at my brother.

He grinned at our uncle. "When do we suit up?"

Uncle Max sighed and wheeled his chair away from the computers. "You two know your parents wanted me to protect you."

"You've done a great job." Dane clasped his shoulder. "We're hunters now and the perfect age to go undercover on a college campus." His eyebrows bounced up and down.

Uncle Max closed his eyes. "All right, suit up."

"*Gracias.*" I kissed his cheek.

He gripped my elbow, and his eyes rounded as he whispered, "Keira, I know you wanted that dragon."

A wave of heat, like tiny pinpricks, spread over my skin. "What matters is that it's dead."

Uncle Max nodded, but it looked like he had more to say. "I just want you to be careful. You've been reckless lately."

"I won't put Dane in danger, if that's your worry. I would never let anything happen to him. Besides, always have your partner's back. Isn't that our first rule?"

"Yes. But my rules and Isabel's rules aren't always the same."

Not this again. "Her rules fit nicely right under yours." I crossed my arms. If this was about my ability to kill a dragon without flinching, he really needed to see them as the monsters they were.

He tipped his head to the side. "I know you looked up to Isabel, but she wasn't always right. She forgot that dragons have as much humanity as we do. Don't you forget that."

Humanity? He was blind. "Safety first, Uncle Max."

My uncle was too soft. I'd follow Isabel's methods until the day I died: no negotiations, no survivors—unless we needed information or smoke—and never trust a dragon.

As I walked out of the lab, I didn't turn back to see the disappointed expression he was undoubtedly wearing.

Dane waited for me by the door, juggling his knives. I didn't stop to acknowledge him, but I heard him racing after me once I hit the hallway. I didn't slow as I headed to the weapons room.

He eyed me sideways. As if I was some fragile, emotional creature who would break at the news.

Yeah. I'd wanted to kill the dragon. I'd wanted to be the one to look him in his eyes and bury my knife in him. Actually, I'd wanted to carve a few more *x's* and *o's* into his chest while I made him tell me what a forest dragon's poison was. What he'd done to Isabel. How my father had died.

Then I'd bury my knife into his lung and tell him how long I'd been waiting for this day. And I'd watch the light fade.

Tears threatened. I squeezed my eyes shut and focused on the anger. Turning the pain of loss into rage. Then I shoved open the door to the weapons' room and headed straight back to the locker room.

Dane got that door for me.

I shot him a confused glare.

He shrugged. "I didn't think this door could take a beating."

I rolled my eyes and stalked to my locker. "Stop babying me."

"I'm not. I'm protecting the things around you from your wrath."

I whirled to face him and his stupid, nonchalant attitude. He was leaning against the wall, tossing a knife in a spiral and catching it.

"You're so indifferent! Do you even feel? Do you even care?"

He sighed, sheathed his knife, and opened his mouth, but whatever he'd planned to say didn't pass his lips. Instead, his eyes rounded, then he waved his hand as if dismissing everything he was thinking. His shoulders sagged, and he walked out of the room. "Be nice to the doors."

I contained a frustrated scream and faced my locker again. But as I opened the door and caught sight of myself in the mirror, I balked. I was on the warpath, and it showed. I scrubbed my hands over my cheeks and rested my forehead on the edge of the locker shelf. Dane was right. I needed to cool off. I needed to contain my feelings. I needed to stop being a loose cannon.

I breathed deeply and straightened my spine. I checked my partially packed bag. Two flame-retardant suits, a pair of boots with dragon-tooth cleats, two cans of smoke, a utility belt, and two boomerang dragon-claw knives.

I touched the hilt of a knife, carved out of dragon bone. This set of knives had been Isabel's. She might have been my stepmom, but people always thought I was her daughter. It could have been the fact that we both had brown eyes and long brown hair—so unlike Dane's light-colored eyes and blond hair. Like many hunter families, ours was another cobbled together with survivors whose blood families were slaughtered by dragons. Though Dad, with his vivid blue eyes was my blood relative, my birth mother was Puerto Rican.

I didn't really know Mom. Isabel had been the mother who raised me. I liked to think I took after both of them.

Except they had been killed by dragons. And Dad too. So who cared whether or not my dragon was dead? Stopping the dragons for good was what mattered.

Pulling out my bag, I slammed my locker door. Good time for some target practice.

I entered the training room and set my bag on a table.

Dane tossed me a can of smoke. "Do you think the old base is still intact?"

"I hope so." I swallowed the lump rising in my throat. Five years and it still cut deep.

I clicked my silver bracelet onto my right wrist—over the tattoo of a tic-tac-toe game. I checked to see that my dragon-claw knives were synced to the bracelet and headed to stand opposite the wall targets.

A new dragon silhouette took up the south wall. It'd be riddled with knife holes when I was done with it. I pulled my knife free and tossed it. The blade sank into what would be the beast's occipital lobe. He'd drop right on the spot. A near-impossible shot to make, unless they turned their armored heads just right.

I flicked my right hand, and my bracelet recalled the knife. I gripped the hilt and aimed again. Throat shot, severing the fire trigger. Its flame would be gone. With a rotation of my wrist, my knife snapped back to me. I tossed again. Again. Harder. Faster. Making easier shots. Ones that would only do damage if the blade was covered in that dragon's poison. Fighting a band of misfits was like fighting a mixed bag.

I could coat my knife with mint leaves to kill a volcano dragon, but that wouldn't hurt an ice dragon. In fact, it tended to make them stronger.

This battle would be won by wit. Uncle Max was right to not want to send Dane and me alone, but there was no one else to dispatch. The other hunters had their own assignments. He'd send some scouts into the area with us, so backup could be called, but by the time reinforcements got to Missoula, these misfits could be gone—or halfway through a killing spree.

Dane walked up beside me, watching with his arms folded. "I'm sorry Lance killed your dragon."

"Why? I'm not." I yelled it at him. I didn't mean to, but I did. I recalled my knife.

"I just thought . . . you always wanted to be the one to kill it."

"It's better dead than alive, right?" I faced my brother and cocked an eyebrow to dare him to keep this *conversation* alive.

He nodded, glancing at the ground. "You can pretend to be okay with this, but—"

"Dane, drop it." I whisked past him and jammed my knives into my bag. "I let that dragon go, and it killed Dad and Isabel. It might be dead now, but it served its purpose. It taught me to never trust a dragon. A mistake I'll never make again."

I zipped up my bag.

His hand gripped my shoulder, nudging me to face him. "Keira, I don't blame you for what happened. You know that, right?"

That—his offer of forgiveness—was *my* poison. I felt it like a jab in the heart. I tried to stay strong. Keep everything contained. Their deaths were my fault. Mine and that forest dragon's.

But that was the thing about Dane—he truly didn't blame me. And he wanted me to forgive myself. My throat tightened. "I don't know what I did to deserve your forgiveness."

"You have to stop blaming yourself."

I finally looked into his eyes. "Not until I avenge Isabel's death."

Not until I atoned for my sins.

"The dragon's already dead, Keira."

"I know."

That's what made this harder. I'd been searching for a way to make it right, and the one thing I'd been banking on was no longer an option.

But there *was* something I could do. I would change my goal. I would still seek revenge. And I would do it with a cool head and deadly aim.

"I have to finish Isabel's work. I'll find out what forest-dragon poison is. Then I'll exterminate the beasts from the globe." I picked up an extra can of smoke from the table and handed it to him, then snatched up my bag and headed out. "You still coming, partner?"

"I always have your back," he said. Then, quieter, "Even when you're being an idiot."

"I heard that."

FOUR

As I lay in bed, waiting for my alarm to go off and tell me it was time to go to Missoula, all of the memories taunted me.

Dad's lifeless body, ripped open by dragon talons.

Claw marks and blood all over the floor.

Isabel gone and a puddle of blood and dragon tracks in her place.

I closed my eyes, but the memories were still there. Tears dripped down my cheeks, slipped into my ears, wet my hair and my pillow. And I let them come as more memories tormented me.

Memories no one else knew I had—not even Dane. Memories from before my training, when I'd been tricked into thinking dragons had humanity. When I'd treated them like people. My humanity had gotten my dad and Isabel killed.

Fresh tears spilled down my face, and I rolled over to stifle a sob with my pillow. *"Lo siento, Papa! Lo siento, Isabel!"* I whispered my apologies over and over, but as always, they did nothing to change what I'd done.

I sat up, wiped my face, flicked on my lamp, and pulled Isabel's journal out of my hunter's bag. With renewed determination to finish her work, I flipped through the highlighted, underlined, dog-eared pages. The second page held her famous list of dragon ten commandments:

> *1. Dragons can never be trusted.*
>
> *2. Never leave a dragon alive if you can kill it—unless you need it for smoke, parts, or information.*
>
> *3. Dragons don't feel pain like we do. Their scales make them immune on the surface, and they heal fast, so cut deep.*
>
> *4. Never threaten a dragon on its own territory; it will kill you.*
>
> *5. Dragons twist their words to lie without letting their eyes reveal that they're lying.*
>
> *6. A dragon doesn't care for anything but itself; don't let perceived acts of kindness fool you. They are incapable of real compassion.*
>
> *7. Dragons can spot a lie in your face. Be like a stone.*
>
> *8. The only thing a dragon will protect aside from itself is its treasure.*
>
> *9. Legend says a dragon's eyes will pulse gold when it's showing its soul—this is a lie. Dragons have no soul.*
>
> *10. Dragons are monsters, and once they decide to kill, nothing will stop them.*
>
> *11. And the bonus commandment: Despite what they want you to believe, dragons are not human.*

Uncle Max had removed these from the wall in the training room and replaced them with the rules of dragon hunting: Always have your partner's back. Trust your training. Don't kill for killing's sake. That kind of rule was dangerous. It fueled hunters like my brother to view dragons as less threatening. Dane's merciful heart would get him killed someday if he couldn't see dragons as monsters.

I gripped a clump of bedsheets in my fist and slammed the journal closed.

Why was Uncle Max so soft? Didn't he care about the thousands of humans whose lives were in danger? My hands trembled. Things had been so different under Dad and Isabel. Well, mostly Isabel. I recalled her and Dad fighting a lot about the hunting, especially that one night.

The memory swirled through my thoughts, overtaking my view of the journal's leather cover and blurring everything until I could envision the scene clearly in my mind's eye.

I was only ten. I should have been in bed, but the roar of Isabel's bike announced her return, and the huge door in the loading dock below the lower floor of the house—beneath my bedroom—that led into the lab rumbled open.

I wasn't allowed in the lab. I raced to my window and peered out, hoping to get a glimpse of the secret entrance. Of the stones she pushed to gain access.

In the fading summer light, I caught sight of a creature the size of a black bear racing back and forth in the cage. It was hard to tell in the dark, but the scales looked to be the prettiest green. Was that a dragon? I'd expected something bigger the way Isabel talked about them. Why did she have a dragon? Then I remembered—sometimes she kept one alive to get smoke to heal hunters. I hadn't realized she collected smoke here in the lab.

Something cold skittered over my skin, and goosebumps raised the hairs on my arms and the back of my neck. Why would she bring a dragon here? What if it killed us? What if it burned the place down?

Fearing for Dane's life, and my own, I decided to go ask her why she would bring such a dangerous animal here. If she'd told Dad. Surely Dad wouldn't let her keep a monster in the lab.

Isabel and some of the hunters wheeled the cage beneath the overhang, moving it from my line of sight, so I crept out of my room.

Light spilled into the upper hallway. The soft glow beneath Dane's door revealed his night-light, which meant he was up reading graphic novels. My toes sank into the carpet as I padded to the railing and grabbed two wooden rails. I pressed my face between them and listened, straining to hear.

Dad asked, "Are you sure you want to do this?"

"Yes." Isabel sounded serious.

"For what purpose? I don't understand—"

"This dragon has the secrets I need. And I will get answers from it."

Answers? How?

"Isabel . . ."

"For one," Isabel said, "it's a forest dragon. We haven't been able to come close enough to one of those before."

"They've never given us reason to—"

"And it's young."

The pause lasted so long I thought they might have left the kitchen, so I stepped down a stair. Then another.

"How young?"

Dad's words made me freeze, and my heart thundered.

"A child. It has to be Keira's age. Perhaps a little older."

"A child? Isabel, you can't possibly keep—"

"Come. See for yourself."

"No. I think you should let it go. What if its mother is looking for it?"

"Do I need to remind you how your wife died?"

My heart stalled a moment before beating again. Why was she bringing up my first mother?

"No." Dad's voice was short and hard. Louder than anything he'd said this whole conversation.

I stepped down another stair, not wanting them to fight. If I had to sneak in and ask for a cup of water or pretend to be scared of something in my room, I would.

"I was there when it happened." The sternness in Dad's voice halted me again.

"It was a forest dragon that took her from you. It was a forest dragon that ripped my husband's heart from his chest and then burned him to ash. And what of that boy of yours? Didn't you find forest dragon scales at the site of his dead parents?"

Dad's words were still sharp. "Along with evidence of other types of dragons. It was inconclusi—"

"Inconclusive, right." Isabel huffed. "Not to me."

I cringed, tears stinging my eyes and nose. Why did the dragons hunt us? What had we done to them? I curled into a ball on the steps, hugging my knees to my chest. I didn't care what answers that monster in the lab had. I needed Isabel to let it go before more of my family was killed.

"Isabel." Dad's tone softened, like when he hugged me after I scraped my knee or fell off my bike.

Her quiet sobs sounded muffled, and I imagined Dad was holding her. I pulled my knees closer, resting my chin on them. Our whole family had the same purpose: protect people from dragons. Maybe I needed to trust that Isabel knew what she was doing.

"I still don't like this," Dad said quietly.

"I'll make sure the dragon won't get out. The children will never even know it's down there. It will be safe. I promise."

"Dragon or not, it's a child, Isabel."

"All I want from it is information about the forest dragons. It won't be here long."

Dad sighed for what seemed like a really long time. "You'll take care of it, then? When it's all over?"

"Of course I will."

I heard a kiss, and then someone walked away. I wiped the tears from my eyes and pressed my face into the railings.

Take care of it. A sense of sadness crept into my soul. I understood that that's what Dad and Isabel did. They killed dragons to keep everyone safe. Yet the thought of killing a kid dragon made me sad.

Then I remembered my mom. I didn't remember much anymore. But I recalled singing. A peppy, upbeat tune. Her voice had been my favorite sound. She talked so fast, but in a way that was completely melodious. Like a song of its own. And she *loved* to cook. I remembered amazing food and the scent of spices and frying *tostones*. The smell of those still made me feel warm inside. When she kissed my forehead at night and told me she loved me in that rich, beautiful accent. And I remembered a smile. Dark hair. Dark eyes. Like mine.

And now I knew what kind of dragon had taken her from me.

"You ready?" Dane appeared in the doorway, shattering my memories and pulling me back to the here and now. I stuffed Isabel's journal into my bag, realizing a tear had escaped and was trickling down my cheek. I wiped it away, hoping he wouldn't notice.

He sat next to me on the bed. "You okay?"

I nodded.

"You know, Keira, you don't have to pretend with me. Your secret is safe. I won't let the other hunters know you have actual feelings." He sort of smiled, but his forehead wrinkled.

I laughed sadly and pushed against his shoulder, but he pulled me in and hugged me.

And I needed it more than air right now. Ever-perceptive Dane. My brother to the core. Even if we weren't blood, we may as well be. Our bond was stronger than blood. I still didn't let him hug me for long, though.

"Come on, we have some forest dragons to kill." I got up, grabbed my bag, and headed for the door, wiping all the remnants of tears from my face.

Dane didn't follow, so I stopped and looked at him still sitting on the bed, his head dipped. I took a few tentative steps back into the room.

"*Lo siento*, Dane." When I whispered it and heard the tiny influence of my mother's accent in my words, my insides squeezed. "I should have seen how this is affecting you. I've been so hung up on . . ."

"Revenge?"

The bag slid off my shoulder, and I crouched in front of him. "It's justice."

"Really?"

I clenched my hands. Dane hadn't trained under Isabel. He didn't see the dragons' terrible nature the way she'd described it to me. He thought, as Uncle Max did, that some of them were worth saving. Not me. I knew better.

I'd made that mistake once. Never again.

I touched his knee. "I know I'm not the only one who lost them."

Dane nodded, his head still bowed. "We'll end this."

I stood up and stared at my hands. The tattoo on my wrist. The reminder that pain and heartache had made me the hunter I was today. "Do you think we're doing the right thing?"

He glanced up at me. "Going after the misfits who want to slaughter hunters and innocent people? Yes. Absolutely. They're monsters, and they need to be stopped."

"Good."

He glanced back down at his lap and pressed his hands against the mattress but didn't get up. I sensed a "but" coming, so I waited. And braced myself.

He sort of winced. "Do you really think they're all bad?"

I leaned over and unzipped my bag. Pulled out Isabel's journal. Flipped to the right page. "Look. She said that once they reach a certain age, they become increasingly aggressive. It's in their DNA, Dane. They. Are. Monsters. I know Uncle Max wants us to leave peaceful dragons alone, but he's wrong. None of them can be trusted. He's so bent on saying that what Isabel and Dad did got them killed. He's wrong. Dragons are monsters, period. They *all* need to die. No matter what."

My throat tightened, but I kept talking. Because if I didn't get Dane to believe this, he could end up being tricked like I had been. "Uncle Max is afraid to do what needs to be done. I'm not. I'm going to make sure they all die. Are you with me?"

He stared at me, his eyes moving back and forth to take in my expression. "Of course. I would think you'd know that. I'm just . . . I don't want you to go off the deep end. You saw what happened to Isabel in those days before—just don't lose who you are."

"Dane, do you have my back out there?"

"Of course." His eyes grew serious, and he stood with a look hard enough to give anyone pause. "I am all for bringing monsters to justice. Make no mistake."

"Then let's go exterminate some evil."

FIVE

I tried to tamp down my rising feelings as Dane and I headed toward our old base—our old home. A place filled with memories, warmth, betrayal, death. The things that had happened here had defined me.

The building was a tall sort of warehouse. A lab and hunter's base, not unlike the one we worked out of now, made up the sprawling underground floor. Our home had been aboveground. One garage door opened to the underground level. Two entrances—one through the house and one through that door, which Isabel had heavily guarded by an alarm system sensitive to heat, motion, and noise. And only she had the access codes.

Dane stopped in the doorway. No reason to open the door to my dad's lab; it had been tossed to the floor. Covered in inches of dust.

"Looks like no one has been here for years." Dane walked into the room. The cut wires on the floor were all that was left of the mainframe computers we'd taken to the new place. I hadn't been here for that. Uncle Max hadn't wanted Dane or me anywhere near here when they went through everything.

Dane trudged in farther than I did. "They didn't find anything. That's why they're drawing us out. They want to know what kind of research Isabel was doing. How many dragon subspecies' poisons she'd found out about. If she was close to finding a way to recreate the fabled, lost all-serum."

We were. We needed one more key component—forest-dragon poison. Then the all-serum, a compound that contained every dragon poison, could be created. No more carrying individual poisons. This supposed serum would be able to tailor itself to a specific dragon's blood, negating the effects of any properties that would make a dragon stronger—like mint for ice dragons—and enhancing the actual poisonous compounds for a specific subspecies. I tapped my utility belt and checked the compartments for various dragon poisons: honey, cayenne pepper, sarsaparilla. Any weapon coated in a dragon's poison would pierce scales as if it were made of dragon claws or teeth—actually, easier. But some dragons' poisons actually supercharged other dragons' defenses.

If we had one poison that worked equally effectively on all subspecies, those monsters would be running scared.

I walked to the top of the spiral staircase that led down to the basement. Where everything started.

"Looks like they got into the lab," Dane said.

Wall crumbled around the staircase. The narrow spiral was supposed to be able to keep a dragon from getting up here in dragon form—in case we were ever under attack. Isabel had created all kinds of safeguards in this place. But it looked like a huge armored dragon had gotten in anyway.

As I stood at the top of the battered staircase, my memory changed it. Broken concrete morphed back to solid walls and a wrought iron banister. It was cold in my hands as I snuck down the stairs in my pajamas, making sure not to wake Dad or Isabel.

The night she'd brought home the young dragon was the night I'd broken the rules for the first time. We weren't allowed in the underground lab— where they kept the weapons and tools and computers with dragon data. Isabel had promised me that she'd bring me down here when I was ready.

That had been enough for me until that night.

Curiosity had lured me. I wanted to see a dragon. The beast Isabel had told me horror stories about. The monster that deserved death. Step by careful step, I walked through the lab to the door at the far wall. The forbidden door.

Would the dragon that sat captive down here truly be harmless in the cage Isabel had built? Surely it could still try to—how had she put it?—charm me with its silver tongue. Catch me if I got too close. But other than that, it couldn't hurt me. Isabel had said so to Dad just that evening.

My insides tingled. My hand trembled as I turned the doorknob. Pushed.

The lights flicked on as soon as the door creaked open, and I froze.

The dragon, smaller than I'd thought—but bigger than a horse—sat in a cell designed by Isabel. It lifted its head, and the black-slitted pupil in its green eye narrowed. I sucked in a breath.

The dragon shrank back, to the other side of its small cell. I gaped. It was . . . beautiful.

I stared at the way the light reflected off its pale-green scales. It shifted, and I flinched, bumping the door closed. The dragon arched its back. The fire muzzle kept it from being able to burn me.

I approached its cage and peered in. "You're smaller than I thought."

The scent of burning leaves poured off of it. Something in its green eyes seemed human.

"Why am I here?" It sounded young, like me. But I could tell it was a boy.

I stepped back, my heart jolting. "You can talk?"

"Of course."

Now I understood why Isabel had told me to be careful of their tongues. "You're a dragon. Doesn't that mean you want to kill me?"

It shook its head, its round eyes pleading. "Why would I want to kill you?"

"That's what dragons do."

"That's not true." It sat up. "We take care of people."

"How? Wouldn't people be scared of you?" I crept closer, completely enchanted by this strange creature in front of me.

"Not when I'm in my other form."

Dragons had another form? "What do you mean?"

"See that blue light on the top of my cage? It's part of a frequency that's keeping me from shifting into my other form. Turn it off, and I'll show you."

A lying dragon's eyes would pulse red. This one's hadn't. Had they? I didn't know for sure, because Isabel had said she'd have to train me on a real dragon. But I thought for certain I would see red if it flashed in those pale-green eyes.

I stepped closer. "What's your other form?"

"I can be human. Like you."

My heart thundered. No red. Could it be possible? "You'll hurt me if I get too close."

"No." It shook its head. No red.

I swallowed. Was Isabel wrong? "Promise?"

It nodded.

Its horns and claws were cut to nubs. It looked scared. Broken. Isabel was right. This dragon was harmless. Still, my body shook as I approached the bars and reached out.

"Careful. Those are electric," it said.

I pulled my hand back to my chest and bit my lip. "Isabel says she wants information from you."

It nodded. "She asked me about my poison."

"What is it?"

Its scaly head drooped. "I can't tell you. I'm not allowed to."

"Why not?"

It shifted closer to me, lowering its head so it was eye level with me. "If you carried the secret to what could kill your whole race, would you tell your enemy?"

"No." The raspy word pierced the silence. I stared at the dragon a few more heartbeats. This wasn't right. Isabel couldn't keep a dragon locked up down here.

I headed to the main control switchboard, right by the door. I glanced over my shoulder once more into its hopeful eyes. Then I reached forward with shaking fingers, curled my hands around the cold lever, closed my eyes, and flipped the switch, turning off the blue light.

When I looked back, the dragon was gone. Replaced by a boy.

I gasped. He must have been a couple of years older than me. My stomach tightened, and I pressed my hands to my mouth. How could Isabel cage a kid?

"How are you doing that?" I walked up to the cage.

He sat near the bars. Freckles dotted the bridge of his nose. "This is who I am."

"How old are you?"

"Eleven. I'm not just human—I'm still a dragon. This is my other form. See. I'm just like you. Well, except you're a girl."

A year older than me. I shook my head. This wasn't right, if dragons were human too. Slowly, I reached up to unlock the cage door.

"I have to get you out of here," I said. "I'll tell my stepmom that you're really a human."

"She already knows."

I paused, something in my insides squeezing. No way. I knew Isabel. She was a good person. "That can't be true. You'll see. I'll tell her." I reached for the lock again.

"Careful." He smiled sadly. "The locks are protected by current too. You have to unlock it from the controls at her computer." He looked up at the door, eyes wide, and moved to the back of his cage, shifting into dragon form. "Someone's coming."

"Keira?" Isabel's voice carried down the stairs.

Oh no. My heart jumped into my throat. I stepped back and stared at the boy. "I'll—I'll be back later."

The light flicked on, and Isabel stood there with a knife.

That was the moment my lessons began. My training.

For the next three years, she ground into my head the true nature of dragons. They were all liars. Monsters. Deceivers. They might be able to look like humans, but there was no humanity in them.

I didn't believe her at first. I'd seen the boy. If only I could make Isabel understand. But the pictures she showed me of the terrible things dragons had done made me cry myself to sleep.

Still, I'd snuck into the containment room most nights to talk to my dragon friend. Something about him was so alluring. Though I never dared turn off the frequency chip again, I knew he was still a boy. And a dragon.

I called him Boy. It reminded me who—what—he was. Isabel could spot a lie, even on my face, so I could never know his actual name. Never see his human form again. We just talked. And laughed. And I wondered why she thought he was dangerous.

That's why I planned his escape.

Now I knew better.

Everything Isabel had told me was true, and everything that dragon had said was a lie.

"Keira?" Dane's voice pulled me free of the memory. I turned toward him, the old anger still burning in my gut.

"Are you okay?" He touched my shoulder, his eyes soft. "It must be hard for you to come here."

"Yeah." I whirled toward the front door. "Come on. Let's get to the safe house. We have college classes to attend tomorrow."

SIX

My stomach churned.

All classrooms smelled the same, U of Montana or not—the sweat of thousands of people, industrial floor cleaner, too many kinds of food to make anything smell appetizing. Overlaid on this one was the faint scent of ozone from the rebuilt campus after one too many dragon attacks in the old wars. I stilled a shudder. Maybe coming here wasn't the best idea after all.

But amid all of that, the faint scent of smoke tinged this room. Not from a cigarette , but the kind I'd been trained to sniff out since I was ten.

I slipped inside, pulled out what looked like a phone, and set a scanner tracker. It would locate smoke in the area and scan it for warmth. Set to silent, it vibrated in my pocket, and I pulled it back out.

I'd been right. Red showed on the screen. Smoke. Warm. That meant recent. Probably one of the students who had come in before me.

Not wanting any dragons in the room to notice, I turned off the tracker. Looked like I'd be taking Humanities 102 for a little while.

I walked to an empty seat and pulled out a notebook and pen. I pretended to check the wall clock behind me while I scanned the room. In the back corner, there was a group of five guys who wouldn't have landed on my radar except that one of them made direct eye contact with me. And he glared.

My heart jumped, and I took note of his backward baseball cap and dark eyes before I shifted my attention elsewhere. Had I done something to tip anyone off? The scent wasn't as strong now, so I couldn't tell if the smoke was coming from his direction or not.

Class started, and I faked taking notes, but my eyes were on the hunt for anything that might give this beast away. Too bad I couldn't keep an eye on Mr. Back Row from here.

A few minutes into the professor's mind-numbing, monotonous drone, someone set a book on the desk beside me.

"Is this seat taken?"

I looked into a pair of green eyes, and my heart did a tiny flutter. *Ay! Que guapo!*

I cleared my throat and tried to recover my nonchalant attitude, but I was pretty sure I'd already given him the reaction he wanted, because he was grinning.

"Umm, no."

"Great." He slid into the chair next to mine, and the scents of hot coffee and amazing cologne wafted my way. "What'd I miss?"

He slipped off his black leather jacket and draped it over the back of his chair. Maybe college wouldn't be so bad after all.

I stared at his biceps a little too long. "Something about Renaissance art."

He leaned over and unzipped his backpack. The subtle hiss of a paper cup against a Formica desktop jolted my reflexes. His elbow bumped the coffee cup, and the container of hot liquid tipped toward my thigh. Muscle memory took over, and I caught the cup as it started to fall, then set it back on his desk. "Don't want to wear that."

His eyes widened. "Nice catch."

Isabel's voice rang clearly in my head: *Never show off in public. A dragon could be watching.*

I glanced around, but no one seemed to be paying attention to me.

Not even the back-row boys. I swallowed hard and shifted my notepad, feigning interest in the details of the Sistine Chapel.

My eyes wandered.

Dark stubble perfectly framed Cute Guy's smile and made his teeth look even whiter. He caught me staring, but something in his grin told me he'd been waiting for me to look his way again.

"I'm Wallace."

Not a name I'd have put with him. I let my amused smile warm my face. "Wallace. Really? What do your friends call you?"

His eyebrows pulled together. "Wallace." He shrugged. "Sometimes Wally."

"Never Ace?"

He let out a soft laugh, and his eyes searched mine as if he was trying to figure me out. At least he seemed to be enjoying himself.

"Sorry, Wally." I smiled. "I'm—"

"Keira?" He pointed to the corner of my notebook where I'd written my name.

"Perceptive."

His gaze flicked to my notebook again. "I see you take good notes."

I glanced at the mindless doodles on my paper to hide the reddening in my cheeks. "I write down the important stuff."

"Hmm. I don't see my name there."

I snorted when I laughed, which earned me a "shush," probably from some overzealous Humanities major, and a seriously cute grin from Wallace.

I wrote "Ace" on the top line. Next to it, I added, "Cocky guy in a leather jacket."

"That's about right." He showed off that white smile again. "But something's missing."

"Should I draw hearts around it?"

"I think you want to."

My cheeks flushed, and I pretended to pay attention to the lecture.

When my eyes wandered again, I caught Ace staring.

He tapped the inside of his wrist. "You got a thing for tic-tac-toe?"

Heat fanned across my chest, and I pulled down my sleeve to hide my tattoo. "It's just something I need to remember."

"Interesting memory." Ace squinted, searching my face as if studying me for a lie.

My breathing stalled for a moment. Dragons did that. Isabel's voice warned me: *Dragons can spot a lie in your face. Be like a stone.*

But there was no danger here. If Wallace was a dragon, I'd have smelled smoke with him this close.

"Sorry, didn't mean to pry." His eyes softened. "No need to hide."

"It's okay." I managed a smile.

We got more than one nasty glare from other students as our playful banter continued, then soon enough, everyone around us started packing up. Class was over already?

Ace stood and picked up his jacket. That woodsy cologne drifted my way again. "Save me a seat on Wednesday?"

Okay. Yes. Absolutely. "If I think about it."

He chuckled. "Well, if you forget, don't blame me when someone less riveting tries to make conversation with you." He walked out, and wind eddied around me. I caught a faint whiff of grease-fire smoke and glanced up to see that group of guys from the back row walking past me. But I tried to act normal. I couldn't blow my cover.

They made it to the door in a hurry, and one of them glared at me before he exited. His lips framed one inaudible word: "Hunter."

I sucked in a breath. Had he seen me catch the cup? I raced out of the room after him, but a line of students trying to talk to the professor blocked my easy escape. I navigated around them as fast as I could.

Finally in the hall, I caught the scent of smoke. My blood boiled as I scanned the hallway. No sign of those boys. I clenched my jaw and pulled out the tracker. It pinged back.

Sure enough, dragons in the area, but the smoke scent was fading fast.

I slipped it into my pocket and called Dane.

He answered right away. "Yeah?"

"Where are you?"

"South campus, following a lead."

"I have one here too. I'm west."

"I see you on my scanner. Think your target's headed this way?"

I pulled up Dane's tracker on my device. He wasn't that far from me. Definitely possible for my guys to be over by him. I headed down the hallway, but Dane was moving still.

"I'm coming to you," I said.

"Good. I think there's more than one."

I looked at the tracker again. I'd been wrong. Dane was headed toward me from the south side. That meant these were two different groups of dragons. I pressed my palm to my forehead, wishing desperately that there was something around here I could kick.

This misfit horde might be way bigger than anticipated. We might need backup if there were too many. That meant Dane and I were screwed if our cover was blown. Not good. My chest tightened. That one guy had called me out already. Time to lie low until we knew exactly what we were up against.

I turned the corner and saw Dane headed toward me.

"Hey!" I laughed and walked right up to him. "You have classes in this building?"

"Keira?" Dane pretended to be really surprised to see me, and it was convincing. No one would suspect we were siblings. Perfect. "How did I not know you were headed here?"

"Small world." Now we were walking in step, side by side. I leaned closer to him. "How many did you see?"

"I can't confirm, but I know three girls and two loner guys to keep an eye on."

"Composite sketches back at the base?"

"Yeah. And we might want to call for backup."

"I agree. I saw a group of five."

He whistled low. "How long before backup can get here?"

I shook my head. "We have to do what we can to stay hidden until Uncle Max sends help."

"Well, good talk," he said louder and headed down a separate hallway.

I smiled and nodded, but inside, my stomach was in knots. I'd dragged my little brother into this mess, and I wasn't going to let him get hurt because of my rashness. Especially because I was certain no other Guardian Tech hunters were dispatch-ready right now.

Taking out a lone dragon or a pair was one thing. If we did that, the rest of the horde usually came out, and we'd call in bigger numbers too.

But this horde had to be massive if they had at least eight in the open.

When Dane finally showed up at home, I'd already uploaded my smoke sensor. Three samples were too weak to match, but one was definitely a forest dragon. That made the rage in my chest flare. How had I missed it?

Dane set his backpack on the couch and headed right to the fridge. By the look of the wet marks on his T-shirt, he'd gone for a run. "Have anything we can work with?"

"Proof of a forest dragon." I swiveled my chair away from the computer screen and held my hand out for his smoke reader. "What kept you?"

"I thought we agreed to meet back at seven. I followed a dragon out by the river."

My eyes had to be popping out of my head. "Are you kidding me? You could have been caught."

He wiped his face with his sweat-soaked shirt, then took it off and headed into the bathroom. "Relax. I was careful. Just a runner in a park."

I stared at the huge scar on his left side. It took up the whole length of his torso, curling from his lower back to up over his shoulder. I blinked away an unexpected sting in my eyes. "Dane, if they caught you and I was far away, that—"

He peered out the doorway, a rueful expression on his face. "I know, and I'm sorry."

I turned back to the computer screen to calm my rising temper as he headed once more to the fridge—oblivious. Focused on food, no doubt.

I looked over at him. "I called Uncle Max. Backup is six days out. He wants us to lie low."

"Of course he does. Then we make do until reinforcements get here. We honestly might be able to isolate some of them. They're hanging out in small groups."

"But if they can call backup of their own . . . we'd be screwed." He didn't respond, just stood at the counter, probably thinking of his stomach—which reminded me. "Did you take your medicine?"

He held up a glass of the disgusting-looking liquid as if offering a toast. "Cheers, overprotective big sis."

I rolled my eyes. "I shouldn't have brought—"

"Stop." He set the glass on the counter with a *clack*. "I'm not a scout, either. And you're killing my pride here." He pressed his hand against his chest as if I'd wounded him. "Seriously, I can take care of myself." He walked over and slid into a nearby chair.

"You're reckless."

"And smart."

I smiled. "You charge in without looking."

"I follow my intuition."

I slumped in my chair.

He downed his medicine and shivered. Then he looked at me. "I'm good at what I do."

"Instigating dragons?"

"Hunting."

To that I had no response, because he was right. And he had the scars to prove it. Scarred instead of dead.

Most of my would-be scars were from burns, so they'd been removed with smoke. But a lot of his were from tail spikes, which killed by venom.

He tapped the table with his hand and stood. "Well, I have an early physics class, so I'm headed to bed."

"Make sure you bring extra tail-spike antidote with you tomorrow."

His laugh followed him down the hall. "Noted."

I stared at the words on the screen, which confirmed that I'd seen a forest dragon. And I whispered, "You're mine."

SEVEN

When I headed out for class, Dane was already gone. I flipped on my tracking device and pinpointed his location. Already on his way to campus.

The morning sun beat down on me from an expansive blue sky. It was so bright here. And cool. The air had this amazing, clean smell that I missed. Nothing like our new base in California. I preferred Montana. Wilder mountains. Untamed forests. Land stretching out before me like freedom.

As soon as I pulled into the school parking lot and turned off my bike, my cell buzzed. Dane. Maybe he'd found something. I answered.

"Hey." His voice was hushed. "I'm tailing a couple of them. Do you think if I can get one separated that maybe we could bring her in for a bit of questioning?"

My blood spiked hot. "Absolutely."

"Great. Stand by."

"You got it." I slipped the phone back into my pocket. My class didn't start for hours, but I didn't want Dane here alone. Looked like I had some time to kill. I turned on my smoke scanner to be sure I didn't miss anything, even though I usually smelled it before the scanner alerted me, and headed toward the campus café.

An old woman with two right shoes and a threadbare sweater was just outside the back door, digging through the trash without seeming to care if anyone saw her. I felt a pang in my rib cage, and I wanted to tell her college kids weren't really into wasting, but then she pulled a pizza box out of the trash. Nothing. Not even crusts.

My heart dropped a little as she picked at the bits of dried cheese stuck to the center of the cardboard, and I tapped my pockets. I had nothing on me to give her.

As she looked up, I ducked my head and walked around the building, so as not to embarrass her with my blatant staring. As I left her line of sight, another tug in my chest gripped me. I couldn't imagine having to pull things out of the trash like that.

"Hey, Keira."

I spun at the sound of my name, hand ready to grab my secret dragon-claw knife.

"Didn't mean to startle you." Ace grinned.

And just like that, my morning got brighter. I laughed awkwardly and took a step closer to him. "Early classes suck, huh?"

"Well, that's the beauty of being able to pick your own schedule. You know?"

"Unless you need a class that's only available at the butt crack of dawn."

"Whoa. Not a morning person?"

"What gave it away?"

He tipped his head toward the coffeehouse. "The trick to being a morning person is caffeine. Want some?" He smiled and pulled the door handle, spreading his leather jacket and revealing his very muscular chest.

Oh, what the heck. He was really, really attractive, and it couldn't hurt to look like a normal student. I walked through the open door, and he followed me inside.

The scent of his subtle cologne meshed with the amazing brew, and I breathed in, thankful at this moment for the smoke detector.

The line wasn't too long yet. And I recognized the logo as the one he'd had on his cup in our late-morning class yesterday.

"See anything you'd like?" He motioned ahead of us, and I realized it was my turn. "I'm buying."

My face warmed. *"Gracias."*

What was wrong with me? I didn't normally get blushy over a guy. But it had to be good for my cover, so I decided to go for it and order something. So did Ace. And he tried to get me to have one of those massive cinnamon-roll doughnuts.

I declined. Several times. Finally he settled on half a dozen.

We walked out together, me warming my hands on my cup. "You must really like those things." I motioned to the brown paper bag.

"They're good." His eyes seemed to sparkle. He set his coffee on an outdoor table and offered a doughnut one more time. "Last call?"

"You don't give up easily."

He shrugged sort of bashfully, almost, which looked very different on him than his normal cocky smirk. Then something a little more honest and intense entered his gaze. "Give me a minute?"

I was about to ask him what was wrong, but he smiled again. Different. Genuine. It touched his eyes more than his lips, and it made me wonder what he was up to. "Sure. Where are you–"

He started to walk behind the café, bag of doughnuts in hand. I picked up his cup off the table and followed. I couldn't help it. Suspicious behavior drew me in like a mosquito to warm blood. I trailed him and peered around the corner in time to see him catch up to the old homeless woman leaving the dumpster. I stood frozen.

He held out the paper bag to her. "Here. I noticed you didn't have anything."

She looked up at him, hesitating a moment before she took the bag. Tears lit her eyes, and she clutched the brown paper as if it were a treasure. "Bless you." A sincerity wrapped those words, and she sniffed. "Thank you."

My heart beat loud and full, and I pressed my warm coffee cup to my chest as I stared, mouth hanging open. Why hadn't I thought to do something like that?

Ace inclined his head in a nod that resembled a tiny bow. "Bless you, too." Then he turned back the way he'd come.

Startled, I tried to decide whether or not I should stay here or head back to the table and wait for him in perceived obliviousness. I backed up a few paces so the wall hid me, and opted for meeting him here.

He turned the corner, and his eyes widened as soon as he saw me.

"I imagine it's too late to change my mind about the doughnuts." I handed him his coffee. "That was a really nice thing you did."

He shrugged and started walking, making me catch up. "I just wish more people were proactive about taking care of the poor."

And suddenly Ace was more than a pretty face, and hanging out with him became less of a cover and more of an actual desire. Weird for me, because I couldn't remember the last time I'd tried to make a friend.

Well, yes, I could. But that mistake didn't count.

After class, Dane and I went full throttle into dragon tracking but hit a bunch of dead ends. Was our cover blown? I reached for my phone to call Dane, when it rang.

I answered.

"Keira?" Dane's voice shook as if he was in pain.

My heart sped. "Where are you?"

"Down by the river. Three left. Bring smoke."

Smoke? "How bad are you?"

"Just h-hurry."

My chest tightened. He was across campus. I raced to the parking lot, jumped on my motorcycle, and buckled on my helmet.

These guys had messed with the wrong person's baby brother.

Clouds of smoke and fire billowed near the riverbank. I parked and rushed through the trees until I spotted the massive yellow head of a grease-fire dragon.

Dane leaned against a tree for cover. Sweat glistened on his forehead, and when I saw his left leg, I pressed my hand against my mouth. Blood-darkened jeans clung to him.

Two piles of ash showed where a couple of dragons had met their fate, but he didn't stand a chance alone against the remaining three. The yellow dragon sniffed the air, drawing closer to my brother's hiding place.

Why had Dane gone after them alone?

Sometimes I wanted to strangle him. But right now I just needed him to be okay.

I pulled out my dragon-claw dagger and ran, nearly rolling an ankle on the rocky ground. Three scaly heads turned my direction: pale blue, bright red, and metallic yellow. I caught their stink on the wind. One smelled like ice, another like volcanic ash, and the third like a grease fire.

Only one reason for three different subspecies of dragon to horde together: they were misfits.

Two dragons headed toward Dane, necks stretched out. The third kept its eyes on me.

I stepped onto the bank in clear view. "Why do you guys always have to gang up on us?"

The dragon's gold scales flashed in the sunlight as it leaned closer. Definitely Grease-Fire Guy.

It chuckled, and smoke poured out of its nostrils. "You're so much fun to play with."

A sound, like the sizzle of hamburger grease hitting hot coals, rose up in its throat—it was loaded. Its neck arched.

My muscles twitched. Focus. Wait for—now!

I jumped to the left, and a blaze of heat scorched my right side as its fire hit the spot I'd vacated.

Close. Too close.

I made eye contact with the ugly beast and cracked my neck.

A low rumble started in the gullet of the bright-red dragon next to Greasy. Five seconds before Volcano Breath would spit burning lava at me. If that wasn't enough, the crackle of thawing ice resounded in the pale-blue dragon's throat. Fire and ice spraying together? Not an explosion I wanted any part of.

I rolled out of the way as they shot flame together. The air crackled. A cloud of smoke stunted my vision. Movement to the left caught my eye—Dane sneaking around a tree and flicking his gaze toward Greasy. I nodded and focused on the red dragon. Its crimson neck arced, and its yellow eyes locked onto me. The gurgle in its gullet told me it was ready to fire.

I clutched my dagger hilt tighter and dipped it into my utility belt—the third compartment on the left. Spearmint coated the blade—a volcanic dragon's poison. Now this knife would break through those red scales with ease, spreading poison as it mixed with the dragon's blood. I just had to be careful to wipe the knife clean before I used it on Icy, because spearmint in its blood would strengthen it.

Volcano Breath tipped its head up, signaling a full-on eruption. I had to get out of range, or I'd be sprayed with drops of molten lava.

I headed farther from the water as burning liquid spurted from its throat like a fountain in the middle of a pond. But I had to stay close enough to make the shot. Volcanic dragons were most vulnerable when they erupted. Well, if anyone could get close enough to their exposed throats.

I skidded to a stop and turned.

Orange lava splashed against my flame-retardant leather jacket. Heat penetrated the material. I stood my ground. Aimed. Followed through. My knife sailed toward its neck.

The blade sank deep into the scales and severed the fire trigger right next to its vocal cord. Lava rained down around me, but I'd squelched its source.

My mind registered Dane throwing his knife. The hiss in Greasy's throat died as the dagger stuck in the back of its head, right below the occipital lobe. It dropped dead. Great shot.

Mouth agape, Volcano Breath lunged at me. It still had talons and a spiked tail coated with poison, but at least I didn't have to worry about being turned into something crispy.

I flicked my wrist, and my bracelet called my dagger back. "Want to go another round? Oh, that's right, no more talking for you."

Volcano Breath snapped.

A crackle, like splitting ice, hit the air, and I glanced at Icy. *Dane better have my back right now.*

Volcano Breath's body arched. I bent my knees and bounced on the balls of my feet. Its spiked tail sailed toward me. I jumped onto the thick, muscular appendage. My dragon-tooth cleats didn't get good enough purchase. Off-balance, I fell, and my head hit stone.

The world shook. Sounds were muffled. I touched the tender spot and felt blood. But the dragon's tail was whipping back. I rolled to my feet and braced for a moving landing. Then I sprang up, and the spikes on my shoes dug into its scaly hide. I tipped forward and gripped the thick tail.

My head throbbed. I focused on what I had to do. Stood. Grabbed a spike at the base where it couldn't stab me with poison, and pulled myself higher. The dragon shook its head as I raced up its back, but my cleats kept me from falling. I reached the crest at the crown of its head and gripped it for balance. Then I plunged my poisoned dagger into its skull.

The long neck wobbled, and I held tight as it dropped, then turned to hot ash beneath me.

I stood and dusted myself off.

Cleaned my knife on my shirt.

A crackle like breaking ice caused me to turn.

Icy swung its thick, armored tail at my brother. Dane's leg was already injured, and he couldn't get away in time. The tail slammed into him and tossed him toward a tree. Dane landed in a patch of rosebushes with a *snap*.

Blood. There was blood on Icy's tail spike.

No.

Dane had been poisoned.

Icy's long neck reached my brother's form in the bush. "I should kill you."

"Why haven't you?" Dane lay on his back, one knee bent, his other leg dragging as he slowly slid back from the dragon and out of the brush. Cuts marred his arms.

I raced across the bank to get to them. Hopefully I'd be in range in time to take the dragon out. I had to be.

Losing Dane was not an option.

The dragon tipped its head to the side. The crackle in its throat died, and its spikes flattened.

"I never wanted this." The dragon's voice shook, and it stepped back.

"This?" Dane's pain was evident in his tone even as he tried to keep it steady.

The dragon shook its head. "They didn't tell me I'd have to kill people."

"Y-you don't have to."

What on earth was Dane doing? He had a shot. Why wasn't he taking it? I ran as the ice dragon seemed to recoil from him.

"You didn't attack us. We attacked you." It stepped back again. Was it seriously letting us go? No. This was a trick. But it bought me the time I needed.

I dashed between the dragon and my brother.

"Keira, wait! This one's different!" Dane tried to stop me.

He was nuts. Couldn't he see the trap?

It tipped its head sideways and shrank back. "I won't hurt you."

I stood frozen for a heartbeat. No red had pulsed in its eyes. No lie. How was that possible?

Isabel's voice seeped into my thoughts: *Dragons have a way with words. A way of disguising their true intentions to fool our ability to see their lies.*

My heart hardened. Maybe it didn't plan to hurt me—it planned to kill me. "You expect me to believe you?"

"Keira. Let him—"

"No negotiations, no survivors." I echoed Isabel's words as I threw the knife.

It opened its mouth in an attempt to shoot frost at us, but the dragon-talon knife cut right into its neck, making it misfire at the trees behind us. The dragon stumbled. Water splashed as its body collapsed into the river. Ice rippled out around it, its breath freezing the surface. I ran over the ice and plucked my weapon out of its blue scales.

"Please." The dragon's eyes met mine. All of its spikes flattened. "I won't hurt you."

No red flashed. Only gold surrounded the huge black pupils. Its soul. It was showing me its soul?

My hands shook as I hesitated. How was that possible?

It wasn't. And if I didn't act now, both Dane and I would be frozen corpses. "Liar!" I buried the blade in its head.

Ash crumbled beneath me. The ice started melting. A pang ate at my stomach, but I ignored it. Icy may have looked sincere, but all dragons were liars.

Cold water seeped through my clothes, and I raced off the sweating ice, pulled the can of smoke from my jacket pocket, and knelt next to Dane. He looked *muy mal*, and my heart clutched.

He leaned back, supported by his elbows. "Keira, I think he . . ." Dane shivered.

"Shh." I helped him lie back. "We're safe now. Let's take care of that burn."

It was worse than I'd first thought. Blood oozed from his clothes along his whole left side. I peeled up his shirt. He cried out, and I pressed the back of my hand against my lips.

Oh, Dane. Charred skin stuck to his clothes, and a deep laceration ran the length of his torso. My stomach flipped. The tail spike had gouged deep, and his bloody jeans told me his left leg was burned badly. The last time I'd seen him this bad . . . no. I couldn't go there. I had to get him the antidote before the spike's poison started to kill him. It was strapped to the bag on my bike.

"How did you manage to help me fight those last dragons?" I prayed I had enough smoke to douse his whole burn. "Hold still, it's almost over." I held up his shirt and aimed the aerosol can at his wounded skin.

A dark shadow spread over my brother.

A deep chuckle followed.

I glanced over my shoulder. Five dragons. The one in front was white with midnight-blue horns—a frost dragon.

"It's time for you hunter scum to die." The frost dragon's horned head snaked closer. Liquid nitrogen poured out of its nostrils.

I gripped my blood-slicked dagger while stats poured through my mind: *Poison—cayenne pepper.* With shaking hands, I dipped my knife in the right compartment on my belt. But even if I got this dragon, there would still be four left. I couldn't count on Dane, nor could I leave him unprotected.

"Not so fast, hunter scum." A horned head rammed into me so hard the world spun as my body rolled across the bumpy earth. I tried to curl into a ball, but a tree stopped my momentum.

I gasped, everything still blurry. Then the pain in my head intensified. I touched the back of my scalp, and fresh blood met my fingers. I tried to push myself up in time to see the frost dragon stalk closer to my brother. Dizziness kept me down.

"No!" I screamed.

Wind eddied around me, sweeping up my hair. Leaves and twigs scattered, and a looming darkness hung over us. Another dragon. Even the frost dragon looked up.

I took the moment to scramble to my feet, and I half stumbled, half ran over to Dane. Then I fell on top of him and reached to activate my shield. A gouge in the bracelet revealed where the button used to be. It must have busted in the fight! I hunched over Dane anyway, and my skin tingled as I waited for a blast of heat. Tears pricked my eyes, and I squeezed them shut.

"Run, Keira." Dane's eyes rolled back, and his head fell limp.

My chest tightened. Not my brother. Not like this. I tapped his face. "Dane?"

Talons wrapped around my waist and pried me off Dane's form. I tried to hang on to him, but the claws tightened and I couldn't. I screamed and fought the dragon's iron grip. Then the dragon scooped Dane up, too, and my heart sank to my stomach as the beast lifted us skyward.

Surely death by fire would have been better than the torture that was about to come. I could only hope Uncle Max had dispatched trackers. Not that I still had my phone on me after that battle.

The only thing I had was my belt, which I couldn't get to because of the stupid claws around my waist, and my knife. That would do nothing now except make the beast drop me to my death.

"After them!" the frost dragon roared.

"Don't worry." The dragon that carried me spoke, and its deep voice vibrated through my body. "They won't catch me before I hit my territory."

This dragon wasn't one of the misfits? Then where was it taking us? And why?

EIGHT

A dozen forest dragons lined the sky in front of us, their wings beating as they dove toward the battle we'd just left. I strained to see, but the dragon carrying me kept going.

"That's my horde. This is a trap for those misfits you were fighting."

"Where are you taking us?"

It chuckled. "My lair. I'm going to cook you over dragon fire until your bones are nice and crunchy." Its voice was smooth and surprisingly sarcastic.

I looked up to see a huge tree-trunk neck. Light green, the color of peridot. Its wing beats sounded like a flag whipping in the wind and sent the smell of burning leaves around me.

A forest dragon.

No! Anything but that! My insides crumpled. I craned my body to see the green-gold scales lining its long neck and the dark-green scaled knuckles that carried me.

The way it carried me made it impossible for me to check the golden-green scales lining its underside—I couldn't see past its boney knuckles. But I forced myself to stop craning my neck anyway. Old habits really did die hard. I'd momentarily forgotten that my dragon was already dead.

Good thing, because I might not make it out of this alive.

Next to me, Dane's limp body hung in the dragon's other clawed fist. He didn't look good.

"*Querido Señor, por favor, no!*" A whispered prayer escaped me before I even realized what I was doing. They'd kill Dane and torture me. I had to do something.

I pounded on the dragon's claws. "Let us go."

"Your friend isn't going to make it without my help."

"I don't want your help!"

It glanced down at me, its peridot eye taking me in. "Good thing you don't speak for him."

So that was it. I'd have to wait and see where it took us.

Maybe I could get this forest dragon to lower its guard enough for me to get some secrets out of it. Maybe transmit them to Uncle Max if I could flip my recording switch, assuming it was still intact.

My head throbbed, and I started to nod off, but I flinched, trying to keep myself awake. I touched the smooth surface of the dragon's claws. Why weren't the talons hurting me? And why did they feel so different than the knife I had—made from a piece of what Isabel had told me was a forest-dragon claw? These didn't seem so sharp.

Cool air beat against me, crisp and fresh. We flew closer to a city on the border of a forest. The dragon stayed high, keeping its shadow from touching the ground—I supposed to avoid scaring unsuspecting people. Typically, if there was a dragon sighting, hunters were called in right away. The general public still didn't know these beasts could take on human form. It was best that way. Widespread panic tended to do more harm than good.

Dismal fog surrounded me as the dragon took us into a cloud. When we broke through, I noticed we'd come closer to the town. Blackened remnants of skyscrapers next to new buildings gave the skyline a jagged appearance.

Was it seriously taking us here? Did it live among humans? Some of them did that, but not usually hordes. A tall building with slight scorching, porches off every sliding glass door, and flame-protective awnings told me this was an apartment building.

This dragon had some guts living with people. And flying to its own balcony. If this was its home, anyway.

It dropped Dane on the balcony but tightened its hold on me as it hovered over my brother's unmoving body.

"What are you doing?" I tried to pry its claws open. "Don't kill him!" I screamed my throat raw.

Smoke poured from its nostrils and bathed Dane.

I lost sight of my brother and pushed harder against the talons. Finally, the dragon released me onto the balcony. I tumbled across the hard floor, my head throbbing. Then I pushed myself up and ran to Dane, smoke stinging my eyes and burning my lungs.

Dane lay on the ground, his clothes covered in blood, his only movement the rise and fall of his chest. His eyes remained closed. I cursed myself as tears brimmed on my lashes.

Why had I left the antivenom on my bike? Now how would I get it for him? I checked his wounds, but every burn had been healed. I sucked in a breath past the lump in my throat.

"You healed him?" I turned around, and the dragon stood there in human form. Air caught in my lungs. "Ace?"

I should have known. Those stupid green eyes. All forest dragons had green eyes. All this time, he'd been getting close to me. For what? What was he planning? And how had I let him slip under my radar unnoticed? I clenched my jaw.

Heat spread through my core, and I looked right at the deceiver. "What do you want?"

"Keira."

I stood between him and my brother and held out my dagger.

Ace raised his hands. His eyes tracked my movements, and he had the audacity to look hurt. "Really? I just saved your lives."

"No." I shook my head, trying desperately to figure out his game. "This is some plan of yours."

He gritted his teeth and motioned to Dane. "He's still losing blood. He needs stitches, and he's been poisoned."

"Don't you touch him! I know how to treat a wound." My voice broke, and I cursed myself for it.

"Okay." He lowered his hands and motioned toward the sliding glass door, way too calmly. "I have supplies inside."

I shook my head again, and it throbbed harder. I bent over and pressed my hand to my forehead. "I'm not going in there."

"You should sit. Your head is—"

I glared at him. "My brother needs an antidote. Do you have—"

"I can take care of him if you—"

"Touch him and I will kill you!"

Ace's eyes narrowed slightly, as if he could possibly be confused by my reluctance to trust him.

I sneered. "You do know I'm a hunter, right?"

He opened his mouth as if he might try again to calm me down, then he just looked betrayed. "I know what you are."

He opened the sliding glass door and walked inside.

I glanced at Dane, and my stomach constricted. At least he wasn't convulsing. There was still time. I just had to think. Maybe I could use Ace's tail-spike venom to make an antivenom. But was there time?

Ace returned with some sort of first aid kit. "I have something to counteract the poison. I just hope it's enough."

Half of me wanted to yell that he get away, but if he really wanted information out of us, perhaps saving Dane was in his best interests—especially if I could make it seem like Dane had information that I didn't.

Ace's eyes widened, and he lunged toward Dane. I tried to stop him, but he motioned to my brother. "We don't have time for this, Keira."

I turned around.

Dane started shaking.

No. Every ounce of air left my lungs. My chest screamed inside, like my heart was imploding.

Not my brother. I'd seen too many hunters convulsing on a table. None of them had made it.

Ace gripped my shoulders and moved me aside with substantial strength. "There's a bottle of dark liquid in the kit. Give it to me."

I dug it out and handed it over, trembling. Dane wasn't going to make it. I cupped my hand over my mouth and sank to my knees.

Ace tore open Dane's pant leg and shirt. The huge tail spike had ripped from his thigh to his abdomen. Why did he get so close to their tails? Hot tears pricked my eyes, begging to be released. I'd told him to stop being so reckless.

Ace didn't seem at all fazed by my undoing or Dane's shaking. He simply emptied the contents of the bottle into Dane's wound. The scent was like black licorice. I knew it well, and this wasn't the antidote we used for tail-spike wounds.

"What are you doing to him?" I grabbed Ace's arm.

He looked right into my eyes, calm, collected, and serious. "He's going to die if you don't let me go." He pushed me aside.

I knelt on the ground and sank as low as possible, watching Dane, whispering about how sorry I was for bringing him into this.

And he stopped convulsing. No. He stopped moving altogether.

Something in my chest broke. No—screamed. "You killed him?" I swung my fist at Ace, desperate to unleash the fury inside.

He caught my hand.

I didn't care. My body shook, and I buckled over.

"Hey, hey." Ace tugged my hand. "Keira? He's fine. See?" Gently, he guided my hand to my brother's neck. A faint pulse tapped my fingers.

I breathed deep and snapped my attention to Ace. Those same compassionate eyes I'd seen behind the café when he'd touched the homeless woman and given her food.

The sixth commandment of dragon hunting flashed into my memory:

A dragon doesn't care for anything but itself; don't let perceived acts of kindness fool you. They are incapable of real compassion.

I smacked his hand away. "You'll wish you'd killed me first, because if you lay a finger on my brother, I will rip out your throat while you watch."

Ace leaned back, slowly, as if I were a wild wolverine that might snap. Wise move.

"What do you think I'm going to do to him?" he finally asked.

"I don't typically play guess-the-torture—it gives my enemies too many ideas."

Ace actually chuckled, though there was a hint of sadness in it. "I'm not going to hurt you."

I glared. "You must really think I'm stupid. What I want to know is how I didn't detect your smoke."

Ace's expression softened. Then he turned his attention toward Dane again.

I shut my eyes for a moment, trying to make sense of any of this. "What are you—"

"Just let me get him stitched up, okay?"

Considering my hands were still trembling from almost losing my brother, and that for some reason Ace wanted him alive, I conceded with a nod. But he hadn't removed my weapons, so I stayed close.

He'd obviously done this before. His hands remained steady, and the stitches were nearly textbook perfect.

My breathing was still tremulous, but at least it didn't hurt anymore. "You the horde doctor or something?" My voice sounded scratchy.

He glanced my direction and smiled sadly but didn't say anything.

I shouldn't have really tried talking to him, anyway. But he was a forest dragon, and he had answers I needed. No reason I couldn't play this hostage situation to my advantage, at least until backup arrived.

My shaking subsided, and the throbbing in my head returned with a vengeance. A wave of exhaustion swept over me, and I leaned back against the patio chair to try and hide it. But the furniture scraped against the ground, betraying me.

Ace looked over. "You okay?"

I just glared.

He rolled his eyes and turned back to Dane, still cleaning and stitching his wound.

Maybe it was time to get him talking. "Why did you save us?"

"Misfits are dangerous. For whatever reason, they've left their own tribe and formed another. Those reasons usually involve killing humans." He turned his gaze to me. "I don't like what they stand for. My horde has been fighting them."

"Are you expecting a thank-you?"

His eyes narrowed in what again looked like confusion. "I don't know what you have against me and—"

"Dragon." I pointed to him. "Hunter." I pointed to myself. Was he really so clueless? "It's not rocket science."

He seemed to be studying me. I looked away, not willing to let him try and see my soul and exploit my weaknesses.

"That's hardly fair."

I laughed in his face. His wounded expression did nothing against my protected heart. Clearly this dragon didn't know how educated I was on his kind and their tricks.

"You're just going to take everything you know about me and throw it out the window because you found out I'm a dragon?"

I leaned toward him. "No. I'm going to pay specific attention to the fact that you're a dragon."

He sort of winced, but it looked like he might be tamping down anger. He must have decided not to retort, as he started putting away his medical supplies. "Your friend will be out for about twenty-four hours, but I think he'll be just fine—once he heals, that is. He's going to have a nasty scar. Let's get him inside, then maybe you'll let me do something about that gash on your head?"

I touched the tender spot, and sticky blood coated my fingers. "Let's not get confused. I don't trust you."

"Okay." He handed me a needle and medical-grade stitching thread. "There's a mirror in the bathroom."

"I'm not going into your lair."

He cocked an eyebrow. "You think I saved you from those dragons to bring you here and let you slowly bleed to death?"

"I had it handled."

He ran a hand through his hair. "Right."

"I don't know what you want from me, but you're not going to get it."

Ace motioned to my brother. "Help me get him to the couch." He tipped his head toward his lair—er, apartment—and I hesitated.

It wasn't like I could get Dane out of here myself. Or stitch up my own pounding head. It would be better if I stalled until help arrived. I lifted my brother's shoulders.

Ace smirked. "She can be reasoned with." He opened the sliding glass door and then helped me carry Dane.

We set him on the couch just inside. From here, I had a clear view into the open kitchen. There was no door to separate it from the sitting room. Off the kitchen to the right was a hallway that likely led to the front door. And to the left, another hallway. Bedrooms, maybe? The place smelled nice, like Ace, and was surprisingly clean.

I sat with Dane while Ace placed the medical supplies on the kitchen counter. I searched Dane's belt but didn't find a trace of his tracker. Must have fallen off when he called me.

Ace turned on the kitchen lights and the faucet and patted a barstool. "Have a seat."

If I had any chance of getting information from this beast, I had to play his game better than he did. That meant playing nice for now. I complied.

The seat gave me a good view of the front door. My way out as soon as Dane was well enough.

Ace gently moved my hair aside and dabbed a cloth against the gash in my head. The water was warm, but it stung. I pressed my eyes closed.

"This is deep," he said.

"Yeah, well, a dragon tried to kill me. What's new?"

He didn't say anything. Just kept cleaning. I stared at Dane's peaceful form on the couch. What would he be thinking if he knew a dragon had us? Would he stay to get information? Try and leave to bring help back this way?

"This might hurt a little." Ace's voice pulled me out of my planning.

I laughed bitterly. "Stop acting like you care."

He paused for a moment and then slid the thread through my tender skin. "I know this goes against everything you've ever been taught."

"Staying with a dragon. Letting one help me. There's so much wrong with this scenario."

He tugged harder on the thread.

"Ow."

"Sorry."

"No, you're not."

He sighed. "You're not the first hunter I've met. It's like you all take this vow to kill any dragon you see without asking questions."

That pretty much summed it up. "I was nice to a dragon once. It killed my parents."

Ace's hand froze. "I'm sorry that happened to you."

"Ha." I wished I'd been facing him so I could've seen his eyes flash red, revealing his lie.

"Keira, I don't know what I did to you that makes you think I'm doing anything other than helping you here."

"I told you already. I'm a hunter. All you had to do to become my enemy was be born a dragon."

His hand stilled. "We aren't all killers."

"Oh please. It's in your blood."

"How would you know?" His tone was harsher that time.

That only made my anger burn hotter. "I've studied your kind my entire life."

He finished stitching my head and set down the needle.

And I whirled to face him. "No snappy comeback this time?"

He started putting away the medical supplies again and set a glass of water and two aspirin on the counter next to me. Then he leaned back against the kitchen counter and crossed his arms. "You mean you studied a couple of cases involving dragons who did terrible things?"

"I studied under Isabel Delarosa, the greatest dragon hunter who ever lived."

He scoffed.

"What?"

"I've heard of Isabel, but I'm not sure what you think makes her so great."

"She killed more dragons than any other hunter. She figured out how to unlock the secrets of different subspecies—their poisons, their weaknesses. She's saved more people from you terrorizing beasts than any other hunter to date. And she taught me everything she knew."

"But you befriended a dragon."

I visibly startled and wanted to slap myself for it. A burst of adrenaline shot through me. "What would you know about it?"

He shrugged. "Nothing. You said you trusted one once, so I—"

"Exactly. You know nothing about me, except for how that ended. So if you turn your back on me, dragon, it's at your own risk."

That searching look overcame his features again, and he seemed to study me. I wanted him to know that I wasn't afraid to let him look into my eyes.

"Looking for a weakness?" I asked while maintaining harsh eye contact. "Let me save you the trouble. I have a hot temper. Means I kill before asking questions."

"Noted," he said quietly, and for the first time in his presence, the faint scent of forest-dragon smoke trickled to my senses.

"How are you doing that?"

"Doing what?"

"Hiding your stench in public."

He straightened his spine and squared his shoulders. "Maybe the dragon has something to teach the hunter after all?"

I just shot him a glare.

He pushed the aspirin and water toward me again. "Dragons only spill smoke in human form for three reasons. Otherwise, you can't detect it." Then he smiled, but this time it looked devious. I knew he couldn't hide behind that mask of pretending to be good forever. And I was slowly cracking that shell.

I pushed the aspirin and water back. "Why?"

"I can't tell you that." Ace stared at the medicine I'd rejected and shook his head. "You're going to have a bear of a headache."

"I'll live. Besides, I'm not planning to stay long."

He shrugged and motioned to the door. "You're free to go, but your friend will likely sleep for twenty-four hours. He took in a lot of poison. You might as well get comfortable."

I leaned my hip against the counter.

"Suit yourself."

I turned away and walked toward the front door, trying to get a feel for my escape routes. "This is a pretty extravagant place you've got here. I thought forest dragons liked trees, not cities."

He chuckled. "We do. I have a great cabin in the woods, but it's kind of far from my college classes."

"Right. What were you doing there, anyway?"

"Same thing you were, tracking those misfits." He opened a cupboard door and pulled out a bag of microwave popcorn.

Seriously? My weakness. And I was so hungry. He lifted the bag. "You want some?"

"No, thanks."

He shook his head and put the bag into an old-fashioned microwave. The kind with buttons to touch instead of a computer that talks. It beeped as he pressed the numbers. "It's just popcorn."

"Probably poisoned," I muttered halfheartedly.

He sighed and bowed his head, quiet while the seconds ticked by in neon green. "I'm trying to help you see I'm not a threat to you. I saved you and your friend. What more do you want from me, Keira?"

I looked right into his eyes, and a fire raged in my chest. My heart beat faster and faster to the sounds of the popcorn kernels exploding. The words boiled up in my throat, and I let them come.

"I want you to die."

NINE

The popping slowed in the microwave.

He stared at me with his eyes wide for a heartbeat, then opened the microwave door and grabbed the bag. Poured the contents into the bowl, all while ignoring me and my words. It was maddening.

He set the bowl on the counter near me. "Does this have something to do with that tattoo on your wrist that you keep rubbing? If it does, you should know—"

"It does." I swung my arm behind my back, unaware that I'd been touching the tattoo. "You can save my brother all you want—you're still the enemy. You still deserve to die."

"For a different dragon's crime?"

"Well, that dragon is already dead. Doesn't mean you're any different."

He paused. His Adam's apple bobbed several times. "So the tattoo is a trophy."

I looked at the mark on my wrist. That dragon had been my friend once. At least I'd thought so. It wasn't a trophy. It was a reminder.

Every time I looked at it, I felt the pain. The heartache of what Isabel had made me do. The thought that *I* was betraying *him,* when in reality, all our friendship had been a lie.

I breathed deep to try and get rid of the ache in my throat. To try and even my voice. "Yes."

Ace stood there with a handful of popcorn frozen halfway to his mouth.

"Dragons are good at lying. All of them. Good at building trust, only to betray."

"We have a way with words, but you can tell if we're lying if you know how to look, which I think you do."

"That's why you've gotten so clever with your words. Loopholes are your own personal challenge."

He grabbed another handful of popcorn. "You sure you don't want any?"

The heavenly aroma was getting too hard to bear. I ate some. "I don't know what your angle is, dragon, but I'll find out. And I'll stop you."

Ace's movements turned slow and deliberate. He set down the bag and tipped his head toward the door. "I need you to hide."

I crossed my arms and leaned on the counter.

"I'm serious, Keira. Some of my horde is coming."

He shoved me toward the hallway that led to the bedrooms. "First door on the left is my room. Hide in the closet."

I braced against the doorframe. "Your closet? Are you serious?"

He made direct eye contact. "Yes."

My heart jumped. "Dane." I couldn't leave my brother out there.

"I won't let anything happen to him." Ace grabbed hold of my upper arms and nudged me closer to his room, tearing my grip from the doorframe. "Your stubbornness is going to get you killed."

"I was hoping it would get *you* killed."

"Keira, please."

"Get your hands off me." I pulled away, and he released me, putting his hands up in surrender.

He leveled his gaze. "As long as you don't interfere, I've got this. Closet. Now. And stay there."

He herded me closer to his bedroom door and reached around me to open it. The scent of forest-dragon smoke encompassed me. My stare snapped to meet his. "They'll smell me?"

"Yes. My room smells strongest of me. Besides, what did you think the popcorn was for?"

I opened my mouth to protest, but he pressed his finger to his lips, then tapped his ear.

They could hear me? Of course they could. He'd heard them.

The doorknob jiggled. There was no way I could make it to Dane without being seen, and even if I did, there was no way out. Dane's best chance now was for me to stay hidden.

I set my jaw and ducked into his bedroom. He pulled the door mostly closed behind me, dimming the light significantly. I tripped over a pile of clothes on the floor and caught myself on the edge of a desk.

That was close. I could have left him trying to explain the noise as some clichéd cat. They probably liked to eat cats, horrid monsters that they were. I tiptoed my way to the closet and stepped inside.

Muffled voices wandered into the next room. I strained to hear.

"Hey, Wally. What's that smell?"

"Popcorn. Nice," another voice joined in.

"This is why I like you, Wally. You always have food ready."

At least three distinct voices. The fridge opened. "Anything to drink?"

"Dude. Who's that?"

Ice chilled my veins. They'd seen Dane.

"He helped me against the misfits. Got hurt real bad. I had to pull him out of there." Ace sounded confident.

A good liar. Even when a dragon was in human form, I could pick up on the color change if I focused. Could the other dragons? Did they know?

Well, it wasn't *technically* a lie, so he probably didn't have to hide anything.

"He's in human form," one of them said.

They thought Dane was a dragon? Oh no.

"Yeah, but he'll pull through now," Ace said.

Why the heck would he say that? They'd never buy that Dane was a dragon. Not for long, anyway.

"Did you recruit him for our horde?"

I sucked in a gasp. All right. Maybe he did have it handled. Nice thinking, *Wally.*

The scent of burning wood hit me. I moved farther back behind Ace's shirts.

"You hiding something?" one of them asked.

I pulled my knife free and clutched the hilt.

"Hide—yes, I'm hiding something. You three devour everything I buy." Ace's voice trailed farther away. "Are you guys going to stick around all day, or did you come here for a reason?"

I leaned closer to the door. What was Ace's game?

"Dad wants to speak to you. In person." The talkative one spoke with his mouth full. "Something about you stealing from the misfits. I'm guessing they're talking about your new friend there. You can't give him back, though. Can you? He's incurred a life debt. He smells like you."

Life debt?

My heart pounded, intensifying the ache in my head.

What had Uncle Max said to Lance about that earlier? My brother smelled like a dragon now? What did that mean?

"It's not safe for either of you here, Wally. Not with the misfits sniffing out your scent. They want you now. They're going to want an all-out war after this."

"They've wanted war for a while, remember? They don't have enough numbers for that."

"Yet."

"Let's keep it that way."

"It'll be worse once they find out who you are. It's time to go back into hiding."

Who *was* he? The misfits wanted Ace because he'd saved us? When was he going to let me in on *that* secret? Pain tightened my chest. I'd let my guard down.

Isabel would already have answers to a few of these questions.

I crept out of the closet, careful not to let the door creak, edged over to the wall, and peered toward the kitchen through the cracked-open door. Ace stood with his back to the living room, blocking the other three from accessing it.

Their backs were also conveniently toward me.

"Come home, or Dad will send someone to get you and your friend. All the sentries saw you cross the line with someone. They all suspect a life debt. I can tell them—"

"I'll come," Ace said. "Just give him some time to heal." He motioned to Dane.

The dragon to Ace's right crossed his arms. "I'll wait while you pack."

"Bran, go. Tell Dad I'm coming."

Bran grasped Ace's shoulder. "You can't risk that. You let this dragon heal, he might take off the first chance he gets. A life debt is a life debt. Do you know how dangerous it would be if you let him go?"

"I know." Ace brushed Bran's hand away.

"I'm not letting you leave without him." Bran took a step toward the living room, and Ace planted a palm against his chest. A cloud of smoke grew like a fog in the room.

Nice. Some stupid alpha-dragon threat display. I held my breath as my heart thrummed.

"You want to make my smoke alarm go off, Bran? Quit your bristling, and let me handle this."

"This could put more than just you in danger." Bran pushed Ace aside, strode to the couch, and motioned for another one of the guys to help him pick up Dane. "Look, now you're packed. Let's go before the misfits get here."

I rounded the corner and held out my weapon. "Put him down."

Bran's eyes widened, and he tipped his chin toward me. "You *were* hiding something."

I ground my teeth. "Give me my brother."

"Brother?" Bran's eyes narrowed. "You don't look—"

"He's adopted. Want to know his blood type, too? Now *vete al garete,* or I'll take care of you myself!"

Bran shook his head. "Vete what?"

"It means get lost." I brandished my knife.

The other two dragons flanked Bran and broadened their shoulders, widening their stances. Yeah, my odds were *muy malas,* but I'd still go for it to save Dane.

Bran's eyes darkened. "Sorry, a life debt is a life debt."

I stared at the dragon, my heart pounding. This was Dane. I couldn't let them take him. I had to do something. Anything.

I lowered my weapon. "Then take me. Let him go, and I'll pay the life debt." I slid my knife into its sheath, despite my mind screaming for me to kill the dragons.

Bran looked at my weapon holstered in my Guardian Tech belt. "A hunter?" He turned his attention to Ace. "Debts can be transferred. Zelda might be willing. A hunter has never agreed to a life debt. This could be good for us."

I met Ace's gaze. "Then let's do it."

Bran chuckled and picked up Dane, slinging him over his shoulders. "Girl's got spunk." One of the other guys opened the sliding glass door, and Bran stepped out, carrying Dane.

"Wait." I raced after him.

He jumped off the balcony, and as he started to plummet, wings spread from his back. He grew larger and longer, and his skin seemed to sprout green scales that covered his entire body like tiny shields scurrying into place. Like a flower in a time-lapse video, his neck elongated, and his face blossomed into a fierce head crowned with spikes. His armored tail whipped through the blue sky.

My mother had told me stories at night of *el cucuy,* the monster who came for children who didn't behave. She always laughed and tickled me under the chin, saying not to worry, *el cucuy* wasn't real.

Little had she known, it was. And it's what had killed her.

Sun glistened off Bran's scales as he rocketed higher and higher on his mighty wings. In the time it would take for three blinks, he'd changed. And yet, I'd seen it so rarely that I found myself enraptured.

I noticed a small, crescent-shaped tear in his right wing. I'd remember the dragon who dared take Dane from me. And he'd pay. I would watch him turn to ash and tell him he'd signed his *sentencia de muerte* when he took my brother.

I glared at Ace. "I shouldn't have expected a dragon to keep his promise."

"You know what? You're annoying." He picked me up, tossed me over his shoulder, and jumped off the balcony.

TEN

Air fluttered through my hair as we fell.

My stomach flipped. I clawed at Ace's jacket, but his clothes faded into green scales—smooth like leather yet hard like a turtle shell. And so many scars. The number of scars actually shocked me.

Then again, they couldn't feel pain very well.

Woodsy brown wings lifted us. I scrambled to turn around on his back and face the direction we were headed, hugging the base of his very large neck, which my arms were not long enough to encircle.

The world below became miniature. Cooler air blasted my face as clouds engulfed us. Ace's wings beat a steady rhythm. This had to be what dogs loved about sticking their heads out of car windows. Maybe I'd enjoy it under different circumstances. This just left me with a sinking feeling in my stomach. "Where are you taking us?"

"My horde."

Great. The lion's den. "The dragon with Dane is your brother?"

"I won't let them hurt your brother." His voice was deep, and it vibrated in his back.

"I don't believe you."

"You've made that pretty clear."

I rolled over onto my back, stuck the cleats of my shoes into his scales, and dug my heels in.

"Take it easy with those." He grunted. "I won't let you fall off, you know." His voice held a slight edge like . . . he was in pain.

Strange. It shouldn't have hurt him. "You felt that?"

"It *is* my back."

I cringed. That didn't make sense. He had to be lying. I shook the thought away and clung to Isabel's truths. He was just trying to rattle me. I wouldn't let him. "You deserve that and more for letting your friends take my brother." I dug the cleats deeper, not believing his pathetic lie, but he flinched. Why? To gain my sympathy?

"Okay. I deserved it, but did I deserve that too?"

Something inside me, still, quiet, and introspective, seemed to awaken. If he could really feel that, was it a forest-dragon thing? Because Isabel's journal had been very clear on the topic. "I thought your scales protected you."

"Well, yeah, but your freaking cleats are made of what?"

Dragon-teeth chips. "Noted. But what did you expect, kidnapping a hunter?"

"I didn't—I'm sorry you're in this mess, Keira. But you offered to accept the life debt."

"Because you let your brother take mine." I crossed my arms, but I also retracted the cleats into my shoes.

Blood welled up from the new gashes in his scales. I stared at the red pools and covered my mouth with my hand. I nearly said *lo siento* but stopped myself.

I shouldn't care.

But he'd saved Dane.

And he could have left me. My heart twisted. What was happening?

Then again, that Bran character seemed to think I was valuable for something. I pressed my hands against my face. How could I possibly consider giving him the benefit of the doubt here? He'd kidnapped me, no matter how he tried to spin it.

Apparently he had nothing more to say, so I just lay there on his back and watched the clouds pass by above us. The subtle rise and fall of his body eventually rocked me to sleep.

I jolted awake and slipped. A leathery wing pushed me back to safety—if the back of a dragon could be considered safe.

Where was I? And how long had I slept? We were starting to descend.

Towering coniferous trees covered the steeply rising hills. In the distance, the Rocky Mountains bordered the woods. The heavy scent of pine and drying leaves rushed up at me. The trees grew bigger every second. I rolled over and hugged Ace's neck, gripping his flattened spikes as I braced for the landing. As soon as we hit the ground, Ace let me slide off his back, and then he donned his human form.

He faced me. "This way." He led me into the wide mouth of a cave.

The others remained dragons. And the one with the crescent-shaped wing tear—Bran—still held my brother.

Lit torches in sconces on the walls sent shadows dancing across the uneven rock, and the scent of burning leaves filtered through the cave. Water dripped from stalactites into a puddle at the base of a ledge.

Bran set my brother down on this side of the ledge. Dane just lay there, limp. I ran toward him, but dragons blocked me. I would've punched one in the stomach, except I didn't feel like breaking my hand. Instead, I held out my palm to block the beast, and it grabbed my arm.

"Stop." Ace's deep voice made the dragon freeze. And the faint scent of forest dragon filtered through the cave.

"Easy, Wally, I wasn't—"

"Just let her go."

I ripped my arm free as soon as its grip relaxed. Thin scrapes marred my wrists where its thick claws had dug in. I glared past the dragon in front of me and right at Bran. "If my brother has so much as a scratch from you, I will kill you myself, *el cucuy*."

"Noted, hunter." Bran's smirk heated my blood.

Ace touched my arm, and I whirled to face him.

He held up his hands as if to say he offered no threat. Yeah. He didn't need to. His motley crew was enough.

"I need you to hand over your belt, communication devices, and weapons," he said. "Zelda won't come in here if you're armed or able to send a signal."

I studied Ace's eyes for any trace of a lie and saw no flashes of red.

Isabel's warning rang clear in my head. *When you're on the enemy's turf, always keep a weapon.* But this time Dane's safety hung in the balance. I handed over everything.

Bran crushed my tracking device and tossed it into a pool of water. His green eyes bored into me, and a satisfied smile snaked across his lips. "You won't need that if you're taking the life debt."

Two huge forest dragons came up from the belly of the cave. They were much bigger than Ace and his friends. Even though they were all forest dragons, they each had differences, nuances. One of the larger dragons was more slender, with a longer neck and golden-green eyes. The other was darker, like shadowy foliage.

Bran's scales gleamed a mossy hue, and his eyes were a bluish green. He also seemed to have a cocky smile that made me want to pull my knife on him. I stood on his left and noticed more scars marring his pretty scales.

Whoa. Pretty? Scratch that thought.

I glanced at Ace for a moment. Why had he turned into a human when everyone else remained in dragon form? If he planned to try to get me to trust him, that was a game I'd play. And I'd play it so well he'd be the dragonfly caught in my web. Not the other way around.

"You wish to take his life debt?" asked the slender dragon with the golden-green eyes. Must be Zelda.

"In exchange for my brother's safety and return home." My words wavered.

The dragon next to me searched my face with narrowed eyes. "We've never had a human take on a life debt."

I placed my hands on my hips and widened my stance. "I've never been saved by a dragon. It's new to me, too."

The golden-eyed dragon nodded. "You are willing?"

"I'm fresh out of options, if that's what you mean."

The dragon's eyes narrowed, searching my face in a way that reminded me of the studying look Ace had given me. I wanted to avert my eyes to stop Zelda from reading my soul, but this was for Dane, so I didn't.

She nodded again. "The thirst for revenge inside you will fuel the bonding."

I did *not* love how she'd seen through me so easily.

She morphed into her human form. It was much less magnificent than when a dragon morphed from human to beast. While that was like a whirlwind of a plant bursting from the ground, this transformation was like a tree withering, almost. Her form hunched low, wings retracting and folding in. She was a blur of scales that melted into a slender, graceful, beautiful form, like a woman with golden hair.

Her dress reached the ground, the light fabric flowing as she raised her arm to beckon me closer. Her eyes were the same color. Held the same depth.

She motioned to Bran, who carried my brother over. With long, slim fingers, she touched Dane's forehead. "The poison is receding. He will regain strength and recover." She looked at Ace. "You rescued him, Wallace?"

"Yes." His voice seemed more regal, somehow, as if the cave walls brought out a richness I'd never heard.

Zelda turned her attention to me again. She held out her other hand, still touching my brother, and her stare pierced me. "If you are certain you will take the burden of life debt to this dragon, give me your hand."

"Burden?"

"You will be bound to remain with him until the debt is paid."

"What exactly is the debt?"

"If you save his life as many times as he's saved yours, the debt will be considered paid. When I transfer the debt, it will be as though he has saved your life once. Your brother's slate will be wiped clean."

Yeah. Or I could somehow get another tracker and lead my band of hunters right into their nest—after I'd discovered their weakness. Not before. That would be suicide.

It might look bad on the outside, but this move could actually be what we needed. Maybe it was my turn to jump in recklessly. I matched Zelda's intense gaze and shot her what I hoped was a challenging grin. "I'm certain."

She looked at Ace. "And you are willing to allow this replacement, son?"

Son? Whoa. Wait a minute.

He glanced at me, and his regal voice cracked. "Yes."

Zelda's gaze latched onto me. "Give me your hand."

Ace's mother or not, I wanted to protect Dane. I put my hand in hers. She tipped my wrist and looked at my tattoo.

I stared at her, refusing to remember that day.

Her eyes searched mine. Then she curled her fingers around my wrist. Heat surged from her iron grip. I tried to maintain eye contact while the pain consumed me. My knees buckled. My leg and side felt like they were on fire. Was this what Dane had felt? Stabbing pain skewered my ribs. I screamed and then saw darkness.

ELEVEN

I opened my eyes to the soft glow of morning and sat up. My head throbbed, and I wanted to lie back down.

A gentle breeze disturbed the thin curtains leading to a balcony bathed in sunlight. I knew that balcony. I'd almost watched my brother die there.

My brother! I spun around to see Dane sprawled on Ace's couch. I was on the loveseat, covered by a blanket. I flung it off and scrambled to my feet. Every movement sent stabbing pain through my skull.

Ace stood at the kitchen counter, and I smelled blueberry muffins.

He smiled. "Morning."

I tried to remember anything about the dragon cave and transfer of the life debt. All I remembered was that it hurt fiercely. I touched Dane's forehead. Checked his pulse. He seemed so peaceful, and his heart rate felt normal. I ran my hand through my hair and recalled the stupid, throbbing laceration on my head. I approached the counter and slid onto a barstool, facing Ace. "What time is it?"

"Seven a.m." He handed me a muffin.

I didn't want his stupid muffins. My hand disobeyed because apparently my stomach was more threatening this morning than my temper. Plus, I really loved blueberries. "You had time to buy muffins?"

"I can bake."

"Am I supposed to be impressed?"

He shrugged. "I didn't set off the smoke alarm."

That cocky smile had returned. If he was trying to charm me into letting down my guard, it wouldn't work. But I actually found myself struggling to hide a chuckle. I ate the muffin. It was marvelous. And Ace set a glass of milk on the counter. I guess if I was going to be his prisoner, I shouldn't starve myself. I had an ulterior motive to pursue. But then he pulled his bottle of aspirin out of the cabinet and shook it.

I stared at it. My head pulsed in time with my heartbeat. "No, thanks."

He sort of winced, as if asking me if I was sure I wanted to lean on my pride for this one.

I shrugged. "I'd rather die poisoned by blueberry muffins than a stupid pill."

He rolled his eyes and put the bottle away. As he shut the cupboard door, I focused on the oven's digital time display. His earlier comment about the time finally registered, and I jumped out of my chair, cursing myself for the quick movement.

"Seven a.m.?" I stood up and scanned the room for my stuff. "Dane needs his medicine. Where's my jacket? I always keep extra medicine in my jacket. Where's—" I pressed the heel of my hand into my temple and gritted my teeth.

"Calm down, Keira. Your jacket, belt, and weapons are all in my car. I'll go get it."

"He didn't have any last night. I need to get him another dose. I—"

"Okay." Ace stood in front of me now. "I was hoping to get Dane home this morning. He should be waking up within the next few hours, anyway. If we get him home, is that enough time to get him his medicine?"

I breathed in and nodded. "Yes."

A low groan from the other couch caught my attention. I rushed to Dane's side as he rolled over and tried to sit up. With a wince, he lay back.

I grabbed his hand. "How are you?"

He breathed in through his teeth as he lifted up his shirt. The huge gash was healing nicely, but it looked awful. He smiled weakly. "I've had worse." His eyes searched me. "You okay?"

"*Sí*, I'm fine." A lump rose in my throat. "You were worse. It was a good thing he had smoke." I motioned to Ace, who my brother could not find out was a dragon. Because I had a plan, and it included Dane being in the dark.

Dane's eyebrows pulled together. "Who—wait. Are you—?"

"He's a hunter." I cut in and then looked meaningfully at Ace, making sure Dane couldn't see my face and Ace understood that I really, *really* needed him to play along here. "And he helped us with those dragons."

Ace's eyebrows rose slightly, but he recovered quickly and stuck out his hand for Dane to shake. "I'm Wall—um—Ace." He smiled at me and bit into a muffin.

"A hunter?" Dane gripped Ace's hand, but a strange look passed between them. That ignited my worry, mostly because I couldn't read it. Which probably meant Dane was headed into protective brother territory. "Nice to . . . meet you . . . Ace."

I motioned to Ace in his T-shirt and perfectly fitting blue jeans. "He's not really dressed the part, but he helped us." Thankfully that gained me Dane's eye contact. I shrugged. "He convinced me."

"That is a feat." Dane looked me over, too, his eyes squinting momentarily as if he was trying to read the situation and failing. This really had to be information overload for him. I put a hand on his shoulder. "We're safe here."

"Right." Dane tried to sit up, slowly.

Ace gripped his arm and helped him. "You must be hungry."

"Starved. How long was I out?" He looked at me.

"Eighteen hours."

"From . . ."

"Poison." I motioned to the wound in his side. My eyes stung, and I squeezed them shut to avoid looking all weak and sentimental. "You were convulsing."

He stared at me with his mouth open.

"Ace had something to counteract the poison." I took a deep, shaky breath.

He glanced at Ace, eyes wide, and shook his head. "Y-you—?"

Ace nodded. "I'm glad you pulled through. Your sister's been worried sick."

Dane seemed quite confused at first, not that I could blame him. It was a lot to take in. But a strange look passed between him and Ace. Dane finally shook his head and let out a sigh. "Thank you, I—"

"I'm just happy to help . . . another hunter."

I looked at Ace askance, and he smiled softly. At least he was willing to go along with my lie. *"Gracias."*

Ace's eyebrows lifted slightly, as if my gratitude surprised him. "Of course." He headed back toward the kitchen. "We should get moving, I guess."

I turned my attention back to Dane. "Let's get you back to base." He tried to stand, and I steadied him. "Are you going to be okay?"

"I'll be fine, Keira." His gaze bored into me. "The other dragons?"

"We didn't get them. Not all of them. Listen, I have a plan. Ace is going to help me. We have a lead on where the nest might be. You are going to rest up and wait for our backup."

They should be here in five days.

"This does not sound okay. I don't need—"

"You'll tear out your stitches, and I'll be picking your insides off the ground. How much medicine did you bring with you?"

Dane's forehead creased. "I have enough." When he was done trying to convince me—with a look—that he could take care of himself, he limped toward the door. "You need to stop pretending I'm worthless as a partner."

Worthless? Did he not understand how much I needed him? "I'm not—Dane, I need someone to man the computers while Ace and I track these misfits."

He looked over his shoulder at Ace, then lowered his voice. "You trust this guy?"

"Not at all." I smiled. "You know me. The only one I trust is you."

"Keira, I—"

"Please? I almost watched you . . ." My throat tightened. I took a deep breath. "Rest up before you try to run recklessly into this."

He nodded. "A couple of days, then I'm in on this team."

Days? I'd felt what had happened to him. "At least a week."

"A week? No way."

I ushered him out the door and into the hallway. "I'll keep you informed."

Ace stayed back to lock his apartment door, so I lowered my voice.

"He did save your life. And he knows where the nest is. I'll need you to watch for dragon activity and communicate with Uncle Max. But don't tell him—"

"That you're running off with a strange hunter and I'm home on sick leave? No problem. But be careful." He glanced at Ace and slipped something into my hands. "And keep in touch."

Heart pounding, I pocketed it. A homing device and two-way. I'd be able to call Dane and text him and Uncle Max. My way out.

Gracias, Dane, for knowing me so well. "And it might be a good idea to stall a minute before calling the cavalry. You know how Uncle Max might try and blow my cover."

"I remember." His gaze betrayed his concern, though. "I also know I won't be able to talk you out of this. Be careful."

After dropping Dane off, I got back into Ace's black Challenger and shut the door. Ace had stayed behind because Dane wanted to have a word with him. But I'd watched their body language from the vehicle. Since Dane let Ace leave and get into the car with me, I was certain Ace hadn't blown my—our—cover. As soon as he joined me, I buckled up. "So, where are we going, captor?"

He frowned.

I shrugged. "If the shoe fits."

He sighed, put the car into drive, and headed down the road. "I have a cabin in the woods."

"That's not creepy."

He rolled his eyes.

"Will I be blindfolded for this trip?"

"Nah. When we get far enough from civilization, I'll change into a dragon and carry the car the rest of the way." His stupid grin made me shake my head.

"Tell me about this life debt. When do I get *my* life back?"

Ace smirked. "You're stuck with me until you save my life."

"Why don't we go find the misfits so I get that over with faster?"

"I see you're bringing your wit with you."

"I never leave home without it."

He gripped the steering wheel with his left hand and dipped his right shoulder closer to me. "The life debt is like a link. You smell like me, so any dragon with a vendetta might track you instead."

"You mean all those misfits?"

He winced a little. "In turn, I know where you are at all times."

He what? *Muy mal.* "Sounds reasonable." I pretended to be interested in my fingernails instead of my internal freak-out. "Maybe I should just kill you and be done with this."

He chuckled. "You can't. The life debt is like a dragon code of honor. It won't allow you to kill me."

I shrugged. "Dragons have honor?"

"You're bound to *me,* not the other way around. I can kill you if you get too annoying."

"Funny." Actually, quite unsettling. "If it's dragon code, why include humans?"

He cocked an eyebrow. "You're the one who wanted to be included."

"I meant my brother, moron."

He cleared his throat. "What was I supposed to say? I saved his life." His brows furrowed, and those green eyes searched my face.

Isabel's voice rang clear in my head: *Never let a dragon stare into your eyes, or it might glimpse your soul. We store all of our weaknesses there.* My breathing quickened, and I turned away from him.

Obviously the whole life-debt ruse had just been part of his dumb plan to keep Dane and me safe when his horde members showed up, but that had completely backfired.

Or had it? Did he actually care about keeping us safe? Maybe he'd wanted to deliver two hunters to his horde. Either way, he wanted a hunter for something.

At least Dane was safe. For now. And I was going into the nest. Once there, I'd find a way to poison forest dragons or die trying.

"Uh-oh." Ace looked out his window, and I leaned forward to see what he'd spotted. A group of six guys motioning toward the Challenger.

I grabbed his shoulder. "They're following us? You can't let them get to my brother."

"I won't." He looked at me. "But they can't know you smell like me."

My eyebrows shot up. "What does that mean?"

"It means we lead them away from here, making these guys think I got what I came for."

"Which is?"

His eyes met mine. "You."

TWELVE

Ace put the car in reverse and backed up. The Challenger jerked as he slammed on the brakes and threw it into first. He gunned it, and the tires screeched, catching the attention of the six misfits sniffing around the base. "I need you to act like you're my prisoner."

"I am your prisoner."

He glared at me. "*Act* like it."

I lowered my window and, as we drove past the guys, screamed.

It worked. They turned their heads and ran around the corner after us.

Ace chuckled. "You call that a scream."

I narrowed my eyes. Then I checked the rearview mirror. "They're following."

"Yeah." He stopped at a red light.

"Now what?" I turned and screamed again.

Ace pushed my head down and yelled for me to be quiet. He was more heavy-handed than I thought he should be, so I punched him in the ribs.

He flinched. "Hey, I'm driving!"

I popped up so I could look out the rear window again. "You're losing them."

"Not for long. See that park? They'll cut through there. They'll tail us a little longer."

"Then what? I'm not seeing much genius to your plan."

"Your base, as you call it, is full of traps specially designed to not only keep dragons in, but also to keep them out, right?"

"How do you know that?"

"Every dragon in the area knows that."

Good point. The car swerved, and I held on to the seat but crashed into Ace's shoulder. He pulled into a parking lot, and the tires screeched as the vehicle spun around. Our pursuers crested the horizon. The scent of burning rubber wafted through the windows as Ace peeled off again.

Now we were far enough from the base and too far for them to pursue on foot. They'd have to change forms to follow us. And they'd want to do that hidden so people in the area didn't suddenly see dragons.

Ace glanced at me. "Recognize any of them?"

I scanned their faces. Sure enough, Mr. Back Row from the college. "Yeah. One—actually, two look really familiar."

"Then the misfits know I have a hunter now."

"Is that good or bad?"

He pulled out his phone and pushed *call*. "Bran? I have a mess."

I watched the world go by as Ace told Bran about the misfits and sped through traffic in the city. Dragon reflexes were something to envy, that was for sure. He finally hung up.

I stared at the phone in his lap. "You called in your backup *corillo* to take care of that?"

Ace glanced at me askance, eyes narrowing as if I'd said something he didn't understand. "Those misfits will change into dragons and chase us. We aren't fast enough in the car. My brother's still in the area. The misfits can't find out I spared a hunter."

"Why not?"

He stared out the windshield, his one-handed grip on the steering wheel easily maneuvering us through traffic.

Finally, he spoke. "Let's just say forest dragons have been the hands on the reins of a very strong, thankfully reclusive, dragon subspecies for decades. If they find out I'm harboring a hunter for any purpose they deem unreasonable, they might be willing to pull hard enough to break those reins."

"What's reasonable?"

He shrugged, but his jaw was clenched. "Keeping you alive in my cabin won't sit well with them unless . . ."

I leaned in, but he didn't finish. "Unless what?"

He glanced at me. "I might have an idea. Your cooperation would be appreciated."

"Why? What happens if they break their reins or whatever? Is this just dragon family drama?"

"It could be an uprising. Mountain dragons have been persuaded to stay out of the world of humans, Keira. Trust me, you want it to stay that way. If the misfits think they can get the mountain dragons to turn on us forest dragons, they'll do it. Humans and dragons? They don't mix very well."

"Because you monsters are always trying to kill us?" I crossed my arms.

"Because we don't take the time to understand one another."

Something about the quiet, confident way he stated that made me end the conversation. He couldn't actually believe that, could he? I turned my attention to the hazy outline on the horizon. Mountains. Ace sped toward them, and the number of cars on the road with us seemed to lessen as we drove.

I'd heard of mountain dragons. Isabel had fought some of them in the past. She'd told me they were dangerous. Massive. And their poison was honey.

"Why would you harboring a hunter be enough to start an uprising?"

He sighed. "It's not the first time my family's done it. Last time, the hunter escaped. Found out mountain-dragon poison. Almost hunted them to extinction."

"Well, good thing you're not harboring me, then."

He breathed deep. And then the car started moving faster.

The Challenger door slamming woke me. Ace was out of the car, and we had come to a complete stop. Trees surrounded us. The scent of woods. Of forest dragon, minus the smoke.

A really nice log cabin sat nestled into a hillside overlooking a gorgeous mountain view. Ace appeared at the passenger door and tapped on the window as I stared out the windshield. This was his cabin?

He leaned one arm on the hood of the car and opened the door. "You okay?"

"I'm in the middle of nowhere with a dragon. What do you think?"

He chuckled. "You should have stayed in the closet."

I pushed against his chest and got out of the car, carrying my belongings, including weapons he'd said I couldn't use against him. Maybe that was just a ruse so I wouldn't try. Easy enough to test.

He reached to take my bag, but I swatted his hand away. "It isn't fair that you can kill me."

"I already saved your life—well, your brother's. And if I have to save your life again, it just doubles the debt." He walked ahead of me up to the cabin. "I don't owe you anything else."

Great. My heart lurched. What had I gotten myself into?

Dry leaves crunched beneath my boots as I shuffled toward the porch. "Then why bring me here? Why not just let the misfits get me?"

Ace shook his head.

The porch stairs creaked under my weight. "Tell me there's running water."

He laughed and went inside. I really hoped that meant yes.

The door opened to a massive foyer with a high ceiling. A stairway sat to the left and a bathroom to the right. The faint scent of campfire mingled with roses. A strange yet pleasant combination.

Ace motioned to the staircase. "There's a guest room upstairs. Second door on the left."

I set my stuff down and scanned my surroundings. The second floor didn't span the length of the entire cabin. Only the left side. The rest was just an open ceiling. Probably big enough for him to stand there in dragon form. Across from me was a kitchen. I walked farther in to see what was to the right of that. A huge fireplace in a great big open room with a TV and sectional. More high ceilings.

The whole west wall was covered in windows, which overlooked a huge deck and a breathtaking view of a coniferous mountainside. Treetops swayed below while mountains rose into rock faces in the distance. If I wasn't a prisoner, I might actually want to be here.

Front door. Downstairs bathroom window. Back door through the kitchen. And I spied a staircase off the deck. Multiple exits. Good.

"You like it?" Ace asked.

"What's not to like?" I brushed past him and picked an apple from the fruit bowl on the kitchen counter. Then I headed toward the stairs. "I'm going to check out my prisoner quarters."

I'd wait to contact Dane until there was a need. The homing beacon he'd given me needed to stay off for now so he didn't suspect I'd gotten here at dragon speed. That might bring him here too soon. I couldn't let him get hurt again.

"All right. I'm going out for a perimeter check." Ace headed toward the back door. "I'll be back in an hour if all goes well."

"Perimeter check? For what?" I changed direction and followed him, stopping by the kitchen counter. When he didn't answer except to look at me askance, I added, "You need a bodyguard? I'm happy to meet my life-saving quota early this month."

One corner of his mouth twitched up. "As charming as you are, I don't think your presence would be appreciated."

"Aren't you afraid I'll escape?"

"I'll find you. Life debt, remember?"

"Annoying." I bit into my apple.

"Hey, you wanted to save a dragon."

"Wanted to?" I set down the tart fruit and glared into his eyes. Heat poured through my veins, starting in my core. "Just so we're clear, dragons will always be my enemy. So, no, I didn't want to. I had to."

He stopped, hand on the doorknob, and glanced over his shoulder. A half smirk grew on his face. "If you think you can last five days, I know how you can save my life."

I crossed my arms. "Can you tell the future? Is there something I should be ready for? 'Cause I gotta say, your death would free me of a lot of hassle."

"The life debt would just pass on to my brother."

Bran? No thank you. "You dragons aren't big on easy outs."

"My parents are hosting the annual Feast of Fire in five days. It's a dragon holiday. Sort of like your Thanksgiving and New Year's all rolled into one. I'll be without a date, yet again. The shame was going to kill me, but now . . ." He spread his arms wide as if to say I'd become his saving grace. That cocky, lopsided grin graced his face. "What do you say?"

"I'm not sure that counts." I took another bite of apple, not hiding my narrowed eyes.

"Clearly you haven't had to survive the taunts of my family members. They're quite—"

"Obnoxious? I know the type." I rolled my eyes.

"Well, you're invited."

Something inside me dared to hope, but I tamped it down. This was nothing but typical dragon deception. "So this isn't a must-attend event?"

He stepped closer to me, a head and shoulders taller. The kitchen light illuminated his green eyes. "You're a prisoner, I'm not going to lie. But your real fate could have been much worse. There's an island where we keep captured hunters. That's where they wanted to put you. You can still end up there—or worse, they could kill you. And if the mountain dragons find out you're here, they'll try, my territory or no."

His territory? How could I be so stupid as to forget that little detail? Dragons became more aggressive in their own territory. Stronger too. And faster. Braver. It helped them to protect it better.

I couldn't let him see my nervousness. "Your threats are expected, dragon. I'm not afraid of you."

His eyes narrowed, and heat flickered over my skin—from him—even as he stepped away. "Not smart, hunter. The moment you're released from your debt, chances are high you'll be targeted. This ball is your chance to show the dragons that you're more than a ruthless killer. It's your chance to make it out of here alive once your duty is fulfilled. I can't protect you forever."

I leaned my hip against the counter while my temper warmed me from the inside. "Good thing I don't need your protection."

"Do you know where you are?"

My turn to let the slow smirk fill my face. That was the thing about dragons. They always thought they were the smartest ones in the room. "Exactly where I want to be."

Right in the middle of a forest-dragon nest.

The way he minutely tucked his chin told me my slight threat had registered. Good.

He shrugged, opened the door, and left.

Cold air swirled around me, and I hugged my middle.

This had better not backfire.

THIRTEEN

Ace's dragon form dashed in front of the windows on the west side of the house. I watched him soar through the air with the mountains as his backdrop, and a shiver skittered across my skin.

Wow. I hadn't expected to find that beautiful.

I tore my gaze from his retreating form. Now I had a chance to see what kind of secrets he was hiding. I headed upstairs. Plush carpet squished beneath my feet.

The guest bedroom was simple: one double bed, one dresser with four drawers, and a nightstand with a lamp.

I set my stuff on the bed and slid on my leather jacket and utility belt. I felt the vial of Dane's medicine in my pocket. I should have left it with him. I set the jar of licorice-scented liquid on the bedside table. Next to that, I put the tracker, still off for now.

I opened the nightstand drawer. Huh? A bouquet of dried roses? I picked it up and pricked my finger. Ouch. Okay, roses with thorns. Seriously, who gave someone a bouquet with thorns?

A petal fell to the floor. I leaned down to grab it and set the whole thing back in the drawer. How many other victims had Ace brought here and tried to woo?

Then I looked through my bag.

Two dragon-claw knives, which I stashed in my belt.

One more set of flame-retardant clothes.

Too bad I didn't have a crossbow and some dragon-claw-tipped arrows.

I headed over to Ace's room. It wasn't like I expected to find a neon sign pointing to his weakness, but I could at least know what to rule out. Like apples.

The room smelled faintly of campfire, but his belongings revealed nothing useful. Except that he did have a crossbow. I made a mental note of where he'd stashed it and headed downstairs.

Likely the poison wasn't spearmint dental floss, wintergreen toothpaste, or peppermint mouthwash, since I found those in the bathroom. So he had a thing for mint. The kitchen was stocked with broccoli, horseradish, and graham crackers—so not those.

I picked up the box of graham crackers and sank to the floor, holding them as a memory consumed me in its cruel claws.

I hadn't stopped seeing the dragon after Isabel caught me.

For three years, I visited him whenever I could steal away. Something about him always lured me back. I knew not to flip the switch to turn him into a human. That alerted Isabel.

But the dragon, Boy, loved graham crackers. It was such a strange thing to watch a dragon eat. I snuck a box out of the cupboard and headed quietly down the stairs. Into the darkness. The cold. Condensation on the metal banister chilled me. The thrill of doing something forbidden warmed me. Slowly, I opened the door.

Boy saw me and looked visibly relieved.

I walked right up to his cage and passed him a package of crackers, careful not to touch the electrified bars. The crackers were thin enough for him to slide into his mouth with the fire muzzle on. The muzzle I'd taken off of him so many times.

While he ate, I snuck to the control panel and turned off the electrical current. I still didn't have access to open the cell door. I needed Isabel's code for that. Soon.

Then I reached through the bars to take off the fire muzzle again. He stared at me with those green eyes as if my kindness was earning him a debt. I ran my hand over his scales. Green. Hard. Warm. Smooth. He sat completely still, and I snapped my hand back.

"*Lo siento*! I, uh, I mean I'm sorry. I wasn't thinking."

"Don't be." He held out his hand, and I placed mine over top of it, palm against palm. His sharp claws had been filed off.

I closed my eyes, feeling his hand against mine, imagining what he might look like as a human now—three years after I first saw him. Three years in a cell. I opened my eyes and looked up at him.

His eyes pulsed gold, and I stared into the depths of his soul. Something about that made my heart jump, and I stole my hand back. "Have you ever had s'mores?" I lifted the chocolate and showed him some marshmallows.

"Is that what the lighter is for?" He laughed and motioned toward my bag.

I blushed. "So what if it is? I can't exactly build a fire here." As soon as I said it, I flinched. A shudder rippled through me, and I glanced at the muzzle on the floor of his cell. "I-I didn't—"

His eyes seemed to squint in a smile, and his lips curved, too. Something about his expressions were so . . . human. "If you've never had marshmallows cooked in dragon fire, you've never had real toasted marshmallows."

My hand shook, and I laughed nervously through my words. "I bet."

"Oh." His smile fell. "I-I'm sorry. I won't do anything. I promise."

I clutched the bag so tightly I squished some of the white puffs. I stared at them and let go, watching them expand. Almost as if my trust inflated with them, I remembered why I came here once a week. I called him Boy. He was a human. I handed him the bag through the bars that separated him from freedom. "I'd like real toasted marshmallows, please."

His eyes rounded as he slowly reached for the bag. "Are you sure?"

I nodded and sat on the ground next to his cell.

He joined me, still holding the bag. I extended my arm through the bars and pressed my hand against his warm scales. The scent of smoke—like wood burning in the stove at Christmastime—filtered through the room.

And I looked into his eyes. "I don't care what she says. You're not a monster."

He sucked in a breath and leaned closer, lowering his head so I could see the nubs that remained of the horns she continually filed away. "Do you really believe that?" he asked.

"Yes." I touched his hand. "Some dragons are, but not all of you. I don't know why she keeps you here." A tear trickled down my cheek. "I'm going to set you free."

He pulled back. "What?" His voice quavered. He stared at me, eyes wide, and shook his head. "Don't—don't joke about someth—"

"I wouldn't. I figured out how to do it. Next week, when the hunters' convention is in town, they'll be announcing that I'm ready to join the other hunters. I'll get a key to the cells, and Isabel will share her access codes with me." I stared into his eyes.

"You're going through with hunter training?"

"Someone has to show them that some dragons are good. Right?"

He gripped my hands in his and squeezed. "Thank you."

"You're my friend." I laughed softly, letting some of my jumbled nerves out. "I don't even know your name."

He smiled. "I'll tell you."

"When I set you free. Until then"—I raised the chocolate bar—"s'mores?"

The hope in his eyes brightened, and he held one of the marshmallows up to his lips. Lightly, slowly, he breathed a tiny flame. Just a soft glow. The marshmallow tanned, impeccably.

He handed it to me, but I couldn't wait. I popped it into my mouth. The gooey center rushed out as I bit down on the thin, crisp outer shell. It was perfect. And woodsy. Like a campfire. I covered my mouth to keep from squealing. "It's amazing!" I spoke as I chewed. "I need another. *Inmediatamente.*"

He chuckled and held up another.

The tiny orange flame flickered out of his mouth, and the door to the room burst open. It slammed, hollow-sounding, against the wall, and I jumped, pressing my back to the cage. "Isabel!"

She stood in the doorway, face contorted in burning rage. "What have you done?"

The sound of the front door creaking open ripped me from the memory, bringing me back to the present, and I spun, my back to the counter.

Heart pounding, I tried to focus on where I was now. I remembered. I was in a dragon's lair, and I wasn't alone. The box of graham crackers fell from my grip to the floor.

Whoever had entered raced to the kitchen and flicked on the light.

Eyes wide, Bran faced me in his human form. "Oh. It's you." He exhaled loudly and braced his hand against the counter. "Where's Wally?"

"Perimeter check."

I glared at him, leaning against the counter across from him and praying he couldn't see how shaken I was. The emotions I'd just relived plus his surprise entry were not a welcome combination. I tried to swallow back all my feelings.

Bran picked up the graham crackers and put the package of crumbling brown rectangles back into the box without taking his annoying eyes off me. "What did he tell you?"

I shrugged. "About what? Things to do for fun in middle-of-nowhere USA?"

He rolled his eyes and crossed his arms. "About your role . . . in all of this."

"You mean that I have to save his life before I'm free to go? Or that mountain dragons hate hunters more than you guys do?"

He nodded, knowingly, which was a slow burn over my emotions, and headed to the high-ceilinged entertainment room. I didn't want to follow, but he flopped on the couch and turned on the TV.

"Are you babysitting me?" I inched a little closer but remained behind him.

He turned around, resting his arm on the back of the couch. "Sure. Let's call it that."

"Why? Where am I going to go? Your brother said he'd be able to find me."

"True. But if you wander into mountain-dragon territory, your scent—my brother's scent—will make them curious. They'll break protocol and come into his territory to have words, which will end in someone dying."

"Not me."

"No, you'd be dead already. As soon as one of them finds out you're a hunter." He dragged his index finger across his neck.

"Oh great." I plopped into a chair with a perfect view of the kitchen and back door. Maybe this had been a really bad idea. "So I'm stuck in this cabin with no comics and a common enemy in the backyard. Doesn't make us friends, Bran."

He leaned his chin on his palm and studied me through slitted eyes.

I looked away, not willing to let him try to read my soul. "Sounds like it's a bad idea for me to be here."

"Sort of. You hate dragons?"

"Wow, Sherlock. You're good at this."

He rubbed his hand over his face and turned back to the TV. "My brother thinks it's a good idea for you to be here. I disagree."

"That makes two of us. Want to help me get out of here? I know. When he gets home, try to kill him, and I'll save his life."

Bran breathed deep, almost like he wanted to say something. Then he muted the volume. He didn't look my way, but his hard, quiet voice made it to my ears regardless. "If you do anything to put my brother in danger, I will kill you faster than you can think up your next quip. Understand?"

"Dragon threats are a dime a dozen."

Now he stared at me, his green eyes cold. "My human side made that threat, hunter."

My heart jolted at that. I'd faced many dragons, but this was the first time in years that one had gotten to me. The back door opened, stealing any retort I might have had, and Ace walked in. "Bran?"

Bran stood and headed into the kitchen. "Dude, I hope you have another plan, because she's hopeless." The look he gave Ace betrayed his worry.

My throat tightened. What were they not telling me?

Ace's gaze met mine, and I held it, glaring. He glanced away and moved through the other kitchen doorway. "It is what it is, Bran."

"Really?" Bran's voice hushed as he followed his brother.

I tiptoed into the kitchen, just close enough to hear them and not be seen.

"It's not like I can change it." Ace sounded quietly defeated.

"You are the *only* one who can change it." Bran paused. "Wally, please. I don't want to lose you."

"I don't want that, either."

"But the curse—"

"Bran, let me handle the curse. Okay?"

I leaned against the counter, heart hammering.

What curse? And what did it have to do with me?

FOURTEEN

I wasn't sure Bran would ever leave, but hours later, he finally did. I headed down the stairs to make sure, secretly hoping that Ace would have left for another perimeter check or something. I was no closer to finding out what forest-dragon poison was, and I was hungry.

That apple had not cut it. And something downstairs smelled divine.

The stairs creaked as I descended, but no one said a thing, so I ventured carefully into the kitchen. My stomach growled. I clasped my hand over it.

"Just in time." Ace opened the oven and pulled out some type of casserole with chicken and rice and amazing smells, and I wanted it.

He smiled. "Hungry?"

"So you feed your prisoners."

He sighed. "Keira, I hope you can learn to make the most of your stay here."

The most of my *stay*? "You mean you'd like me to forget that I'm here against my will?"

"You chose the life debt." He set the casserole dish on the stovetop and turned off the oven. With his back to me, he pulled plates out of the cupboard.

I turned around and headed toward the stairs, but I swiped the box of graham crackers Bran had left on the counter and took them with me.

"Keira?" Ace's voice followed me. I walked faster, trying to open the cracker package. The brown plastic ripped and sent broken pieces flying across the wood floor. I swore under my breath.

Ace's warmth heated my back as he crouched next to me, picking up the larger pieces. "You could've just told me you're a vegetarian."

I spun to face him. "I'm not."

"You don't like chicken?"

"I don't like you!" I stepped back, but he grabbed hold of the graham-cracker box. I tugged, but he wouldn't let go. Just stared at me.

"What do you want?" I demanded.

"I'd like it if you joined me for dinner."

Not a chance. I let go of the box and crossed my arms. "No. And if you really want me to starve, fine."

"I don't—" He cut himself off with an exasperated sigh and tried to give the crackers back to me.

I wouldn't take them, curse my stupid stubbornness.

"I don't want you to starve, Keira. Please."

I whirled away and headed up the stairs. "I'd rather starve than have a meal with *el cucuy*."

"What does that mean?"

I glared at him, then raced up the stairs as I yelled, "It means you're a monster." I slammed my door on his reply.

When the first rays of sun peered through the window, I opened my eyes. My angry stomach greeted me, and I hurried down the stairs to see if I might be able to steal some food before Ace woke up.

I crept into the kitchen.

The coffee maker was percolating. Blueberry muffins sat on a plate on the table next to a box of graham crackers and a note that said, *Suit yourself.*

I really wanted a stupid muffin, and starving myself would be dumb when my goal was to take down the forest dragons.

I gave in and unwrapped a muffin. It was still warm.

Where was he, anyway? The shower wasn't running, and his bedroom door had been open. Another perimeter check, maybe?

Oh man, these muffins were good. Where did he learn to bake? It reminded me for a moment of my mother's cooking. I remembered little of her, but I couldn't forget two things: the stories and the food. One of my most favorite possessions was a cookbook she'd made for me full of recipes and stories. Something to make and a story to tell my daughter someday in my own kitchen. When she made my father's favorites, like blueberry muffins, they tasted almost like this. I wolfed down three of them and took the box of crackers up to my room in case he tried to get me to join him for dinner again tonight.

If he thought I would soften because of some cooking, he had a lot to learn. Crackers hidden and stomach filled, I decided to continue my search for the elusive forest-dragon poison.

So far, a bunch of items to cross off the list. Most of them strange food items. Saffron? Whatever that was. Apple cider vinegar. Cumin. The dude had fresh basil in a potted plant—which I only knew because the little identification tag was still on the pot. He was seriously into cooking.

I pulled a chair over to the counter and climbed up to check the cupboard above the fridge. Dusty containers lined these mostly bare shelves: honey, cayenne pepper, crushed spearmint—all other dragons' poisons.

Interesting. Why were they separate? And why did he have them? Well, the honey was clear—if he really had a tight rein on the mountain dragons— but the rest . . . did dragons really fight each other with their poisons?

I mentally catalogued all those and came to something I didn't recognize as a dragon poison. A box of herbal tea—the same brand Isabel liked to make.

The smell of it brought me back to that one night she'd made it for me. I started shaking uncontrollably.

I banished the thought, closed the cabinet, and got off the counter. Just thinking about that night made my chest ache. I'd been so lost then. So confused. But I knew how to press dragons for answers now. I wasn't a scared girl anymore. I glanced at my tattoo and sank to the floor as that night flooded back to me anyway.

She'd caught me with the dragon.

I could still taste the marshmallow in my mouth.

I hadn't eaten one since.

She strode into the room, and I leaned back against the cell bars, knees trembling. "Put your muzzle on," I whispered to Boy.

"It's too late," he whispered back.

No. My heart hammered. She'd know it was me. He couldn't take it off himself. I had taken the key from the drawer in her desk. I alone had unleashed his flame.

He would kill her if I moved.

She would kill him if I moved.

I didn't know what to do except stand between them like a buffer. But how would I get the dragon to put the muzzle back on with her standing there?

Isabel walked closer. "Keira, I need you to move. You're in danger."

"No."

She held up her dragon-claw knife. "Step away from the dragon, Keira."

I shook my head, squeezing my eyes closed.

"Keira, I need you to remain safe. This is for your own safety." She placed her hand on the button that would turn the electricity back on the cell bars. "Move. Now."

She wouldn't. Would she?

I looked into her deep, dark eyes. Sad eyes. She wanted me to get out of the way.

"No! He's not what you think!"

"Not what I think?" Isabel's eyebrows rose. Then they twitched into a look I'd seen when she talked about going hunting. It sent a shiver through me. "How much has it poisoned your mind?"

"He's different. I swear!"

She stared at me for a long time. "This *friendship*"—she said the word as if it tasted *muy mal*—"might work to our advantage, Keira."

"What?"

"Move, darling."

I swallowed and stood firm, tears blurring my vision. "You'll kill him!"

"I won't. I need something from him. And I think you're the one who can help me get it."

"What?"

"Move, Keira." Her finger started to press the button.

I opened my mouth to ask her what she was doing, when the dragon pushed me forward. The slight shock of electricity jolted into me for a moment, then I sprawled against the floor, staring up at Isabel. She held her gun up to the dragon.

I screamed and jumped at her. She pushed me down and clicked something on the weapon. "Keira, I'm sorry. This is for your safety."

She aimed the gun at me and shot a dart.

It embedded itself in my neck with a sharp prick. With hazy eyes, I tried to reach out to her. To tell her to stop. But my tongue felt like cotton. And my eyelids started to close.

All I saw was her aiming the weapon at the dragon. And pulling the trigger.

Fire shot out at Isabel.

I tried to scream, but nothing came out. Then I saw darkness.

When I woke up, the real nightmare began.

FIFTEEN

Isabel had moved me away from the dragon, and I woke on the living room couch. She sat beside me—her left arm was bandaged to the shoulder, and angry, red skin peeked out. Her right hand was bandaged, too, and her shirt was a bloody mess.

I sat up, and my voice shook. "Wh-what happened?"

Her sad eyes tracked my face. "Do you not trust me, Keira?"

"Of course I do!" My words came out in sobs.

She bowed her head, eyes closed. When she looked at me, tears brimmed on her lashes. "I know I'm not your real mother. I know I'm not—"

"It's okay." Tears blurred my vision. "You don't have to be. You're who you are, and that's good enough."

"I hoped that you'd at least understand that I want to protect you."

"Of course I do!" My nose stung.

"Then why would you break my rules? Why would you remove a dragon's fire muzzle?"

Her harsh words made me flinch back, but she closed her eyes again.

I leaned toward her. "He's a good dragon. He—"

"Deceived you." She motioned to her burned skin. "Before I use the smoke to heal it, I want you to see what he did to me. It took three of us to get him back into containment."

I gasped. "No."

"Yes. And James was nearly killed."

I covered my mouth as fresh tears rolled down my cheek.

Isabel shook her head. "I wanted you to know the danger you put us all in before this gets more out of hand. That dragon deceived you. That's what they do."

"I-I . . ." I stared at her bandages. "No." I breathed out through the word. "*Lo siento.* I-I never meant for that to happen. I'm sorry."

"Truly?"

"*Sí!* But I think if you give him a chance—"

"Enough!"

I stared back at her, stunned.

She stood, taking a deep breath. "Do you know why I brought this dragon here, Keira? He is the most dangerous deceiver known to hunters. He was born in a different hunter's facility—did he tell you that?"

"No." In fact, he'd told me he was born in the forest with his family. That he had siblings.

She started pacing. "Did he tell you that he got the other hunters to trust him? That they did? That they let him out, and he killed three of them?"

My heart slammed against my rib cage, and it ached. Everything inside of me ached. "I-I didn't see a lie," I whispered.

"You will tonight."

"What?"

She walked away. "Let me go take care of these burns. Then we will go question him together, and you will learn a thing or two about dragons."

"Question? You mean torture?"

Isabel whirled to face me, pausing in the doorway. "Is that what he told you?"

I swallowed.

"That is true. We do torture here. Because they are monsters and have information vital to the survival of humans. But he tried to kill you tonight, Keira. You!" She motioned to her arms. "Do you know what could have happened to you if I hadn't stepped in? You need to learn what these monsters really are. I can't wait so that your father trains you and Dane in his soft ways. I will train you myself. And it will start now." She marched into the other room, and I sat numb on the couch as silence swallowed me.

My dragon had tried to kill me?

I couldn't believe it.

And after I'd told him I planned to free him?

Something inside my chest crumbled. And I sobbed.

When Isabel returned later, healed, she brought me into the room beyond the cells. Boy was there, chained to a wall, fire muzzle back on. He looked at me with sad eyes. I wanted to cry all over again.

"You tried to kill me?" I whispered.

"No!"

"Lies already?" Isabel walked up to him with her knife. She drew a line across his scales.

He screamed. "No! I didn't!"

"You never lied to her?" She pushed the knife in, and I turned away, my stomach heaving.

"No!"

"Look at the red that pulses in his eyes." Isabel's voice called me out of my sadness.

Red? I stepped closer, the shock of betrayal igniting something deep inside of me. I wanted to cry. I wanted to scream. Tears rolled down my cheeks, and half of them were from loss, the other half from hatred. "You lied to me?"

Tears dripped down his scales.

"Answer her! Did you ever lie?" Isabel yelled.

"No!" Red flashed through his irises.

Red.

And something in my heart shattered.

I squeezed my eyes shut, trying to pull myself out of the depths of the memory, but I couldn't. I'd come too deep into it to walk away now. The darkest moment poured into my thoughts unbidden, and I was back in that room.

My voice turned deep, bold, hurt. "You betrayed me."

Isabel pressed the knife she'd been using to slice through his scales into my hand. Leaned close to me. Her cheek touching mine, she pointed to the bleeding gash in the dragon's chest. "That's right. Because all dragons are monsters. Now, make him pay. Like this."

I still felt the hilt, sticky with blood, in my hands as Isabel helped me drag it across the dragon's stomach.

"Long, slow strokes, Keira. Dragons don't feel pain like we do, so you have to make it last."

"What if I don't want to?" My voice trembled.

"Then we'll never get our answers. Do it."

I slashed his skin, and the dragon cried out despite the fire muzzle holding his jaws shut. Blood trickled over his green scales. Tears coursed down my cheeks. He'd betrayed me, but this still wasn't right. It didn't seem right. How could it be?

"Keep cutting until he's ready to tell you what we want to know." Isabel's steady hand covered mine. Tightened my fingers around the hilt. Pushed the knife deeper. "Pretend it's a game of tic-tac-toe." She drew a deep *x* with the knife. "Now, make him tell us how to kill his kind."

I looked into my dragon's wet, sad eyes. My only friend. How could he betray me? "Tell me what your poison is," I said in a choked whisper.

His eyes flickered gold—he was showing me his soul—and all I saw in him was fear and pain. How could that be a lie? Isabel was wrong. There had to be an explanation for all of this.

I dropped the knife. "I can't!"

"You can. And you will." She forced the hilt into my hand and pressed the blade deep into the dragon's flesh. I closed my eyes, but that didn't drown out his muffled screams as she made me draw the next letter.

I tried to let go.

Tried to make her stop.

Make her listen.

My two-way chirped, pulling me back to the present. I wiped tears off my cheeks and checked to see who was calling. Dane.

The tic-tac-toe tattooed on my right wrist peeked out at me from under my sleeve, and I pulled the material over it to hide it. That memory was forever seared into me. Making me who I was today. Reminding me of the price of befriending a monster.

I breathed deep to loosen the tightening in my throat and stood up. I didn't need Wally the border guardian coming home mid-conversation, so I went out the back door. The sky was blue and clear, with silhouetted mountains in the distance.

I headed down the thirteen wooden stairs, memorizing the creakiest ones. The misty air filtered through my jeans, and my boots crunched fallen leaves with every step. I settled at the base of a tree and tapped my two-way.

"Keira?" Dane sounded hurt.

I stood up fast, trying to recall where Ace had left his keys. "Are you okay?"

"Yeah. Where are you?"

I leaned back against the tree, relief coursing through me. "You don't sound okay."

"You sound like you've been crying. Are *you* okay?"

I swallowed as my throat started to tighten again. "I'm okay. I'm at an old lair."

"With that hunter?"

"Ace. Yeah. We just got here, so I don't have any news yet. Did you sort things out with Uncle Max?"

He groaned as if in pain, then let out a long breath. "Yeah. I told him we were on the trail of some misfits and not engaging yet."

"I hope you didn't sound like you were in as much pain as you do now."

"Nah. I sent him a message. He had a lot of questions, though."

"Are you sure you're okay?"

"My sister went off with a strange hunter, and I have no idea where she is because she hasn't turned on her tracker. No. I am not okay."

"Dane." I used my stern voice.

"I'm healing up, Keira. Thanks to you. But I really need to know where you are so I can sleep at night."

I considered telling him, but the way he sounded, I just needed him to be okay. "I think I'll leave the tracker off for now, in case Uncle Max gets some harebrained idea to come after me. I can't have him scaring off my leads like he did in Minnesota with the ice dragons."

"I hear you. But I'm getting antsy."

"You're the other reason for my secrecy. You have to get some rest. That wound was awful."

"In two days I'll be stir-crazy, pain or no."

"You'll have my location by then."

"I'd better."

"You will. I promise."

He paused. "Stay safe."

"You too." I put my two-way in my jeans pocket. A familiar flapping sound caused me to freeze. Ace had found me?

"It's not nice to play hide-and-seek," a deep, gravelly voice boomed.

Not Ace.

A shiver skittered over my skin. It was—oh crap—someone who thought *I* was Ace.

SIXTEEN

A growl shook the tree I was leaning against, and I clutched my dragon-claw knife. Smoke that smelled like scorched rock surrounded me.

"You are not whom I expected to see."

I whirled to face the beast. Its scales, all shades of gray, resembled the sharp, rocky features of a mountain's face. Its eyes—dark red, like blood—locked onto me, and a look of pleasure snaked across its face.

"Coming out alone in forest-dragon territory was stupid. But you smell of dragon." The largest dragon head I'd ever seen slithered toward me, bending smaller trees as it descended. Smoke poured out of its nostrils. "Why is that?"

I held up my knife.

"Puny weapon."

"It's made of dragon claw. It'll cut through you just fine."

Its pupils narrowed. "I've seen a knife like that before, with a hilt carved from dragon bone."

"Maybe my stepmother killed a monster you know. It was her weapon."

"You took it from her?"

"Isabel's dead. A dragon killed her. I don't have a lot of patience for your kind."

"You're a hunter?" It cocked its head, and its huge eye searched my face. If this dragon lied, the pulse through the iris would be black. I recalled this much from Isabel's journal. She had a whole section on mountain dragons—beasts most other hunters had never seen.

The dragon let out a heated breath. No flame, yet the air left condensation on my skin. I backed away a step, scanning for a tree to hide behind.

The red eyes tracked me. "Isabel deserves death for what she's done, but she lives."

My heart stalled. "She died."

"One of my horde saw her not three days ago."

No black pulsed around his pupil. I couldn't breathe. How could this be? "You know Isabel?"

"Every dragon around here knows of her. Don't play games, hunter. You must be aware of her anticipated appearance at the Feast of Fire. I imagine that's why you're here. But why you smell of the dragon who lives on this land, I am curious."

The feast? Was that the feast Ace had talked about? My heart thundered. I was right. He wanted me here for some strange reason. "Why will she be at this feast?"

The scent of coal fire drifted nearer. "Come closer, and I'll tell you."

I held up my dagger. "Smell honey? How close do you want me?"

The dragon lifted its head so its long neck towered above me. "I see you brought more than a sharp tongue."

"Tell me about Isabel."

It chuckled, a sound like rocks rolling down a hill, gaining speed. "Tell me why you smell like a dragon."

"It's the best way to move through here undetected. Why are you in a forest dragon's territory?"

"Which question matters more to you, tiny Isabel?" The dragon grinned, and a flash of teeth told me it was about to open its mouth. I rolled toward the nearest tree for cover as a spurt of flame rained down around me. My pulse sped. This was the longest flame spurt I'd ever witnessed!

Heat ripped through my sleeve, and I cursed under my breath as I batted my arm against the ground, putting out the flame. By the time I stood up, the dragon's face was in front of me again. It chuckled, dark and mysterious. "I can't have you attempting to free Isabel or any other hunters before the Feast of Fire."

My blood pumped cold through my veins. That's what this celebration was all about? Slaughtering hunters? I knew it. And that was exactly why Zelda and Wallace wanted me there. To kill me.

I had to find a way out of here. To warn Uncle Max and save Isabel. Ace said the Feast was four days from now. That wasn't enough time unless Dane had called in swarms of backup.

He hadn't.

That meant the backup we had coming didn't stand a chance unless I could figure out forest-dragon poison.

The dragon in front of me chuckled. "Young hunters are so clueless." It opened its mouth again, and flames shot out. I barely had time to duck behind the tree. Heat seared my clothes from all sides.

The the fire stopped sooner this time.

A snarl shook the ground, and I turned. A green dragon crouched low, back to me, facing the mountain dragon that was three times larger. It approached the gray beast, smoke pouring from its nostrils. "You're trespassing."

I knew that voice. Ace.

"You're harboring a hunter?" The mountain dragon's neck stretched upward. "The Council will not be pleased."

"Who said anything about harboring?"

"You intend to bring this creature to the Feast of Fire? As your prisoner?"

My heart hammered. I wanted to make a run for it. Maybe we could still defeat them without the forest-dragon poison. If there was a chance to save Isabel and stop the dragons, it was during this feast. I could get to Dane and tell him.

"This hunter—"

"Smells like a life debt. If you've thrown your lot in with their kind, the Council—"

"The Council will never know, since trespassing is punishable by death." Ace's voice took on a dark tone that made me shudder.

I knew enough about fighting dragons on their own territory. It made them stronger. More aggressive. Isabel's words rang clear in my mind: *If you threaten a dragon on its property, be ready to kill it. If you don't, it will kill you. All dragons are territorial in a way they can't control.*

"Not informing the Council of hunter sightings is also punishable by death." The mountain dragon lowered its head.

"Since when?"

"Since now. Well, it's cause enough for me to kill you."

Ace growled. "Are you threatening me on my property?"

A snarl reverberated in the mountain dragon's gullet, and its gaze locked onto me. The charred tree I stood behind was hardly shelter now. Its weight shifted, and I knew it was ready to pounce.

"Run, Keira." Ace lunged forward and pinned the mountain dragon to the ground.

I darted for cover, then turned. It was hard to make out everything with the trees obscuring my view, but the larger mountain dragon was clearly struggling as Ace pushed it to the ground on its back. I wanted to run, but the fact that Isabel had been so incredibly right kept me planted. Ace's strength seemed to surpass the other dragon's. He lowered his head and grabbed the mountain dragon's throat in his jaws. It whimpered.

Ace's teeth dug into the dragon's neck, and everything went quiet.

My heartbeat revved. I *had* to find the forest-dragon poison. But perhaps I wouldn't find it here. Maybe this was the most dangerous place for me to be. This . . . this monster was clearly hungry for death.

Blood, dark and wet, seeped out from the trees, running downhill. And the mountain dragon turned to ash.

The red pool remained.

Ace grew smaller, completely hidden behind the pines, and stepped out as a man.

I stood, frozen. I'd never seen a dragon kill another dragon.

"Let's get home." He walked past me.

I stared at his back. "You have more in common with hunters than you think."

Ace kept going. "I killed him because he was on my property. And he threatened me."

"Dragons are more brutal than I realized."

He shot a glare over his shoulder. "He was going to tell the Council I'm harboring a hunter. It could have started a war."

I followed after him. "Why? Does your horde value hunters?"

He snarled, and the sound was incredibly dragon-like.

"Are you teaming up with them? I mean, you brought me here. What do you want with the hunters?"

"I want them to stop hunting dragons."

I had to jog to catch up with him, and he quickened his pace. "So we should just leave the dragon-killing to the dragons?"

"You have no idea what the other dragons would do to you."

"Bring me to the Feast of Fire like they're doing with Isabel? Is that why you want me to come? So you can have a hunter of your own? Will I be a bargaining chip, or is there some special torture session I should be getting prepared for? Or maybe it's a group burning-at-the-stake? Is that it?"

That got him to stop walking, but he didn't face me.

"I know about Isabel. The prized hunter who will be at your Feast. You must have heard of her. And let me tell you something, dragon. If you so much as bring me anywhere *near* that feast of yours, be prepared for me to try and rescue her."

His shoulders heaved in a very slow, controlled breath. "You have no idea what kind of monster she is."

I knew exactly what kind of monster she was. And I was about to find out how much of a ruse this life debt truly was. I caught up to him, grabbed his collar, and pulled.

"She's my stepmom." I placed my knife against his side, between his ribs. Old hatred spurred my actions now, and I embraced it. My blade pierced clothes and ripped into skin. "I might not be able to kill you, but one more inch and I hit your lungs. That'll take your fire long enough for me to run before you heal. Now, I thought Isabel was dead, so you're going to tell me everything you know about her."

Ace said nothing. He just stared at me, a look of pain contorting his features. Almost as though he was trying really hard not to fight back. "D-don't . . . threaten me, Keira."

"Or what?" I pushed the knife in further. I wanted to kill him. Make him pay. My pulse pounded. If the life debt truly prevented me from taking his life, this was a death wish, and I'd jumped in headfirst.

A splitting pain shot through my skull and blurred my vision. I cried out, my own screams echoing in my head. My lungs started to contract, but I needed air. Couldn't get any. I doubled over. A sense of free-falling overtook me, and I landed on my back in the dirt.

Finally, I could take a breath. Something strong pushed against my shoulders, anchoring me to the ground.

Ace's face filled my vision, morphing, changing into a dragon's. White fangs protruded from a long, rough muzzle. A growl so loud it shook my chest ratcheted through my body. Heat encompassed me. I trembled. My heart couldn't beat fast enough. My lungs—I couldn't breathe. A sob clogged my throat. I was staring *muerte* in the eyes.

"Don't ever threaten me on my property again." His voice shook me—a quiet growl that sent a shudder through my body. And I stared at his irises. No red. No lie. He was dead serious.

Was he going to kill me now?

Slowly, the snarl faded, and he morphed back into a man, let me go, and stood up. His hands shook as he walked away.

I lay on the ground and clutched my knife tighter. Blood wet the blade.

Ace's. I'd stabbed him. My chest squeezed tight, and I tried to calm my breathing.

I'd signed my own death sentence.

And yet, he hadn't killed me.

Still shaking, I sat up, replaying the whole thing on a loop. His face morphing into a monster's. His fangs. The heat on my skin. *El muerte.* I'd thought I was about to die.

Isabel had said they couldn't control it.

I glanced up to see Ace striding back to the cabin. His hands still shaking. Blood staining the side of his shirt. I breathed in. I was lucky to be alive.

My body started quaking, and I pressed my hands against my head and let myself sob.

It was almost as if his instinct had taken over and he'd fought it off.

Why?

What did he need me for?

SEVENTEEN

I stared at my boots, finally composing myself enough to think through the situation. If Ace needed me for something at this Feast of Fire, I should probably stay away. But defeating the forest dragons forever was almost in my grasp.

I had two choices. I could try and make Ace trust me—and play the biggest con of my life—or I could abandon this and convince the other hunters to come in and save Isabel.

Right now, I was Isabel's best chance of rescue.

But I was also our best chance of completing her work so we could make the all-serum.

A series of unfortunate events had given me this once-in-a-lifetime opportunity to what we needed. Or I could very easily die here if Ace took me to the Feast as his prisoner.

Which meant I'd have to change plans and agree to go as his date.

I shuddered as a shiver raced through me. A dragon's date. That was against everything I stood for. And Ace would know that too. Which meant I had to make this "change of heart" convincing.

As soon as I heard the distant sound of the cabin door slamming, I stood up, dusted the dirt off of my pants, and made a break for it.

If he was telling the truth about this life debt enabling him to track me, he'd hunt me down, no problem. I'd head back, kicking and screaming. He'd already made me dinner and breakfast and tried to play nice to me, so as long as I could get him to show me one more act of kindness, I could pretend his little plan was working on me.

I raced through the woods, toward the mountains, which I assumed was the enemy's territory. He didn't even shout at me to stop. Twigs scratched my face and pulled at my clothes. Still, I saw nothing in the sky. No ugly shadow. No hideous beast following me.

Did he not care that his little prize was gone?

Did he think I'd come back on my own?

At that thought, a harsh laugh huffed out of my chest, and I ran faster. He'd clearly underestimated my stubbornness.

I ran and hiked and picked brambles off my clothes for what seemed like hours. Maybe he'd lied. Maybe he couldn't track me at all. I tossed another stupid burr to the ground.

"You know your base is the other way?"

I whirled around and found Ace leaning against a tree, hair wet. He smelled like the amazing, clean scent of a bathroom right after a shower. He'd changed, too, but he still wore that black leather jacket.

I put my hands on my hips, not even wanting to think about the state of my hair right now. "Maybe I wanted to throw you for a loop."

He smirked, all cocky and annoying. "I told you I'd be able to find you."

I curled my fingers into a fist, but at the all-too-fresh memory of not being able to stab him, I let out a frustrated growl instead. "So you thought you'd let me run through the woods for hours so you could prove a point?"

His smirk turned into a pleased grin. "Sounds about right."

In frustration, I spun in a tight circle and ended facing him again. Unable to control my anger—at myself for falling for his taunting—I pointed my finger into his muscular chest. "That was . . . very unnecessary."

Oh great. I'd apparently lost my wit while out here proving *my* point.

He looked down at my finger and then tipped his head as he took in my expression with obvious delight. "Don't blame me for your *unnecessary* exercise. You took off. I had a wound to take care of." He touched his side, right where I'd stabbed him.

I backed away, the reminder sending a pang I didn't expect through my heart. I had used my dragon-claw blade, but it had to be half-healed by now. "Well, I hope you didn't expect an apology."

His green eyes dulled for the slightest moment. "From a hunter? Of course not." He pushed off the tree, striding closer to me. "I decided to have lunch, work out, shower." He jerked his thumb over his shoulder. "I left the house ten minutes ago."

Heat boiled in my blood. It couldn't be that easy to track me.

He shrugged, still sporting that pleased-with-himself grin. "Care for a lift back?"

I opened my mouth to retort, but thankfully I stopped myself. First of all, I could still work this whole thing to my planned advantage and make him feel like I was warming up to him. I breathed deeply and bowed my head while I regained my composure. Then I looked up, with a sparkle in my eyes that would dazzle him—hopefully.

The momentary dilating of his pupils told me I was about to show him my con game rivaled his.

I sighed. "Look, I took off. *Lo siento.* It's not like this situation is ideal for either of us. I just—I had to try. You know?"

He stared at me for a heartbeat. "I do." He motioned over his shoulder. "Come on. Let's get you back. And I promise to be more hospitable." He paused. "I don't want you to feel like a prisoner."

"Well, I am one." I hardened my gaze. Then I closed my eyes with what I hoped to be a good show of emotion. "But I haven't really been fair to you." I held out my hand. "To a fresh start?"

His eyebrows rose, and he opened his mouth. Then that suave smile took over, and he took my hand—not in a handshake. He turned it slightly and leaned over to kiss the back.

"Milady." He looked up at me and started to rise, keeping hold of my hand. "I can say with the utmost sincerity that I do hope you will be willing to see the real me."

"Charmed." I snatched my hand back, the tingle from his skin against mine still pulsing warmth into my blood. "I hope you don't expect me to be impressed."

He smiled again, that crooked slant of his lips trying to eat away at my cold heart. "I did come all this way to rescue you."

I planted my fists on my hips. "First of all, I am no damsel in distress. I got myself into this mess, and I will rescue *myself* from the dragon. No prince needed." I looked him over as if scrutinizing art. "And you're no Prince Charming."

"That I am not." He actually waggled his eyebrows. "But I *am* pretty irresistible. Don't be surprised if you're not only impressed but also a mite addicted."

I laughed bitterly. Oh, this was good. If I could get him to fall for me, that would be even better. He'd have no choice but to let me go. I gave him a coy smile. "Not gonna happen. But I'll start with giving you a chance."

At least my eyes didn't pulse red when I lied.

"That's all I ask. Now, would you like a ride back?"

I had him hooked now. Time to reel him in. "I'd love one. *Gracias.*"

The wind picked up, and a huge shadow covered us as a green dragon descended. I noticed the crescent-shaped hole in his wing. Bran.

Ace shrugged. "Good. I asked Bran to give you a lift back to the cabin while I check the perimeter again."

"Bran?"

Ace winked. "He won't hurt you." He looked at Bran. "He gave me his word."

I scowled up at Bran. His huge claws wrapped around me, and he didn't seem to care about jostling me as he scooped me up.

I pounded my fist against his claws as he took me up, soaring above the trees. "Let me go!"

"You sure?"

"No," I grumbled.

He laughed.

I trailed my finger over his claw. My knife was made from this substance, but it was sharp to the touch. His claws weren't.

"They're covered in an invisible casing. If I didn't do that, they'd rip right through you and your designer blouse."

That was actually pretty cool. I shook my head. "Yeah? And why haven't you just killed me?"

"Don't tempt me, hunter." A growl rumbled in Bran's chest and sent a shiver through me.

"Whoa. Someone got up on the wrong side of the—"

Bran let me go, and I plummeted to the porch. I rolled toward the cabin but was able to stop myself before I slammed into the outer wall. "Hey! You gave your word not to hurt me!"

He landed on the deck beside me as a man, a glare heating his eyes. "You stabbed my brother. You deserved that." He walked past me and opened the door.

I got up and dusted myself off, ignoring the stinging scrape on my elbow. Then I followed him inside. "Your brother is keeping me prisoner here."

Bran whirled around and got in my face as the back door slammed behind me. "To protect you!" He turned away and walked farther into the kitchen. "Not that you're worth it. I honestly don't know what Wally sees in you."

Sees in me? I stopped at the counter, staring at Bran's back and trying to make sense of that comment. "What do you mean?"

Bran breathed deep and met my gaze. "You're a hunter. There's nothing to see. But my brother seems to think you're different."

My pulse sped. "Why?"

"Because he's an idiot."

I fingered the design on the apple bowl as I tried to piece everything together, heart pounding. "He wants me for the Feast of Fire."

"Yeah." Bran laughed. "He thinks you're the key to breaking his curse." His eyes filmed with what looked like tears, but he smacked the counter with his palm and brushed past me toward the back door. "I'm going to help him on the perimeter check."

"Wait. What curse?"

Bran faced me and swallowed. "You'd have to ask him about that."

"Let me come with you?"

"No way."

Something wasn't right. "Why would you help him with the perimeter? Is there something going on?"

Bran paused, opening the back door, enough hatred in his expression to cause me to back away. "You stabbed him."

"You heal fast. Don't act like I know nothing about dragons." The pleading in my voice was unintended.

His eyes narrowed. "The curse I was talking about? He can't heal as well now." Bran flinched toward me as if he might grab me around the neck, but he stopped, bowed his head, and dropped his hand to his side. "Just listen to what he has to say, please?"

Blood coursed through me twice as fast, and my heartbeat echoed in my ears. There was something going on here, and I didn't have the whole picture. "About the Feast of Fire?"

"Yeah."

"He asked me to go with him."

Bran looked up at me with what seemed to be hope in his eyes. "And?"

My throat bobbed. "I'm considering."

Slowly, Bran's eyes widened. "Really?"

What on earth was I getting myself into?

EIGHTEEN

I was just about to ask more about this Feast of Fire when a gunshot pierced the silence. My heart jolted, and I stared wide-eyed at the open back door.

Bran glanced at me, his eyebrows pulling together. "Stay here." He ran, jumped off the deck, morphed, and took flight.

Two more shots echoed through the trees. I clutched my jacket closed as I stood on the deck, scanning the darkening sky. Hopefully whoever was wielding that gun didn't hunt dragons by scent. As I waited, orange and magenta descended closer to the horizon. A pang stabbed my heart. Had Ace been killed?

If he was dead, would Bran come and find me?

Did I have time to leave?

At a *thump* on the deck behind me, I grabbed my knife and turned. Ace stood in human form, visible in the lights from the house. His dark hair looked windblown, and he was holding something furry.

"Keira, can you turn on the porch light, please?" He sounded breathless.

I sheathed my knife, raced to the door, and found the light switch on the kitchen wall. I crept back outside to inspect what Ace had laid on the deck. It looked like a coyote with red-stained fur.

I inched closer, a sick feeling in my stomach. "Dinner?"

The coyote growled.

Ace stroked its head, and a soft look filled his eyes. "She won't hurt you. She only hunts dragons."

"Sometimes deer." I knelt down, keeping far enough from the canine's jaws. A huge gash on its stomach oozed blood. I pressed my hand against my mouth. "Someone shot it?"

"Her. Someone shot her." He motioned to the cabin. "There's a basket of medical supplies in the downstairs bathroom. Would you—"

"I got it." I raced inside and returned with the medical supplies and water. I set everything near Ace. "What can I do?"

High-pitched whimpers stopped me, and I turned to see three pups ascending the stairs. My heart melted. "Oh."

"Bran just dropped them off," Ace said. He smiled slightly. "Would you mind keeping an eye on them while I tend to their mother?" His green eyes met mine, and I sensed the concern deep within them.

I stared at him as if he'd asked me the strangest question in the world. In reality, he sort of had. Since when did dragons care about anything? This whole thing was surreal.

"Keira?"

I shook away my state of surprise the best I could and glanced down. The three pups approached me, sniffing shyly at my boots. I reached to touch one, but the mom growled. I looked into her eyes, noticing for the first time how much intelligence, emotion, she held in them. "I won't hurt them."

"She's a friend," Ace said. The coyote grumbled, and Ace chuckled. "No, she wasn't kidding about the deer."

I couldn't help but smile. "You can talk to them?"

He glanced at me and smiled sadly. "That's part of what a forest dragon does. I care for this forest here. All the animals, the trees. They're my responsibility."

One of the pups nuzzled its little, fuzzy head into my palm.

The mother whimpered as Ace pressed a wet cloth to her wound.

"Sorry, girl." Ace winced. Red coated his hands.

Three warm pups pushed up against me, shaking. Poor things. I sat down, and they piled into my lap. All of them faced their mother, their tiny bodies quivering. Ace glanced at them, and compassion filled his expression. "I'll do everything I can. Okay?"

My heart squeezed, and I trailed my finger over one of the pup's soft fur. He sighed. My emotions grew stronger, like a constrictor on my heart. That small gesture—my touch—had helped comfort the pup that much? Slowly, softly, I began to pet them. Their fluffy bodies stopped trembling and, one by one, they fell asleep in my lap.

I watched their little sides rise and fall in tiny breaths.

"Thank you," Ace whispered.

I glanced up, about to protest that I hadn't done anything, but he was too focused on helping the mother. The crease between his eyebrows started to fade away, and he pulled out a bullet, holding it up so I could see. The relief in his eyes was evident. "Got it."

The pups stirred in my lap. One of them whimpered.

That tugged my heartstrings, and I hugged them close, nearly choking on the emotion in my throat. "Looks like your mom's going to be okay." One of them licked my cheek. That made me smile.

The four of us watched while Ace stitched up their mother. His hands moved confidently, steadily, as he deftly sewed her wound. He spoke softly to her. Reassured her. Touched her soft head as she closed her eyes.

"All right, girl." He finally put down the supplies. "What you need now is rest. You can stay in my shed until you're feeling better."

All I could do was stare openmouthed at this—this dragon who had a gentle side. A caring side. How was it possible?

Her pink tongue touched his hand.

"I'm just glad I found you in time." Ace glanced at me and sighed, looking, for the moment, like he'd found the support he needed. "Do you think you could grab a blanket from the supply closet under the stairs?"

"Of course." I extricated myself from the nest of sleeping pups, and they woke, making their way over to their mother while Ace instructed them to be gentle. When I returned with the blanket, Ace took it from me.

"Thank you." The sincerity in his expression made me freeze. He scooped up the mother coyote and carried her down the deck steps while I thawed from my momentary surprise. The pups followed them. I stood on the porch, hugging myself.

Did all forest dragons care this much for the animals in their territory?

As he ascended the steps on his return, his gaze caught mine. Heat flushed my face. A smirk tugged at his lips, and I turned away and bent to pick up the supplies.

He helped me, and his hand brushed mine. "You did great."

I recoiled. "I didn't do anything."

His green gaze bored deep. "You made her pups feel safe. That meant a lot to her." He grinned. "If you don't mind cleaning that up, I'll warm up some milk for the pups."

"Of course." My airy voice followed him as he headed into the house. I watched him through the window.

It was dark now, so I could easily see him standing beside the stove and pouring milk into a pot. The way he rubbed the back of his neck and bowed his head spoke of someone who had nearly lost something—someone—they genuinely cared about.

How could someone so terrifying have such a soft side?

I took the supplies inside and put them away. Then I joined him in the kitchen and started washing the tools he'd used to stitch up the patient.

He glanced over at me, and his face softened. "You don't have to do that."

"I know." I couldn't face him right now. Not while everything I'd learned about dragons seemed to be spinning through my mind, trying to connect somehow with what I'd witnessed of dragons. At least of this dragon.

How did it fit together? My throat ached, and my hands started to shake. I held them under running water. None of this made sense. I thought of the old woman he'd given the doughnuts to. This couldn't be normal. He had to be different.

Ace sighed.

I glanced over my shoulder again. "You okay?"

"Yeah." He poured the milk into a huge bowl, but the look on his face wasn't very convincing. I cocked an eyebrow, and he opened his mouth. Paused. "It's just . . . that was close. I'm really glad you were here for those pups." He smiled sadly and held up the warm milk. "But, so far, it's worked out. Now we need to make sure she pulls through."

We. That word made me pause. I shook away the strange feeling that I was part of this. "Just another day at the office, huh?"

He sort of laughed as he headed outside. "Yeah."

And I watched him as long as I could while hot water reddened my skin and Isabel's sixth commandment echoed in my mind: *A dragon doesn't care for anything but itself; don't let perceived acts of kindness fool you. They are incapable of real compassion.*

But . . . what if she was wrong?

NINETEEN

Morning light spilled through the windows. I rubbed my eyes. The guest bed had been much more comfortable than expected. I barely remembered Ace nudging me awake on the couch, telling me it was time to turn in.

What a day.

Thoughts of that poor coyote made me want to throw on my clothes and head out to check on how she was doing. But the aroma of bacon brought me to a seated position. My stomach grumbled, and I realized I'd forgotten dinner last night.

I headed down the stairs, knife in hand. Then I stopped and looked at the weapon. After everything that had happened, everything I was trying to make him believe, did I really need to be walking around holding my weapon? Slowly, I put it away and entered the kitchen.

Ace stood at the stove, wearing a T-shirt and jeans, cooking bacon and pancakes. "Morning, sleeping beauty." He held up a spatula topped with a pancake and donned that charming smile. "Hungry?"

Was he serious?

"Relax, I'm not going to poison you." He put a short stack on a plate next to a pile of bacon and handed the dish to me.

I took the plate and sat at the table, still trying to understand what kind of game he was playing–if he was playing one. If I'd gotten a glimpse of the real Ace. "I guess if I'm going to be in prison, I should make the most of it."

"That's the spirit."

He stacked the last of the pancakes on a plate, set them in the middle of the table, and joined me.

I cut through the fluffy pancakes and took a tentative bite.

Best. Pancakes. Ever.

Was that cinnamon? Oh my word. I would not let him see that I was enjoying these.

He smirked behind his glass of orange juice.

Apparently I'd failed. "What?"

"Nothing." He shoved food into his mouth.

"How's the coyote?"

His smile turned genuine. "Better. She's still on the mend, but she should pull through."

He resumed eating, and an awkward silence hung between us. I tried to place the source. Maybe because I was having breakfast with the enemy. Maybe because–

He glanced at me out of the corner of his eye and sort of winced. "I wanted to apologize for yesterday."

I stopped, bite of pancake midway to my mouth. "Which part?"

He granted me a knowing grin. Then his expression turned serious again. "Threatening you."

The image of his face, inches from mine, morphing into a dragon, the memory of his fire-hot breath and fangs, rushed through me. I lowered my fork as I stared at him, mouth open. He'd done that because I'd *stabbed* him.

My voice came out softer than intended. "I shouldn't have threatened you in your territory. Every hunter knows it's a death wish. And, I'm sorry I hurt you."

His smile was rueful. "Every hunter also knows dragons are good for a bargain."

As I tried to conceal my shock, I swallowed my food and searched his face, trying to read him. "I'm listening."

He popped a bite of pancake into his mouth and chewed while I waited for him to continue. "I'll answer three questions."

My heart pounded. This was it. This was my moment. I was about to win. "What do I give you in return?"

He pointed at me with an empty fork. "You let me teach you to dance."

A giggle wanted to burst forth from me. That was it? No way.

There had to be something else behind this. Something more. He wouldn't give me that much for so little unless it meant something more to him. It was a trap.

I settled back in my chair and crossed my arms. "I know how to dance."

"Formal dancing."

"As in, ballroom?"

He nodded with that cocky smile that I was really starting to hate that I liked.

I took another bite of breakfast. "You're making me go to this Feast of Fire?"

"If word gets out that I'm harboring a hunter, you won't be safe here alone."

Sarcastic laughter escaped me before I could stop it. "And you care because?"

He narrowed his eyes, and all the friendliness vanished. "You're on my property. That means you're in my care."

Of course. I was under his care like the other forest creatures. As soon as I was free, I'd be hunted. And on my own.

"Do we have a deal, hunter?"

I nodded. "We have a deal, *el cucuy*."

He flinched, and I felt a pang of regret. He cleared his throat, recovering quickly. "Good. You'll have to let me know when the time for asking your three questions begins. That will be up to you, but once it begins, you must ask all three. So choose your words carefully."

"I always do."

He left the table to bring more warm milk out to the coyotes. When he returned, I decided to help him clear the breakfast dishes and clean up the kitchen.

I dried the last plate and hung the towel over the handle on the oven door. "So, now what?"

He glanced over his shoulder and smiled. "I'm going to fly the perimeter."

"It's like OCD with you and your perimeter flying."

He chuckled. "It's my job."

"Who was doing it while you were off in misfit land?"

"My horde pitched in. Mostly Bran." He shrugged into his leather jacket and headed for the back door.

"I want to come." My words stopped him.

He glanced over his shoulder, and a hint of a smile spread his lips. "Really?"

"Yes."

He seemed to think about it for a moment, his eyes searching my face. "Are you going to do as I say?"

"Is that a stipulation?"

"Yes. And you'll have to trust me."

Now that was a bit stickier. I tapped my finger against my lip. Learning as much as I could about forest dragons was advantageous to my hunting them later. And I had to make him think he was earning my trust. I could pretend. "Trust?"

"As soon as I leave here, count to five, then walk to the edge of the deck and jump off."

"Is this some kind of dragon trust exercise?"

His pleased smirk was more of a challenge than anything. He opened the door and walked out. "Leave the cleats."

One.

My adrenaline started pumping as I looked down at my hunting boots.

Two.

He better catch me. He would. Why go through all the trouble of protecting me if he was just going to let me dive off the edge of a cliff?

Three.

Who was I kidding? I wanted this. The thrill of jumping on a dragon's back?

Four.

I walked out into the crisp morning. Leaves rustled against one another, sending a soft *hush, hush* sound through the air.

Five.

I strode to the end of the porch and jumped off.

His body snaked beneath me, spikes retracted, and I landed on his back. His scarred back. I gripped one of the flattened spikes, and he glanced over his shoulder and smirked. Strange. Even under the dragon scales, he still looked like Ace.

"I wasn't sure you'd come." His voice rumbled through me when he spoke, his chuckle vibrating my bones. So strangely different from the deep, threatening voices I was used to hearing from dragons.

"I don't back down from challenges."

The wind kissed my face, fresh and clear and full of morning mist. It smelled like sunshine and rain together. Pale yellow bathed the mountaintops. "This is fantastic. It's like riding a motorcycle."

"A motorcycle's got nothing on flying. Hang on."

My stomach dropped, and for a moment, I felt weightless. Then we plummeted toward the trees. My stomach jumped up to my chest, squeezing my heart for dear life. It was thrilling and scary and amazing. I hung on tight as Ace swirled through the air, effortlessly.

"Can your bike do that?"

"No. This is better." I bit my lip and waited for a response. I wasn't supposed to admit that I liked flying.

Ace didn't say anything, but I imagined he was up there smirking.

"So this is why you fly the perimeter, huh? To get away from the prisoner in your home?"

His wing beats changed. Instead of the glide-and-flap rhythm I was getting used to, one wing beat harder, changing our direction. I grabbed hold of his neck as we coasted lower, closer to the trees. "What's wrong?"

"This is why I check the perimeter." He took us smoothly between trees and to the ground.

It made sense to me now why forest dragons were smaller and more slender than other subspecies. He landed, and I slid off him. He morphed into a man, his back to me, as if blocking me from something.

"Remember, you promised to obey. No sudden movements."

I stood perfectly still, trying to peer over his shoulder.

He walked a few steps away from me, and a frantic rustling in the brush caught my attention.

"It's okay." His voice was soothing, like it had been with the coyote. This was no coyote, though—it was a wide-eyed, skittish deer. And it looked trapped. I saw then that a snare had hold of its hind leg and had left a raw, red cut beneath the sharp wire.

Ace walked right up to the animal and untangled the snare while I stood frozen in place except for my pounding heart. Instead of bolting, the deer stood there. Poor thing had to be too scared to move. It nuzzled into Ace, and my jaw dropped.

"You're welcome," Ace said. Then the deer saw me and snorted.

Ace chuckled. "Yeah, she's a hunter, but don't worry. I've told her to leave you alone." He paused, listening. "I'm keeping her fed. She seems to like bacon and pancakes." His deep laugh didn't frighten the deer. "No, I don't suppose you do."

With that, the animal bounded into the woods. Ace yanked the snare from the dirt and faced me. "Ready."

"You free deer?"

"They are in my care."

"It trusted you."

"Yes. *She* has no reason not to."

Ace turned his back to me and hunched over. Before I could ask what he was doing, he morphed into a dragon again. "Climb aboard."

I did, cleats retracted into the soles of my shoes. It made the climbing a bit trickier, but he had asked me to leave them, and I was starting to think that maybe dragons could feel pain more than Isabel had thought.

"So, what else do you like? Besides bacon and pancakes," he asked as his massive wings lifted us from the ground.

"Haha. Trying to win me over with your cooking?"

"I might as well. As you may have noticed, I'm rather good at it."

"Not until you can make arroz con gandules, you're not."

"Arroz con . . . what is that?"

I breathed in, for a moment smelling my mother's kitchen. Hearing her spunky music. Feeling her grab my hands and twirl me around the linoleum floor only to stop and taste whatever she was making on the stove. She'd tell me to close my eyes and open my mouth. I could almost feel the warm wooden spoon against my lips. Taste the amazing food. I'd open my mouth and exclaim, *Me gusta, me gusta! Es muy bueno!* Her eyes, her sparkling eyes, would light up.

Pulling from the warmth of my memory, I said to Ace, "It's my favorite." My voice came out dreamier and more distant than I'd expected. "It's not good arroz con gandules unless the *pegao* on the bottom is crispy perfection." My father had never mastered it. Neither had I. Not yet.

"Maybe you should show me how, then."

I breathed in sharply. Just the thought of trying to make her dish again brought back a pang. "Maybe."

Silence took over.

As he flew, I studied one of the huge scars on his back. Trailed my finger over it. "What's this from?"

"What?"

"This scar?"

He was quiet for a while.

I wondered if he'd even heard me.

"I don't know. Maybe some fight with a mountain dragon or a misfit."

"You don't know?"

"It's not my only scar, Keira."

Right.

As soon as we landed on the porch, he let me slide off his back, then changed into his human form. So unlike the other dragons, even those I'd met here. Maybe he didn't like being one.

Or maybe he just didn't like being one around *me*. Perhaps that was all part of his plan to make me start to like him. To see him as more human. To keep me from facing him as the monster he was.

He went inside, and I followed him. The warm smell of hazelnut blasted my senses, and I noticed a full pot of coffee. "When did you put that on?"

He chuckled. "Morning routine. Perimeter check, then coffee. Want some?"

"Please."

"Cream? Sugar?"

"Both."

He handed me a full mug that smelled amazing and pushed the cream and sugar toward me. Then he leaned back against the counter, crossing one ankle over the other. "So, that's what a forest dragon does. We're not here to terrorize people and kill them."

I leaned against the opposite counter, across the room from him. "Unless they're hunters."

He stared at me for a beat, his eyes narrowing. "Have you ever stopped to think that maybe the reason dragons hate hunters so much is that we're being *hunted* by them?"

"Of course I have. But it's not the hunters who started it, Ace. Dragons were around long before."

"That's right. We peacefully lived among people, Keira." He straightened his back and punctuated his words with a chopping motion.

"Peacefully. In secret. Until some dragon fell for a human, and she found out and betrayed him."

"Is that the sob story you're going with? Towns feel safer with hunters."

Ace crossed his arms and set down his mug. "We have our purpose, but we're being hunted. And many of us for no reason."

"No." I couldn't believe what I was hearing, and my voice rose in volume. "Maybe because of your *violence*. You kill people for no reason."

"Some do, yes." Ace's voice remained steady. "So do serial killers. Does that mean we should wipe out all humans because of a few bad eggs?"

Why was he making sense? Why did he look like the one being attacked? I shook my head. He was trying to poison my thoughts. "Dragons are not humans."

The growl in his throat told me I was getting his hot button good. "Close enough."

And there it was. The temper. "How can you be with no humanity?"

"No . . . ?" His eyebrows pulled together, and he stared at me as if I'd gone crazy. "Do you really believe that? Or are these just lies other hunters are telling you? When are you going to learn to think for yourself?"

"For myself?" My blood was practically boiling now. What did he know? I was thinking for myself, wasn't I?

I swallowed, thinking of all the things he'd done in the short time I'd known him. Then I remembered all the dragons I'd stopped from killing innocent people.

"I've seen it, Ace."

"Right—this one dragon you trusted who betrayed you. I'm sorry that happened to you—I really am—but it shouldn't mean a death sentence for all dragons." He pointed his finger at me. "*That's* a lack of humanity."

"You're accusing *me* of having no humanity?" I slammed my finger into my chest. "I protect people. That's my job."

He scoffed. "Can you seriously stand there and say that I have no humanity? Even after what you've seen these past few days?"

I blinked. Everything Isabel had told me came crashing in. Alongside everything Ace had done. Two opposites battling one another, and I couldn't process it. I shut my eyes and shook my head, trying to figure out what I believed. Then I stared at Ace, hugged my middle, and brought the warm mug close to my chest to hide that my lungs hurt.

Only one thing was certain now: I wasn't sure what was true anymore.

He moved to my side of the kitchen, and I jumped, snapping to a defensive stance. The mug went crashing to the ground.

He put his hands up, backing away. "I'm sorry. I didn't mean to make you jumpy. I shouldn't have done that."

"Done what?" My words came out shaky as I stepped away from him, trying to calm my pounding pulse.

"You're a hunter, I'm a dragon. Dragons make hunters jumpy, and vice versa. I should have known you'd react." He crouched down and picked up the pieces of the mug. I grabbed a paper towel and helped mop up the coffee. A piece of glass hidden under the edge of the cabinet sliced my finger, and red blood mingled with the liquid.

I sat back, staring.

Thinking.

Shivering.

Truth. Lies. All mixed up together.

I didn't know what to believe. Who to believe. It seemed like everyone told lies among their truths, mingling the two like cream in coffee. Like blood in water. Once a drop infiltrated it, the whole cup was contaminated. If someone lied to me, did that mean I couldn't trust anything they said? Or would I have to accept a little blood in the water?

"You're bleeding." He touched my hand, and compassion filled his eyes. "Sit down."

He handed me a paper towel. Then he tossed the mess into a brown paper bag and threw it into the trash.

I sat at the table numbly, holding my bleeding hand, trying and failing to make sense of everything. Watching the red overtake the paper towel he'd given me. Blood in the water. Lies in the truth.

Something had to give.

It was going to have to be me. Ace was right. I was going to have to think for myself.

He crouched near me again and set his first aid kit on the floor. "Isn't it clotting yet?" He pressed the paper towel against my finger and lifted it. New blood welled up. He winced. "That's a pretty deep cut."

I didn't say anything. Just watched him take care of my hand like he'd taken care of that coyote. The deer. I was another subject in his care. I didn't even know what to feel anymore.

I looked up at him. At his worried expression as he tried to close my cut. "If I leave the forest—after the debt is paid, I mean—will you still care for me? Or will you no longer be obligated?"

He stared at me for a beat, then resumed putting Steri-Strips on my finger. He swallowed a few times. "It'll all depend, Keira. If you go back to fighting me, I'll have to defend myself. But I truly hope you'll come to understand what kind of person I really am. I hope you'll see that I'm not your enemy unless you want me to be."

My throat tightened. "So we could remain friends?"

He looked at me with those soft eyes and smiled. "I think so."

A hot tingle shot through my skin. How? I'd have to rethink . . . everything. "But you're a dragon, and I'm a hunter. How would that even work?" My voice trembled.

One corner of his mouth darted up. "You could stop killing dragons just because they're dragons."

That went against everything I'd ever been taught. It took me back to that moment in the basement, sitting outside a dragon's cage and laughing at his jokes. Listening to him tell me that we could be friends. That we *were* friends. That we weren't so different. I'd believed him.

And he'd killed my dad.

I'd seen him dead on the floor.

In a puddle of blood.

Dragon-claw marks marring his skin.

No. This wasn't right. This had to be a lie too. Just like before. I was being played again. As much as I tried to force myself to believe those words, part of me wouldn't.

Tears threatened. I couldn't let him see me lose it.

"*Gracias.*" I pulled my hand back and stood.

"Where are you going?"

"I need air."

More than that. Ace was right. It was time to figure out for myself what I truly believed.

TWENTY

During lunch, I barely said a word except to tell Ace that he was an excellent cook. He hardly responded but did manage a small laugh. Then he'd asked if I was okay. I . . . didn't have an answer for that. Because I didn't know.

He just kept staring at me, waiting for me to answer his question.

And I kept avoiding.

I was starting to want to trust a dragon again, and that was a new form of agony. Trying to make myself hate him when I didn't.

Finally he took his plate to the sink. "Remember our agreement? Dancing lessons on the deck in an hour. How about I answer your questions then?" He walked out of view.

"Looks cold out there."

He leaned out far enough that I could see his head and that alluring smirk of his. "Dragons are pretty good at keeping others warm, you know."

"No, thanks. Have a coat I could borrow?"

He shrugged. "Don't really have a need for anything more than a jacket." Then he ducked out of view again.

I called after him, "Maybe I'll make some tea. Have a favorite mug I could break?"

He popped around the corner again, wearing his leather jacket, and headed for the back door. "I don't have tea."

"Yes, you do. Up there." I motioned to the shelf that held all the dragon poisons.

Ace opened the cupboard door and tilted his head. "None of this is mine."

"That shelf is loaded with honey, cayenne pepper, sea salt—all poisons for other dragon subspecies. If it's not yours, whose is it?"

His gaze locked onto me, serious and intense. "Is that one of your three questions?"

I sat up straighter, pulse quickening. "Yes."

He nodded slowly. "My parents once thought this a fitting place to keep a certain prisoner named Isabel. It's one of the reasons there's so much contention between us and the mountain dragons. They don't trust us, because we put a hunter here for safekeeping. We didn't kill her. Now we're doing it again. That's why you're in so much danger now."

Air rushed out of my lungs. A thousand tangled thoughts flooded my mind.

That mountain dragon had said she killed one of his family members. I should have known. The room wanted to spin, but I needed answers. I shook the emotions away. "Isabel lived here *with* you?" Things clicked together. "That's why you know who she is."

"No. I mean, all dragons in this area know of her—who she is by name—including me. I was never here with her, though. This hasn't always been my cabin. She did, however, kill my uncle when she escaped."

I gasped, but I wasn't surprised. "Forest dragons murdered her husband and son before she met my father. They killed her family in front of her and left her for dead. Then they took my father's life too. I thought she was dead until yesterday. She spent her whole life trying to figure out your poison."

"Sounds like you share her ambition."

My mouth froze open. Heat filled my veins as I recalled my purpose. "I do."

He nodded once. "You still have a question."

"You promised me three."

"You asked who lived here and if I was here with Isabel." He held up two fingers.

Stupid, literal dragons. I clenched my hands and breathed deep, knowing I wouldn't win that argument.

Didn't matter. I knew the one question I wanted an answer to. "Fine. What's a forest dragon's poison?"

He breathed in, and the hope drained from his eyes. "If I answer that question, it'll kill me."

I shrugged. "That's okay by me."

He looked away, head bowed.

Something tugged painfully in my chest. Why? Why did I suddenly care if I hurt him?

Not wanting him to know he was getting to me, I cocked an eyebrow. "Bargain, dragon. You said you'd answer my questions, and you know when a dragon makes a bargain, it must keep to its word."

"I know," he said softly. "I can tell you a story that answers your question indirectly."

I crossed my arms. "I'm listening."

"First, I have to check the perimeter. I'll tell you the story when I teach you to dance." He flashed a smile, but all the normal cockiness had left it.

"Fine. One hour."

He opened the door, and I turned my attention to the windows. In moments, his streamlined form flew into view and darted up between the clouds. He dove and skimmed the water's surface, then jetted off. Show off.

Still, goosebumps covered my skin.

I'd never taken the time to really watch dragons. I'd always been hunting them.

That thought sent a shiver through me, and I pushed it aside, determined not to let my acting skills soften my heart for real. I was luring him in, and I almost had the poison. In one hour, he'd give me everything I needed.

My skin warmed in anticipation. I was so close to finishing Isabel's work.

And then my heart sank because a piece of it—a really big piece—didn't want to hurt him. I needed more time here. To really understand.

Then there was the problem of Isabel possibly showing up to this Feast of Fire like that mountain dragon had said.

If I knew the poison and showed up to the Feast—with backup—the dragons would all be done for. I raced upstairs to grab my phone and contact Dane. Probably good timing, since my two-way phone showed six missed messages. Five from Dane and one from Uncle Max.

Swallowing hard, I listened to the one from Uncle Max first: "Keira, I need you to check in. Dane has informed me that the misfits are talking of war, and I need to know that you two are lying low. Your brother is dodging the question, and I'm starting to think he's gone rogue."

I called Dane.

"Where have you been?" he demanded, his voice simultaneously angry and nervous.

"It's only been a day since we talked."

"Did you get any of my messages?"

"Listen, Dane, I've stumbled onto something very important here." I kept my voice low in case Bran or Ace came in unannounced. "I am an hour away from figuring out the forest-dragon poison."

He was quiet for so long I wasn't sure I still had a connection, but then he cleared his throat. "That's great. We have problems here, though."

"You're not asking me to come back, are you? I'm so close."

"Keira, the misfits here are talking about some strange forest-dragon custom. It's a celebration of sorts. It happens this month."

My heart seemed to stall. "The Feast of Fire," I whispered.

"Yeah. That might be it. What do you know about it?"

"It's in two days. We need to strike then."

"We won't be the only ones. They were talking about a hunter. Is that guy—Ace—is he okay? Is he with you?"

My mind raced. If the misfits planned to strike at the Feast of Fire, we needed every available hunter at the celebration. And I needed to break out Isabel. Or maybe it would be best for me to break out Isabel and get out of here—secrets intact. We could let them wage their war and then attack the survivors.

I needed to think.

"Keira, I—"

"Wait." I let the thoughts form. "Dane. I have a plan."

"Don't you always?" I could practically hear his eye roll.

"Listen, if they're declaring war, I'll get out of here, but not until I get what I came for."

"The poison? Keira, listen to me. If a war breaks out and you are anywhere near it, I'm hitching a ride on one of the misfits and coming after you. Do you understand? Uncle Max is starting to believe we aren't together."

"Okay. I need until tomorrow night."

"You need your tracker on." His harsh tone surprised me.

"I will turn on my tracker tomorrow."

Dane paused. "Keira—"

The tremor in his voice melted my resolve. "I need you to trust me. I'm safe right now. Ace—"

"Can you really trust him?"

I thought back to the way the coyote had looked at Ace. How he'd cleaned and stitched her wound. The way the deer had calmed when he approached her. I looked at my own bandaged finger. Everything inside of me told me this was the real Ace. I swallowed. "I'm being careful."

"Just tell me where you are. Please."

"I'm right outside a forest-dragon nest."

"Uncle Max will call in the cavalry to find you. You know that, right?"

"Tomorrow."

He sighed, then fell quiet for a long time. "Tomorrow morning."

"Thank you!"

"It's only because you're holding all the chips."

"And you're injured."

"I wish you'd let me protect you, too. I'm not as fragile as you think."

Pain stabbed my chest as I remembered how my brother had gotten the huge scar that covered his side. How I'd almost lost him. "I know you aren't."

"Text Uncle Max? Tell him you're with me?"

"I will."

"All right. If I don't get a text from you by tomorrow night, I'm going off-grid to find you."

"Off—Dane! You can't—"

"Then don't let me down."

TWENTY-ONE

A *thump* on the deck told me Ace was likely back from his perimeter check. I rushed downstairs and found Bran there instead. His little visits were getting old, except this time he wasn't wearing his normal I-hate-you glare. His eyes were wide and wild. "Where's Wally?"

I opened my mouth and shook my head. "He should be back soon. What is it?"

"The misfits he saved you from are after us, and one of our boys confirmed a mountain-dragon sighting. They think we're harboring a hunter. I have to get you out of here."

"What?"

The back door burst open, and Ace strode in. "Bran? What's wrong?"

Bran relayed the same information, but Ace casually placed himself between us, widening his stance and crossing his arms. His calm demeanor sort of reminded me of Dane right before he issued a threat.

Ace didn't seem the type to threaten Bran, though. Either way, the room started to smell like dragon smoke, and my hand flew to my knife.

Ace shook his head. "You're not taking Keira anywhere."

"It's not safe for anyone if she stays here, including her. Not right now, anyway."

Ace nodded and glanced at me over his shoulder. "I have an errand to run. Would you be up for coming with me?"

"You can't take her there." Bran leaned closer to his brother.

Ace just shrugged. "Why not?"

Bran pressed his hand over his eyes. "If—the—it's not . . . actually, it's a good idea." He finally looked up at Ace. "But I don't like it."

"Why not?" I leaned casually against a closet door and pretended to be more interested in filing off a fingernail than their vague conversation. In reality, I hoped my relaxed demeanor put Bran at ease. Wherever Ace was planning to take me, it sounded secret. Like, forest-dragon-only secret. And I needed to get there. The more I knew, the better. My insides were practically jumping off a cliff.

Bran's glare returned, and I met his gaze to let him know he didn't scare me. "Because you don't belong there, hunter."

I pointed at him with my knife. "Maybe you should have thought of that before you agreed to let me smell like your brother."

Bran huffed and straightened his spine, ignoring my threat. "I hope you know what you're doing." He pointed at me but kept his eyes on Ace. "Because the way I see it, she isn't worth the trouble."

Ace held out his hands as if to calm Bran down. Then he led Bran into the other room, lowering his voice. "If it's true, and the mountain dragons are doing a flyby, it'll be best if I'm not here. Besides, once our horde gets word of the flyby, the increase in border security should put them back in line."

"You're too optimistic."

"Only if they don't see her. The things that are supposed to go down at the Feast of Fire should appease the mountain dragons enough."

My heart jolted. What was he planning to do with me? With Isabel? Was he lying? I hadn't seen any evidence of that. I closed my eyes. I was being careless.

Maybe I should turn my tracker on before the Feast of Fire—tonight, even—and ask Dane to get here a little early.

Bran exited out the back, shooting me one last glare.

Ace winced. "I'll have to postpone the dance lesson and storytelling. But only for a few hours." He nodded toward the door Bran had left open. "Care to join me for a little flight?"

"Let me guess. Jump off the balcony in five?"

He chuckled. "You catch on quick."

I rolled my eyes, but for the sake of getting closer to what I wanted—to save people from dragons . . . well, the bad ones—I nodded. My mother had always told me there's a risk to every jump. But, then, she said some jumps were worth it. I wondered if this one would be. "I'm ready when you are."

Ace winked and walked out the back door. I counted to five, raced to the edge of the deck, and jumped. Exhilaration flooded me as I fell toward the gorge. A green dragon darted beneath me, and I landed on his back. Ace glanced at me and smiled. Strange. I could tell he was smiling.

The smile reminded me of my dragon, and I wondered if I had any other genuine dragon smiles to even compare it to. Of course I didn't. I'd never tried to make friends with other dragons. "So, where are you taking me?"

"A little place we like to call the garden."

"That's cryptic."

His laugh reverberated through his back. "You'll like it. Hang on." He started to descend, and I clung to him as he dove between the trees. "Here we are."

As soon as I slid off, he shifted back into a man and turned to face me, but there was something vulnerable about his smile. About the way he bowed his head and walked forward with his hands in his pockets.

I followed, peering around and noticing what looked like a huge park in the middle of the woods. A playscape for kids—and there were a lot of kids—and benches in the shade of trees. But there were no roads leading here, which meant . . .

"They're all dragons?"

The sparkle in Ace's eyes caught me off guard. "I thought maybe we could hang out here for a little while—just while the mountain-dragon search blows over."

"What makes you think it will blow over so quickly?"

"Bran and some of the guys will be there to make sure it does. When it's all clear, they'll let us know."

"And what if it doesn't?"

"Well, that's one of the reasons I brought you here."

"What is this place? Dragon school? There are so many kids."

A young woman approached us. Her hair was fiery red and her eyes brilliant green. About five kids followed her, and three of them rushed past her to give Ace a hug.

"Wally!" they chorused.

"That's *Prince* Wally." The young woman laughed. Then she looked up at him with her smiling eyes.

Prince? What the heck?

"Welcome, Your Highness. I am so glad to see you again." She curtsied.

Curtsied!

I stepped back and stared at Ace with my mouth hanging open. The prince? Even my thoughts stuttered. What on earth? How had I . . . ?

I almost laughed from shock and surprise.

Ace shook his head and waved his hand as if to ask her to stop. "Please, Liz, the formalities—"

"Are good for the children to learn." Then she looked at me. "Who is your friend?" Her eyes widened. "Oh. Are you accompanying Prince Wallace to the Feast of Fire?"

"I . . ." I recalled how he'd asked me. How he'd joked that I'd save him the humiliation of having to go alone.

It made sense now. He was the prince. Not having a date to his kingdom's Feast would be pretty awful. I glanced at him. The small wrinkle on his forehead and hopeful look in his eyes softened my heart a bit. I didn't want to admit to that, but I was supposed to be playing the part of someone who was starting to let down her defenses, so what the heck.

I turned to Liz. "Yes. I am."

"That's wonderful!" She clapped her hands. "I'm so glad he's—"

Ace motioned to me, and he paused before he spoke, seeming to choose his words carefully. He rubbed the back of his neck. This new lack of confidence made me stare at him.

"Liz, this is Keira."

Her face broke out into a huge grin. "A pleasure to meet you." She clasped both of her hands around mine. They were so warm. She tugged me away from the tree line and into the canopy-covered clearing where the children were playing. As soon as they noticed Ace, they started squealing with delight and running in our direction.

Ace chuckled and crouched down to give them his full attention. "How can we help today?"

His smile was so . . . happy. I couldn't help but stare.

The children jumped up and down, shouting out ideas. "Read us a story?"

"Please, make your amazing chicken noodle soup!"

"Can you fix Mr. Wiggles?" A small girl held up her stuffed rabbit in one hand and the rabbit's tail in the other.

Ace opened his arm, inviting her to sit on his bent knee. She crawled onto his lap, and he held her while the others kept spouting ideas.

Ace's eyes practically sparkled. "I think we can manage most of that."

As the kids clung to Ace's fingers and arms and tugged him deeper into their play area, Liz stayed next to me. She paused, biting her lip before her cheerful voice bubbled out. "I'm so glad he's found someone to bring with him to the Feast." She turned her attention to me, her eyes searching my face. A strange look of worry morphed into intrigue. "You're not a dragon."

My eyes widened. "No."

"I always wondered why he was so adamant about going to the human college. Now I know."

What a strange thing to say. But I didn't want to say anything that might blow my cover here, so I resolved to bring it up with Ace later. "I guess you do." That came out more breathless than I'd anticipated. I nodded toward the kids, who were now sitting on the ground, circled around Ace. "Are you a teacher?"

"No." She raised her eyebrows. "Didn't he tell you about this place?"

"Only that it was a surprise and that he thought I'd like it." I hoped my nervous laughter sounded genuine.

Her attention flickered back to Ace and the kids again. "They're all orphans."

"Orphans?" A twinge twisted my heart, and I sucked in a breath.

She nodded. "Most of their parents were killed by hunters. Others by misfits. It's sad, really. All we're trying to do is keep the peace."

A lump grew in my throat, and I looked at the kids. I never thought of dragons as having . . . families. My chest tightened.

She looked at me. "It's nice to know a human who doesn't see us as monsters. It makes sense that Wally would fall for one of your kind. He wants nothing more than to stop the hunters from coming after us."

Fall for . . . ?

My pulse skipped a beat. Then again, I *had* just agreed to be his date, so of course she would jump to that conclusion.

I stood with her for a little longer, and she told me a bit about the program they had there. How the king had made it Ace's job, and how Ace had overseen the building of the place. All the while, my heart swelled, and my thoughts battled one another.

Finally, Ace looked up as if searching for me. When he found me, a grin broke out on his face and he waved me over. "They want to meet you."

"Oh." I started to shake my head, but Liz nodded toward them, beaming. I swallowed hard and headed over to where they sat on the ground. Ace patted the space next to himself. I settled in and looked over at the book he was holding.

He leaned closer to me so that I could see it, and our arms touched.

He didn't move away. Neither did I. He jiggled the book. "Do you want to read for the princess or the evil queen?"

"Princess!" the kids yelled in chorus.

Evil queen? I shot Ace a very subtle, slightly playful glare. "I want to read for the hero. You can read for the princess."

The little girl who'd brought Ace her Mr. Wiggles fell back on the ground laughing, and I noticed that her stuffed rabbit's tail was already attached.

Ace smiled. Then he said in a high-pitched voice, "As you wish."

That triggered a new round of laughter from his audience. I couldn't help but stare at him while he opened the book and began to read. The joy in his eyes. The softness in his expression. This was a dragon? When it came time for the princess to speak, he used the same high-pitched voice that made the kids laugh hysterically.

I took him in. The dark stubble, longer than normal, because he'd stayed up late last night stitching up a helpless forest animal. The way he made expressions with his face when he read the different characters. Who was he?

How could I have been so wrong?

Everything paused, and he looked at me.

I found myself drawn in by those green eyes. My heart pounded. Heat flared in my cheeks when I realized he'd caught me blatantly staring, but he just raised his eyebrows as if expecting me to speak.

I had no idea what to say.

He wiggled the book. "And the prince said."

Oh! I glanced at the pages, trying to catch my breath. Then I let out my gruffest, deepest voice. "I shall save the fair maiden from her prison and defeat the evil . . ." I stopped, stomach sinking. "Why is the dragon evil?"

"He's not!" the girl holding Mr. Wiggles said joyfully.

"Don't spoil the story for her," a young boy said.

Ace glanced at me. His gaze held something. Something hopeful? "Don't worry. It has a happy ending."

"Happy? Does the dragon get the girl?" Why, oh, why on earth had I asked that? I wasn't thinking. And my face had to be on fire.

Ace's eyes rounded, and he blinked several times, mouth agape. Then his face softened. "No. But the prince doesn't slay him." We remained that way—gazes locked—for three very loud heartbeats that echoed in my ears.

Ace started reading again.

A shiver skittered over my skin as I looked out at the boys and girls. And I remembered my dragon. There was a time I'd called him Boy to remind myself that he wasn't just a dragon. He was also like me. Human. I'd believed that until Isabel set me straight.

And now I didn't know what to believe.

TWENTY-TWO

After supper, we said our goodbyes to the children. They all hugged Ace, and some of them shyly hugged me, too, telling me they wanted me to come every time Prince Wally visited. With a lump in my throat, I asked how often that was.

The overwhelming response was, "All the time!"

Liz gave me a hug, which I didn't expect, but since she wasn't letting go, I slowly wrapped my arms around her. She finally released me, her eyes sparkling. "You'll make a beautiful princess someday."

Qué susto! The shock had to be registering on my face even as I tried to school it.

Ace laughed nervously. "Okay, thanks, Liz. We're heading out now." He cleared his throat, and when I turned around, he was already in dragon form, lying down.

With retracted cleats, I climbed onto his back, waved goodbye one last time, and hung on as he took flight.

The sun broke through the heavy clouds, and golden rays painted the horizon. I sat in stunned silence amid my changing thoughts. "So, it seems really important that you have a date to this Feast of Fire."

His long pause made me wonder if he'd heard me, but he finally responded, "Yeah. As you saw, Liz is under the impression that we . . . that you and I are . . . well, she'll think . . ."

As fun as it was to listen to him struggle, I decided to rescue him this once. "That you're *mi corazón, mi vida, mi alma.*"

Even as I said the words—my heart, my life, my soul—in jest, I couldn't help but feel a strange tug. Probably because I heard them in my mother's voice. She'd said these things to my father.

Emotion choked me, and I had to stop. "She believes—erroneously—that we're a couple. I get it. I'll play the game. *For one night.*"

"You sure you still want to come?"

"I'm not going back on my word."

"If you don't want—"

"Do you need a date or not?"

He was quiet for a moment. "I do."

"Then you have my word."

"Thanks. I was starting to wonder how I'd explain to those little ones that I'd managed to lose you by Feast day."

Something hard and cold sank into my stomach. "Those kids will be there?"

Ace chuckled. "You sound so nervous. Don't worry. They loved you. It's my parents and Bran that you'll really have to impress."

This changed everything. I couldn't allow my team of hunters to slaughter children. And the way Liz had looked at me, I couldn't imagine her being a killer. "Why is it so important that you have a date?"

"I told you. Humiliation."

"There's more to it than that."

He sighed. "Yes. There is. At the Feast of Fire, the horde will be celebrating that their prince has come of age, and that I will become king when my father decides to hand over the title. It is customary, as the heir, that I bring with me my . . . intended."

My heart nearly jumped out of my chest and off the dragon's back. "I'm sorry, what?"

"Obviously, you're not willing to—"

"Of course I'm not! When were you going to tell me this?" I was *so* close to releasing the spikes in my boots.

"Tonight. At the dance lesson."

"With a proposal?" My shouts echoed off the mountains.

"Well, it's not like I expected you to take it seriously. My father—"

"Oh. Good. Well, as long as we're clear." My sarcasm was dripping with acid.

"Crystal."

He fell silent. But he'd nearly brought up his father—the king of forest dragons. That was probably someone I needed information on, so I dared to probe. "What about your father?"

"You'll have to impress him." He looked over his shoulder and winced.

I cocked my eyebrow. "You know how I am with impressions."

He chuckled warmly. "I know. But if you're to play the part, you should know some things about my father. Namely that he—well, I'm sure he wishes I wasn't his oldest son."

Perfect Ace? "Why not? Your heart too soft?"

"Something like that."

Oh. I'd meant that as a tease. I leaned forward, placing my palms on his scarred back. "Too soft for what?"

"To be a king someday. To make decisions."

"Like killing humans?"

"No." He glanced at me, his expression showing hurt that made my stomach sink. "I told you, we protect people."

"*Lo siento.*" It came out before I realized what I was saying, or that I meant it.

"Anyway, I'm sure you don't want to hear about my problems with my fa—"

"What would you do as king?"

Even flying through the air, I felt Ace gasp softly. He looked back at me again, as if shocked I'd asked. Then his eyes pulsed golden as he said simply, "Hopefully I'd save my people."

All I could do was stare while my heart fluttered, and it had nothing to do with the fact that we were landing.

Ace dropped me off—I slid off his back and onto the deck. He dove down below, and moments later, I could hear him coming up the steps. I stood on the deck, one hand clutched over my heart. I turned to face him.

He stood in front of me, head bowed. "Are you still willing to go through with the ruse?"

I stared at him, opening my mouth. Ruse. Right.

He continued, "Once you save my life, there will be nothing tying you here. A breakup would be easy to explain. No harm done."

"No harm . . ." The hard look in his eyes told me it wasn't a topic of discussion he wanted to pursue. I actually couldn't blame him.

And now that I knew the children would be at the Feast, I knew what to do: Get him to tell me about the poison. Save Isabel. And leave.

I couldn't bring myself to slaughter innocents. But, in order to get to Isabel, I had to show up at that feast. "I guess you're right."

"I am?" He shook his head. "Did you just admit that I was right?" He held up his finger. "Furthermore, are you saying you'll still—"

"I'll accompany you. Just make sure I don't make a fool out of myself on the dance floor."

Ace's green eyes connected to me on a level too deep for me to swim in right now. I needed to find my way to shallower, safer waters. I cleared my throat.

He stared at me a few more heartbeats before he tore himself away and shook his head. "Yeah. Good. Thank you. Er, *gracias*, er . . . whatever."

"Er, whatever," I repeated, bobbling my head side to side to hopefully give him some sass. But I could tell he was trying to connect with me. Show off a bit. Guys had tried this before in flirting with me. Why did he have to seem so *normal* right now?

He cringed and rubbed his forehead. "That's not what I meant." He bowed his head and glanced up at me. "I'm sorry. I was trying to—"

"Speak Spanish."

"Yeah. Sorry, I don't know much." The apologetic look he gave me warmed my heart. No way was I going to let him wiggle his way into my good graces. Prince or not, this dragon was still my captor. Still keeping secrets. Still probably a liar.

Only he didn't seem like one.

"So, lessons?" I tried not to seem interested.

"I will. But I have one more perimeter check first."

I placed my hands on my hips. "You're going to leave me here alone?"

He held up his phone. "Bran texted. He says the enemy flyby yielded nothing for them except a warning to stay out of here." He pocketed the device. "Unless you want to come with?"

I rubbed my hands over my upper arms. "It's getting a bit chilly. I think I'll have some of that tea and warm up." Really, I needed to contact Dane and update him. I wasn't out of this yet, but the more we could appease Uncle Max, the better.

"As you wish." Ace's dashing smile warmed my insides, and I hoped he couldn't see a flush in my cheeks. He turned to leave.

"Ace?"

"Yeah?"

I still didn't know what his plans were for this feast. What kind of trap I'd be walking into. I looked right into his eyes, making sure I'd see if he lied. "Will I be safe at this Feast of Fire? I mean, I'm a hunter, and—"

"Keira." The intensity of his gaze captured me. "No one will hurt you. You have my word."

No red. No lies. All I could do was nod. He smiled softly, then jumped off the deck. I stood there staring for a few moments before I broke free of my trance. I raced inside to find my phone.

I texted my brother. *Hey! I am about to get the secret of the poison.*

I really wish you'd tell me where you are.

I'm safe. Don't worry.

I think you should call me.

The words stared back at me. He wanted to know if it was really me texting him. But I'd have to keep the call short or he might figure out where I was. I pressed the button for Dane's two-way.

"Keira?" He sounded worried.

"It's me."

"Why are you whispering?"

"Just in case Ace's younger brother comes over. He drops in sometimes. Listen, I'm going to do what you want. I'm staying out of this war."

"Good." He sighed. "You have no idea how happy I am to hear you say that. Please tell me where you are, and I'll come get you."

"I still need time, Dane. But I'll leave before the war starts. In two days, I have to attend the Feast—"

"Not a good idea. You—"

"Please trust me?"

He was silent for a few moments. "I do."

"Meet me here in two days. I'll turn my tracker on tomorrow."

"Tonight."

I paused a little too long for his liking.

"Keira?"

"First thing tomorrow."

He sighed. "Fine."

"Don't call in the cavalry. Just tell Uncle Max we're on our way home soon."

"Be careful."

"I will." I started to hang up but put my phone back to my ear. "And Dane?"

"Yeah."

"*Te amo.*"

He paused. "I love you too. But why are you saying that? Are you okay?"

I had to laugh. "I'm fine. Can't I just tell my little brother how I feel?"

"Yeah. Just tell me to my face. You know? When it doesn't sound like you're headed on a suicide mission."

"Lo siento. I didn't consider that. I'm just—we're about to have everything we've been looking for."

"Okay. Just come home safe. It's not worth dying for."

"I don't plan on it."

We hung up, and I sank into the couch, heart in my throat. Hopefully, I'd dodged putting hunters in the middle of this war.

A *thump* sounded outside. That wasn't long enough for Ace's perimeter check. I slipped on my boots and peeked out the door. The scent of coal fire carried on the wind.

Mountain dragons.

I crept onto the deck and scanned the area, the boards creaking under my boots. "I know you're here."

"Then why come out?"

The voice sounded young. Still, I clutched my knife. "Show yourself."

"You'd like that, wouldn't you?"

Smoke rose up between the wooden slats of the deck, and a dragon flew higher, level with me. He landed. Compared to the one yesterday, this dragon was small. Probably a juvenile.

I stepped closer. "Do you know how dangerous it is to be here?"

The dragon's red eyes widened. His spine arched as he backed away.

I twirled my knife. "Don't you know I can kill you? Probably before you make it into the air."

He inched toward the edge of the deck, making himself small like a scared coyote pup. "Th-that's a hunter's knife."

I glanced at the blade in my hand, and my tattoo stared back at me from beneath the bracelet. Tic-tac-toe. He looked younger than the dragon I'd set free. Perhaps as young as those little ones we saw today. Dragons whose parents I might have actually killed. An ache flared in my chest. Ate away at my anger.

"I won't hurt you. I'm like you. See?" The dragon morphed into his human form. Big brown eyes stared up at me. He couldn't have been more than seven. Younger than I had been when Isabel made me . . .

I swallowed the lump in my throat and sheathed my knife. "Go home and don't say anything about this, okay?"

His eyes grew round. It was as if he wanted to trust me but was afraid.

"I'm letting you go," I said quietly.

"Thank you!" He ran to me and flung his arms around me. "You're not a mindless killer like they say you are." He looked up at me with those eyes. A tiny circle of red rimmed his pupils. Not from a lie. From his mountain-dragon eye color.

They thought *I* was a mindless killer? Of course they did. Just like I thought they were. I felt numb as I pried his arms loose. "Hurry."

He changed into a dragon and hovered above me for a second. He was bigger than Ace's dragon form, but still small for a mountain dragon.

He dipped his head closer to me, and I saw gratitude in his features. Dragons were expressive. How had I missed this in so many that I'd hunted?

"Thank you," he said again. And I caught a faint smile. "Thank you for seeing me." He started to reach for my hand.

The wind picked up, and from the west, a green dragon zoomed toward him. Before I had time to give a warning, the green dragon slammed into the young mountain dragon.

Together, they fell below my line of sight. I raced to the edge of the deck to watch the twirling forms fall into the gorge as one tangled mass of necks and tails.

No. Ace would kill him. Heart hammering, I raced down the deck steps and took off down the chasm in the direction they'd fallen.

I clung to branches and jagged rocks as I hurried down the sharp decline. Each footstep stirred dirt, making it harder to find footing—making me slip. I touched the sides of my shoes and released the cleats, but they helped little against the unstable, shifting ground. I jumped down one more dip, landing on something rocky and solid, and there, a scaly green back with massive brown wings sat in front of me.

Ace bent over the mountain dragon, securing the small neck in his huge jaws.

The mountain dragon's expression changed. Wild. Scared. Desperate.

Isabel's voice rang in my head: *Dragons are monsters, and once they decide to kill, nothing will stop them.*

But Uncle Max's voice echoed louder than hers: *Sometimes Isabel forgets that dragons have as much humanity as we do.*

Was he right? Was it possible to appeal to Ace's humanity? Even at this stage? "Let him go." My words came out shaky.

Ace froze for a moment.

"He's a kid. And he's scared."

Ace released the kid's neck. But he kept his teeth close to his prey. "He was going to kill you. He'll tell the others about you."

"I-I won't say anything." The mountain dragon seemed so small and desperate. "She didn't hurt me. I won't hurt her."

"He's telling the truth." I looked at Ace's back and noticed his scars again. What kind of life did these dragons live? Did they have to? "Let him go. Please."

Ace snarled.

The mountain dragon squeezed his eyes shut. "P-please? I can prove it." His eyes cracked open, making any lies visible. "At your Feast of Fire, someone plans to ambush you afterward. They'll be waiting outside the northern and southern tunnels."

"Who? How many?" Ace's voice was a growl.

"They plan to attack. They'll surround the palace, and they know where your escape tunnel is. They will have dragons waiting. I-I don't know how many."

"What do they want with me?"

"You're the king's son. They want to start a war. The misfits joined us. They want all the hunters dead. You're keeping one alive."

A low rumble thundered in Ace's throat. "If you tell them about her—"

"I won't! I promise!"

"He's telling the truth." I stared at his eyes, which had started to pulse gold.

Another one of Isabel's warnings filled my mind. *Legend says a dragon's eyes will pulse gold when it's showing its soul—this is a lie. Dragons have no soul.*

My stomach tightened. How could I still believe that? I couldn't. I didn't.

Ace's wings folded and melted away. He stood facing the dragon as a man with clenched fists. "Go, before I change my mind."

The mountain dragon scrambled onto all fours and glanced at me, then Ace. Then he took flight.

Air rushed out of my lungs, and my knees weakened as I realized the sensation coursing through me was relief. I never in a million years would have believed Ace would actually let that dragon go. Isabel had said . . . I started trembling.

Ace faced me. When he opened his eyes, they were soft. The corners of his mouth tipped up. "Why, Keira, you do have a heart."

His smile sent a tingle through my blood. Then a spike of ice shot through me. I was getting too good at this game I was playing, if I was starting to actually feel that this ruse was truth. That I might actually have feelings for him.

I turned away from those soul-searching eyes, still not ready to fully trust him, and certainly not ready to trust myself. Or these new emotions.

"Don't think this changes anything." I headed back to the cabin.

But there was no way around it.

I'd lied. It had changed everything.

TWENTY-THREE

Ace gave me a lift to the deck and dropped me off. "I need a minute." He flew around to the front of the house. When he came out the back door moments later, he didn't look like he'd just busted through a bunch of trees and branches down a mountain—like I did. His hair was perfectly windswept, and his jacket no longer had dirt smudges.

I looked down at myself. "You could have told me you were going to freshen up. I could have done the same."

He motioned toward the house and grinned. "Go ahead. I actually woke up like this."

I rolled my eyes and looked down at my clothes. For that, he was going to have to deal with me, scuffed boots, scratched palms, and all. I crossed my arms. "Why did you let him go?"

"Are you going to dissect every little thing I do?"

"Yes."

He sighed. "If a dragon hunter sees no reason to kill a dragon, why should I?" He held out his hand as if asking for mine. "A bargain is a bargain. I owe you one more answer. I'll tell you the story while you take a dancing lesson."

"Fine." I left his hand hanging and walked to the center of the deck.

He followed. The sun was high but hidden behind gray clouds. No warmth. The mountains looked pale and cold in the distance. I trembled from the chill.

"This'll warm you up." Ace stepped in front of me. "Put one hand on my shoulder. Here. And the other here." He held out his palm again and shot me a dashing smirk. "Don't worry. I won't bite."

I placed my hand in his. Then I rested the other on his very broad, very muscular shoulder, and a shiver shot through me. This one had nothing to do with the cold and everything to do with the fact that a warmth seemed to be filling my heart.

Why was my heart fluttering?

His left arm wrapped around my back.

Heat coursed through me.

My pulse quickened.

I swallowed.

"Don't be nervous." He threaded his fingers between mine and pulled me closer. "Just focus on me."

I looked up into his eyes. Green eyes. Soft eyes. This close, I noticed a ring of hazel around his pupil, which gave them a green-gold look. His pupils dilated. I sucked in air while my uncontrollable heart fluttered again.

"You okay?" His eyebrows inched up.

I nodded, afraid my voice might betray me if I spoke. Seeing his humanity was one thing. Falling for him was something else entirely. And completely unexpected. I wasn't ready for either. I mentally chastised myself, but my stupid heart wasn't listening. It was trying to open up.

He smirked. "You warm enough?"

"Yes." My voice cracked.

"Good." He led me through the dance steps, his grip on my waist firm and gentle. I couldn't recall the movements if I tried, but with him leading, I didn't have to. All I did was focus on his touch against my back. His hand holding mine. The warmth pulsing between us. And his eyes. His golden-green eyes.

He kept repeating, "One, two, three, one, two, three," and effortlessly moved me around the deck as though it were a dance floor. And I never once ripped my gaze from his.

He spun me into his side and dipped me back. "You're a natural." The cocky smirk had vanished. Just a soft smile remained. He towed me back to standing and let go. His hand swept a stray hair behind my ear, and his thumb trailed against my cheek. "You like dancing."

The thrum of my heart tripped on a new rhythm. "How can you tell?"

His eyes were so close they moved back and forth, taking in my face. "You smiled. I mean, a real smile. And that tough-Keira front vanished."

I stepped back and crossed my arms. "It's not a front. I am tough."

"I know. That's not what I meant." There was that soft look again. "You let your wall down." His eyes pulsed gold.

I gasped. Was he letting me see his soul?

His Adam's apple bobbed, and he looked away. "Would you like to practice the dance again?"

The flutter in my chest returned, going into overdrive. What on earth was happening to me? What was I seeing? Feeling? Were dragons just as vulnerable as humans? I nodded, which brought another smile to his face. Not a cocky one—a real, uninhibited smile. He held out his hands, inviting me back into his personal space to dance again. Part of me longed for it. To touch him. To be close to him. And the rest of me reared back in fear.

I stepped closer.

Placed one hand in his and the other on his shoulder.

Tingles spread over my skin as he touched my back, strong yet gentle. "Ready?"

He led me through the steps again. Heat radiated between us. His hand on the small of my back, guiding me through the motions, felt natural. I almost forgot I was moving at all.

I let myself lean closer to him, attempting to regain some composure. I tried a smirk this time. "I think you're avoiding my third question."

There was a slight hitch in his step, but he recovered. "No, just waiting for the right moment. Which I guess is now."

His smile melted something inside of me.

"Once upon a time—"

I laughed, more nervously than I'd intended. "You did not just say that."

"That's how it starts." He dipped me back and held me there, looking into my eyes. "Dragons are patient. I can wait."

I smiled. "No. Please, keep going."

He set me upright and pulled me closer than before as he continued to lead me through the dance. "Once upon a time, in a garden full of every kind of plant imaginable, there was a young gardener. She loved plants, most of all flowers. They were much more fragile than she was, however. And she wanted nothing more than to be able to give them a longer life, make them more resilient. She longed for her flowers to be able to talk to her and walk with her. So she sang them a song. One they'd never heard. Her songs were like water to their very souls. In response, the plants sprouted living blooms, free of roots and stems. The gardener called them dragons.

"She named one dragon, born of a fiery-red rose with a light-green stem, forest dragon. He was intelligent and strong, a mighty protector who could devour anything."

"Oh, I see this story has been embellished by forest dragons over the years." I grinned.

Ace actually laughed. "The gardener gave her forest dragon authority to rule the forest lands. Daily she walked and talked with him in the garden. Until one day when he did not meet her.

"The gardener searched for him and found him hiding behind a tree, spying on a human girl. When the dragon saw his creator, he ran to her. 'Please, dear gardener,' he said, 'make me able to take on a form pleasing to the human girl. I want to talk to her and walk with her, and I don't want her to fear me.'

"The gardener saw the longing in her creation's eyes and knew it was the same she'd felt for her blossoms. The longing for companionship. 'Is my love not enough for you?' she asked him.

"'Of course it is. But I also wish to be loved by someone I can love in return. Someone I can be with all the time. Forever.'

"Crushed that the creation she'd made especially for herself craved such affection from someone else, the gardener said, 'Let me think on it.' And she walked away.

"The dragon did not walk with her. Instead, he stayed and waited for the beautiful human woman to return.

"'Why do you look so sad, dragon?' The shrill voice of a water sprite startled him. 'I can make you a man.'

"'How?' the dragon asked.

"'Water makes all the plants grow. Go to the garden and pluck a rose from the bush the gardener used to create your kind. Bring it to me, and I'll do the rest.'

"The dragon, aware that sprites never gave anything away for free, wanted to know what he'd owe for such a favor. 'What would you ask in return?'

"'That your fiery breath not be able to devour my home.' She motioned to the lake.

"This seemed reasonable to the dragon, so he plucked a rose and gave it to the nixie. She breathed on the flower. The petals flew off and whirled around the dragon. When they fell to the ground, he looked like a man.

"'Thank you!' the dragon cried. Then he waited. The gardener found him first. She looked as though she'd been weeping.

"'What's wrong?' the dragon asked her.

"She held up a rose. 'See?' The smooth, green stem had grown thorns. 'You did not wait for me, and now you have been cursed.'

"'Cursed?'

"'If you choose to reveal your true heart to a human who does not love all of you in return, evil will take root in your heart. It will grow like thorns and poison your soul. You will lose that which makes your heart human. Then no human will ever find you beautiful inside, and you will always be hideous and alone.'

"Understanding that the nixie had tricked him, the dragon fell to his knees at the gardener's feet. 'Save me, my dear gardener. Please.'

"'I cannot remove the curse, but I can give you a way to break it: if you choose to give your love to a human who loves you for who you are—dragon *and* man—the curse will be broken. If not, the poison in this flower will take hold and kill you. Or, you can choose to be with me instead, forever.'

"The dragon chose to reveal his secrets to the young woman."

Ace fell quiet but kept dancing. The gentle sway of our bodies in tandem reminded me of the times I'd ridden on his back. Except I found myself gravitating so much closer to him.

It seemed he wasn't going to finish the story. I looked into his eyes and found him already watching me.

"What happened to him? Did the human fall in love with him? Did they live happily ever after?" I asked.

His green gaze entrapped me. "He showed himself, and the human woman thought he was hideous. She said she could never love a monster. When he returned to the gardener, he found that the water sprite had collected all the gardener's tears and put them in her lake, then she hid the gardener inside. The dragon's fire could not devour the prison. He was cursed and alone, forever."

I expelled a breath. "Oh, it's a tragedy."

One side of his mouth darted up in what looked like a sad half smile.

"So a forest dragon's poison is tears?"

He chuckled.

No. Roses. I stood rigid against the gentle pull of the dance steps. My stomach lurched. My pulse sped. I knew.

He stopped. "You okay?"

I let go of him and backed away, my throat tightening. *"Lo siento."* I looked right into his eyes. I knew. I had the answer to Isabel's lifelong search. And tomorrow, I'd be in their nest.

If that mountain dragon was right, Isabel would be there, too. And the mountain dragons would be starting a war. Everything inside me trembled.

Did Ace know Isabel would be there? Would he tell me?

Ace squinted, trying to read my face, no doubt.

My head spun. I just wanted to go inside. Get away from him so I could think clearly. Because right now, I wanted to keep this a secret. I wanted him to feel like he could trust me.

"Well, I guess that's enough practice for one day." The crease between his eyebrows deepened.

I didn't know what to think. How to feel.

This secret was a weapon, and I wasn't sure I should share it. Killing a dragon who murdered innocent people was one thing. Unleashing this secret about their poison to Uncle Max and all the hunters was quite another. If dragons were more human than I'd thought, they were worth saving. Not killing. In two days, I'd meet all of them. At the Feast of Fire, I'd know for sure. In the meantime . . .

I looked up at Ace and his concerned face. I tamped down all my worry, but it just sat heavy in my gut.

"*Gracias,* for the dance lesson. And for answering my question the best you could."

"Of course."

"And for not killing that dragon."

His eyes opened wider for a moment, and then, slowly, one corner of his lips curved up. "Thank you for stopping me."

I turned away, heart thumping wildly, and headed toward the house, but Ace stayed put. I whirled around. "You're not coming in?"

He pointed over his shoulder. "I have to—"

"Fly the perimeter." I finished his sentence with him.

He chuckled and rubbed the back of his neck. "Yeah."

"So this Feast of Fire is in two days?"

He nodded slowly.

"What am I going to wear?"

His eyebrows rose. Then he shook his head. "Umm . . . there's a dress in your closet."

"You bought me a dress?"

"No." He laughed. "My mother, Zelda, did."

Zelda was his mother? The queen? And she'd expected me to come. Something inside of me seemed to still. As if the whirlwind of warring emotions in my gut held its breath for a moment. Was this a trick? Was he playing me? How could I be sure?

The turmoil inside of me churned again. "That was nice of her."

Autumn air swirled around me, and I hugged myself against the chill.

"You're cold." He put an arm around me and ushered me toward the door. "Sorry I didn't notice sooner."

My heartbeat quickened despite my best effort to calm it into submission with my reanimated suspicion. "You make a pretty decent heater, actually."

"Well, in that case, you're welcome." His smile caught me off guard. The way he tilted his head closer and locked his eyes onto mine stole my breath.

There was one way to get answers. To tell if he was lying. "Would you change? For me?"

He froze. "What do you mean, change?"

"Into a dragon."

He backed away. "You've seen me."

A glimpse of him towering over me, teeth bared, raced through my memory, as did all the times I'd ridden on his back. "You always change into human form when you interact with me. It's like you hate to remain in dragon form when I'm around. You're hiding that part of yourself."

"Well, you are a hunter."

"Right now I'm just a girl."

He closed his eyes. "You don't want to see me like that."

The words of the story echoed in my mind. He didn't want me to see him as a monster. A hideous monster. "I shouldn't have asked. *Lo siento.*" My fingertips touched his face.

He opened his eyes. Didn't turn away from me. So close. So warm.

The scent of campfire surrounded us. I couldn't tell how much of this was an act anymore. It all felt real.

His finger trailed the length of my jaw, sending a tingle through my skin, pulling me closer to him like a lure. I closed my eyes, and lips, soft and warm, met mine. Heat flickered between us and coursed through my whole being as if I stood in the midst of a fire that heated but didn't burn.

This couldn't be a trick, could it? I tugged his jacket, and he responded by pulling me closer, deepening the kiss.

It had to be real. And I knew now: it had become real for me. That scared me more than anything. His eyes met mine, intense and full of desire and heat. My heart leapt. Soared. And my hands shook.

I touched my lips and backed away. A dragon. I'd kissed a dragon.

He stared at me with those soulful eyes. Gold pulsed in them like a heartbeat, warming my blood. No, he hadn't deceived me. This was Ace, true and exposed.

I closed the distance between us again.

His chest swelled. "I want to tell you something."

I caught myself searching for a flash of red in his eyes but shook the old habit away. "Then we can dance more?"

His gaze flicked to the ground. "If you still want to dance with me after what I'm about to say." He swallowed. "At the Feast of Fire, it's tradition to recognize dragons who have come of age over the past year. As I said, this year, I'm that dragon. This means I'll be expected to follow in my father's footsteps and become king. Tomorrow, they will present a prisoner and share that prisoner's crimes. It will then be my duty to decide the prisoner's fate—be it punishment or freedom."

"I had no idea. I didn't even get you a gift."

The start of a smile turned into a wince. "I don't want to proclaim fate on the prisoner they've chosen for me. I want it to be you. I want to release you of your debt."

My stomach flipped. I could hardly breathe. "Y-you're planning to set me free."

He touched my cheek. "Yes."

"Why would that make me not want to dance with you?"

His Adam's apple bobbed. "Because the prisoner they've brought in for me to pronounce judgment on won't get judged. And that prisoner is Isabel. She will be returned to that island I told you about. Where we keep the hunters. I didn't know until I got here. I'd planned to set you free, but then you told me who she was, and—"

"Set Isabel free." My heart pounded. I couldn't breathe. I didn't have to take anything I wanted. He could give it all to me. And so much more.

His eyes squeezed shut.

I sucked in a breath and backed away from him, everything inside me chilling like an explosion of fire meeting ice. "You'd sentence her to death?"

His eyes scanned my face. "She killed innocent dragons. She tortured them, Keira. Young dragons. Children. Like the one you asked me to spare today. Like the ones you met today."

I glanced at my tattoo as my heart fought for sanity. The permanent reminder of the darkness I had to pull from in order to save lives.

But was it really that?

Was all that pain and suffering really in the name of good? I had no one but myself to blame for setting free the dragon who killed my father and took Isabel. Still, anyone with a shred of humanity would have done the same. Isabel had done cruel things. But she'd been my mother. She'd kissed my scraped knees. She'd made me Christmas cookies. Taught me everything she knew. She—she loved me. And I loved her.

"Isabel did bad things, but are you any different if you kill her?" I asked.

"I'm still struggling with that."

"So setting me free is an easy way out?"

"No." He gripped my hands, and I didn't pull away. "It's the right thing to do."

"Even though I'm a dragon-killer?"

His eyebrows scrunched together. "Still?"

A lump grew in my throat. "I guess I'm still struggling with that." I breathed deeply, calming my warring emotions. "*Gracias* for telling me about Isabel. For wanting to set me free."

I leaned closer, wrapped my arms around his neck, and kissed him again. His hands slid up my back and pulled me closer. My body pressed against his, and all of my senses died away except for touch. Every inch of me felt everything.

And then he pushed me back, just a bit.

I looked into his eyes.

His chest heaved. "There's something else I want to tell you." He gripped the edge of his shirt and started to pull it up.

All my senses rushed back to me, and, startled, I placed my hand on his. "Wait, I'm—"

A streak of fire shot through the western sky. The muscles in Ace's jaw flexed as he stared up at it and cursed. He looked at me, regret clear on his face. "I'll tell you when I get back, okay?"

"Yeah." I nodded. "Go."

He raced to the end of the deck and jumped. I followed, standing at the edge just in time to watch him zoom past me. My heart beat faster. My hair whipped around my face as the wind picked up speed. In moments, all that was left of him was the black silhouette of a dragon in the blue sky.

I wrapped my arms around myself. He'd told me why Isabel was going to be there. He'd promised no harm would come to me. But he wouldn't free her. He wanted her to pay for her crimes.

Now I was faced with a choice. If he set me free, could I truly leave Isabel to rot in a cell guarded by dragons or to be sentenced to death? Did she deserve it? Maybe I could talk to her. Get her to see what I'd come to understand these past few days.

My phone vibrated, and I checked it. A text from Dane: *Hey, how's it going? Two days till I visit the nest.*

He messaged me back fast. *Flip on your tracker before you go, or I'll kill you. Got it.*

I stared at the message for a long time. Dane was my brother. He'd do anything for me, and I for him. He was the only person I could trust. He deserved to know what he was walking into tomorrow. Time to come clean. *I have to tell you something about Ace. He's not a hunter. He's a dragon.*

The pause before his response grew. Just when I feared he might be too angry to reply, a text came through.

Turn on the tracker. I'm coming now.

No! Please. I know this sounds crazy, but I know the poison. He told me. And Isabel isn't dead.

It took another long moment before he messaged back. *Is he lying?*

No. I'm going to rescue her. Once I get her out of here, I'll need an escape route.

GIVE ME YOUR LOCATION. I will come and get you out of there. Please. Let me help you.

I'll turn my tracker on tomorrow night.

You can't keep postponing this. Are you saying you trust this dragon?

I'm saying

I paused, not hitting "send" yet. Did I trust Ace?

I'm saying you might be right. Not all dragons are monsters. I can't risk Uncle Max and the other hunters making the all-serum yet. And before you ask, yes, this really is me.

No te creo. Esta noche estas como una cabra.

Of course he didn't believe me. And he was right—I did sound crazy.

But I knew just how to reply. *Lol. Venga, güero.* I used the term of endearment that my mother used to call my father and my father then used on Dane. *I know I sound crazy, but I think Uncle Max may be more right about el cucuy than we thought.*

Dane paused for a very long time. I started to get nervous when his text finally came through. *I think you should be careful about Isabel. She doesn't think that. Remember what she made you do?*

I know. I'll be careful.

Together, I'm sure we can keep her contained. Please wait for me.

I will.

TWENTY-FOUR

I pocketed my phone and blew out a heavy breath.

Ace flew across the sky, and a massive dragon followed him. A mountain dragon.

My heart jolted. Ace was being attacked. I raced inside and upstairs to where I remembered seeing the crossbow and quiver. If those were mountain dragons come to play, they were in for a rude awakening. And maybe I'd be able to get myself free of this life debt, and Ace would have to set Isabel free.

Maybe he'd condemn her anyway.

One problem at a time.

I snatched the crossbow and bolts and headed back downstairs. A sinking feeling settled in my gut as I pulled the honey down from the shelf. Isabel's shelf, from her time here.

This was my fault. I had convinced Ace to let that mountain dragon go. They knew I was here, because of my stupidity. One by one, I started coating the dragon-tooth arrowheads in honey. I loaded one in the crossbow.

How could I have asked him to do that when he clearly knew it would spark a war?

War.

That's what these dragons faced because of me.

A *thump* on the deck caused me to spin around, loaded crossbow ready.

Ace stood there in human form. He raced inside and paused when he saw the crossbow. "You saw them?" His eyes were huge.

I nodded.

He plucked the crossbow from my hands. "They're looking for you." He handed me the car keys. "I can cover you if you leave."

"Where is the rest of your horde? I thought they were protecting us."

"They are." He headed toward the front door. "From misfits." He picked up the quiver. "Did you put honey on these?"

"It's a mountain dragon's poison."

He grabbed a dish towel and started wiping the honey off.

"What are you doing?" I pulled at his arm. "That will spread into their blood and kill them."

"I can't use a poison on another dragon. It's part of—we aren't allowed. It'll kill *me*."

I tugged at the quiver. "Then let me."

He shook his head. "On my count, make a run for the car."

"I'm not leaving." I reached for the crossbow, but he pulled it away. I put my hands on my hips. "What am I going to use?"

"I can't defeat them all in dragon form. I have to take them down this way. You run."

"I thought *I* was supposed to save *your* life."

"This isn't funny, Keira." He sighed. "I never should have brought you here."

"A few minutes ago you were going to take off your clothes."

He glanced at me. "That's not—just forget it. You're here now, and I have to make sure you get out safe."

I wasn't going to leave him alone. "How many?"

"Three big ones."

I eyed the weapon in his hand. "You're faster than they are. The car isn't. Give me the crossbow. If you can get them to chase you, I'll pick them off."

A shriek boomed outside. He looked out the window.

"You don't have time, Ace. Let me help you."

Ace held out the honey-laced arrows. I grabbed the quiver, but he didn't release it. His gaze bored into me. "Keira, if things go badly, you run. Understand?"

I tugged the quiver, but he didn't let go until I nodded.

"Be careful." He went out back. I opened the front door and walked out onto the porch. It was unusually quiet. I hesitated when I reached the steps. The hair on the back of my neck prickled.

Shrill and shattering, a dragon's roar ripped through the quiet.

A huge gray-scaled body flooded my vision. Its shadow darkened everything. Adrenaline pumped through my veins, and I welcomed the hot prickling on my skin. I aimed my honey-coated arrow at its chest. Another body shot up between us, half the size of the mountain dragon. I only saw the back of the green torpedo. Ace.

He rammed into one of the dragons, and the two of them plummeted below the tree line. That left two for me. One was in my sights. I pointed the crossbow at the closest lithe body and shot. It hit the mark—right behind the dragon's ear. The beast fell.

Blood pumped hot through me. Muscle memory guided my movements. This was my game, and I was good at it. I stalked closer to the edge of the front porch, where the tiny roof would no longer offer me great cover—but it also wouldn't inhibit my vision.

I scanned the sky, searching for movement above the trees. Nothing. Where was the other one?

The scent of hot coals filtered around me. The sound of rock hitting rock told me he was loaded, but echoes in the mountains prevented me from triangulating his location. Heat fanned across my back. I whirled around as fire pulsed toward me from between the trees.

No.

Bracing myself for the flames, I hit the deck and crawled to hide behind a rickety chair, fumbling to activate my shield. My finger found the busted button on my bracelet. Oh no! *Muy mal!* Dread collapsed my lungs. I had no protection now. Sweat broke out over me, cold and clammy. But no fire touched me.

The air actually seemed cooler. I grabbed the chair and turned to where the torrent of flame had been coming from.

A dragon shape—wings outstretched—shielded me.

Ace.

Blood pumped through me twice as fast. He was saving my life again.

When the heat died out, I turned toward the enemy dragon, ready to fire, but Ace still stood there, back to me.

A huge gray shape like a massive rock formation descended from above, blocking the sun. It towered above trees and shook the ground. I looked up, and the darkness seemed to press against me from all sides. My hands shook. I'd never seen a dragon that big. I didn't even know dragons could *get* that big. Its talons wrapped around Ace's middle and squeezed.

A scream ripped from my throat as I raised the weapon I hadn't even realized I'd lowered.

I shot an arrow.

It glanced off the dragon's cheek. Huge red eyes snapped up to look at me. They narrowed. Smoke poured from the dragon's nostrils.

It tossed Ace with so much force that he torpedoed through the forest, breaking three trees and falling at the base of a massive cedar.

He didn't get up.

TWENTY-FIVE

My heart thundered as the sound of rocks grinding together bubbled into a roar. "I see you, hunter." Its deep voice shook my bones.

It opened its mouth, and I aimed right where the ball of orange light was forming in its gullet. I shot. The arrow hit its mark. The dragon screamed, writhed. There was such a small amount of honey on the arrow. I wasn't sure it'd be enough to kill.

I loaded the crossbow again. My hands steadied as muscle memory kicked in. I fired again. This arrow sank into its neck, near the fire trigger.

Heavy winds bent the treetops and stirred up dirt and leaves as the great gray beast took flight.

I dove to the ground for the best angle. Flat on my back, I released another arrow. This one hit the dragon's chest. Its wings missed a beat. Its body descended, skimming the trees. Then it dipped lower, disappearing into the gorge.

I scanned the sky. Calm. Quiet. For now.

I scrambled to my feet.

My eyes shifted to the tree where Ace's body lay—in human form. Human? My heart beat faster. My stomach tied into a knot. No, no, no. This couldn't be happening. Had he received a killing blow? I raced over to him. "Ace."

He tried to sit up and groaned. "That was some good shooting."

I reached toward his jacket and opened it. Blood wet the whole right side of his shirt. I pressed my hand against my mouth. Breathing hurt. "Why aren't you healing?"

He managed a weak laugh and sat up. "Dragons don't just heal, Keira."

"Yes, they do!" My desperation surprised me.

"I'm pretty sure that's not the case. At least it's never been for me." He moved and groaned. "This'll take some time. And stitches."

I sat there, staring at him, willing this to be a lie. Why had Isabel said . . .

My eyes stung with tears. I blinked them away. Isabel had lied. All of it. Everything she'd told me about them was a lie. I should have trusted my gut. I should have listened to my heart.

I'd just wanted a mother so badly.

I closed my eyes and willed myself to focus. I couldn't fall apart right now. I needed to help Ace. Then I could beg for forgiveness. But right now, I had to pull it together.

"I'll stitch you up. You'll be okay." I looped my arm around his back. "Can you stand?"

He nodded, and I helped him up. He gritted his teeth and cried out in pain, swaying. I steadied him. Slowly, we started walking toward the cabin. He leaned on me more than I'd expected him to.

Then he stumbled and fell to his knees, taking me down with him.

"Are you going to be okay?" My voice broke.

His gaze was rueful. "I've had worse."

"Really?" I helped him back to his feet. We were almost to the cabin now.

He managed a chuckle. "Actually, no. But I'll be fine."

I remembered what Bran had said about Ace not healing as well as normal, and my stomach squeezed. "How much time will it take you to heal?"

His smile was weak. "I'll still find you."

"What?" I stared at him.

"If you leave. As soon as I'm better, I'll be able to track you."

I swallowed. I hadn't even considered running. But I wasn't going to tell him that. We made it to the porch, and he gripped the railing with his bloody hands. I helped him up the steps and inside, my stomach churning as he dripped red everywhere.

He unwrapped his arm from my shoulders and leaned against the door to the bathroom.

I never should have told him to change into a dragon. I should have let him fight on the ground with me. This was all my fault. A sob clawed inside of me, but I held it in.

"Can—are you going to . . ." How was I going to ask this? "Could you change into a dragon now?"

"This isn't going to kill me, Keira. But, no, I won't be able to change for a little while."

"Why not?" The words trembled.

"If I change now, it'll rip me open worse in the process. My dragon body could handle it, but not my human form. I need both to survive." He shuffled into the bathroom.

I followed, but he shot me a wary glance over his shoulder.

"I got this, Keira." He clutched his side, leaned against the sink, and closed the door.

I crossed my arms and stared at the door. He'd need me sooner or later. There was no way he could take care of that alone. I thought of all the scars I'd seen on his back, and my arms unfolded. Maybe he could.

I headed to the kitchen and ran the hot water until steam rose from the sink and heated my face. I'd killed a dragon today. Before, this was normal. A monthly occurrence. Today it was different. An ache gnawed at my stomach. Because dragons were no longer just dangerous animals. They were people.

Tears dripped down my cheeks. Alone for now, I let them come. I was a killer. I was a mindless killer. I let the guilt constrict my stomach. How had I ever believed Isabel?

I splashed hot water over my face and turned off the faucet, standing at the sink for what seemed like an eternity. A loud crash came from the bathroom. I ran to the door. Locked.

Of course it was.

I pounded on it. "Ace? Are you okay in there?"

"I'm fine, Keira." His voice sounded strained.

I ran upstairs and pulled a lockpick from my bag. Maybe I should keep this on me. I raced back down and started on the lock.

"What are you doing?" he asked.

"Nothing. Just leaning against this door until you let me in."

"Stop trying the knob. I—"

Something clicked. Unlocked. Good thing I still had a lot of old skills. The door creaked as I slowly pushed it open.

"Keira, please."

"Are you so stubborn even now? Just let me help you." I didn't mean to yell, but I was rattled. My thumping heart wouldn't calm. I pushed harder against the door. Medical supplies were scattered all over the bloodstained floor. Ace knelt beside the tub, red-soaked towels balled up next to him. His shirtless back was to me.

"Keira, please, you shouldn't—"

"I think you mean *'gracias* or something.'" I sank to my knees and reached for the needle he was holding, noticing again the thick scars on his back. I gasped in spite of myself. How many times had dragon claws sliced into him? Two of the deep gashes on his side were nearly stitched up. One left.

I put my hand on his shoulder and tried to coax him to face me. "This would be easier if—"

"Keira, don't do this."

I barely heard him.

I knew he'd said something.

I couldn't hear anything anymore. All I could do was stare. And try to breathe. I couldn't breathe. My lungs constricted.

Tic-tac-toe.

The old slash marks marred his chest and stomach. Clear as day.

"You're dead." My chest tingled. Tightened. I—I couldn't breathe. My hands went numb. I shook my head, trembling. Everything inside of me ached. "You. You're supposed to be dead." I scrambled to my feet and backed away. "You killed my father."

Now he looked at me. "Keira."

"No." Tears burned my eyes. It hurt to breathe. To swallow. To think.

"Keira, please. I know this looks bad. But I didn't—let me explain."

I shook my head and held out my hand to tell him to stop following me. "You betrayed me," I whispered, wishing I'd yelled it.

He didn't stop following. His steps were slow, and he held his hands out in front of him. "Keira—"

"Stop saying my name!" I'd backed into the banister. I pulled out my knife. The scars. I couldn't take my eyes off of them. My hands shook.

The room spun. I clutched the banister, trembling. "How did you do it? You faked your death? And Lance. He was in on it? I don't understand."

Did Uncle Max know?

Ace took a step closer. "I'm not sure what you're talking about."

I groped around the side of the railing and held up the knife as I backed up the stairs. "You were *dead.*"

"I don't know who told you that, but—"

"*Basta*! Shut up!" Every word seared my throat. He'd done it again. He'd held my heart in his hand and crushed it. "Isabel was right all along. I can't believe I questioned her. I can't believe I was falling for you."

Ace sucked in a breath. "Keira, will you please listen?"

"No!" I didn't want to hear a word. Not one more word out of his lying mouth. "Dragons can never be trusted."

"You know that's not true. You can trust me. You—"

"Stop!" I covered my ears. "Never leave a dragon alive if you can kill it."

"Just yesterday, you—"

I stood taller, finding my strength as I continued to recite Isabel's commandments. "Dragons don't feel pain like we do. Their scales make them immune on the surface, and they heal fast, so cut deep."

Ace flinched. He would remember that one. She'd repeated it over and over as I gave him those scars. As she forced my hand to cut him so deep. My knees weakened. *I'd* given him those scars. Hot tears spilled out of my eyes anew.

I'd tortured him.

Because he was a monster, I reminded myself as the betrayal eroded everything I'd started believing again. He was playing me!

I kept reciting. "Never threaten a dragon on its own territory; it will kill you."

But he hadn't killed me. My crumbling heart ached as it tried to continue beating. The rest of Isabel's commandments came back to me, and I tried to dwell on the truth of them:

Dragons twist their words to lie without letting their eyes reveal that they're lying.

A dragon doesn't care for anything but itself; don't let perceived acts of kindness fool you. They are incapable of real compassion.

But the coyotes. And the orphans.

Dragons can spot a lie in your face. Be like a stone.

I stiffened my spine and tried to stop the tears. To stop feeling.

The only thing a dragon will protect aside from itself is its treasure.

Ace had just saved my life.

Why?

Why!

What did it mean?

Legend says a dragon's eyes will pulse gold when it's showing its soul—this is a lie. Dragons have no soul.

Dragons are monsters, and once they decide to kill, nothing will stop them.

I shook my head and closed my eyes. It was all a plan. An elaborate plan to lure me in. I wanted to scream.

Ace had tried to make me question these very truths, but I could see through him now. He wouldn't deceive me so easily again.

I clenched my hands.

Straightened.

Glared at the monster before me.

I would go with him to his precious Feast of Fire, but I would also call in the cavalry. And he'd never see it coming. Because I knew one thing for certain: *dragons are not human.*

I stuck my hand in my pocket. I had to get a message to Uncle Max, somehow.

But could I even trust him? He had to have been in on Lance's lie. What did Lance care if I hunted a certain dragon? Uncle Max cared, though. He'd hated my obsession. I backed up the stairs until I was out of sight.

"Keira?" Ace sounded so unsure.

I ignored him. I had to do this before he caught me. I texted Dane. *I'm in the nest. I found their poison. Roses. Send backup for their celebration in two days.*

And I flicked my tracker on.

TWENTY-SIX

The floorboards creaked as Ace came closer to the base of the stairs. He could hardly move. I didn't want him to think I feared him, so I walked back down the steps I'd retreated up in order to send my message to Dane.

My heart thrummed. It was a matter of time now. Life debt or not, Dane would figure out how to get me out of here, and he'd kill as many dragons as he had to in order to save me.

I looked right into Ace's eyes and made my stare cold. "You're silver-tongued liars. All of you deserve to die."

His eyes narrowed. "Is that why you let me go that night?"

My heart dropped to my gut. "Don't you dare! I was a kid."

"So was I." Gold flashed in his eyes.

I sucked in a breath. She'd made me torture a kid. A boy. No. A dragon. My fingernails dug into my palms, and I screamed, "You killed my father!"

He held up his hands, taking a step closer. "I didn't kill your father. He was already dead. I just took Isabel."

How could he expect me to believe that? It didn't even make sense. "Stop lying!"

"I'm telling you the truth. He was already dead." Ace's eyes pleaded with me. He was close enough to lean against the banister now, and he stood there, clutching his injured side, looking ready to fall over.

"I saw the claw marks!"

He looked up, eyes round and sad and broken. "You know, there's a way to tell if a dragon is lying."

"Of course I do, but you'd have to be in dragon form for me to believe you." I pointed to his freshly stitched injuries with my blade. "And, conveniently, you're too wounded to change now."

His breathing shook, and he looked me right in the eyes. "Promise not to be scared?"

I stood tall and clutched my weapon, my blood boiling. "You don't scare me, dragon. In fact, I'd prefer to look at your face in that form."

He winced. "All right." He backed up a few paces.

My heart pounded. "You're changing now?"

"You need the truth."

"Wait." Why on earth had I said that? I needed to think. "Changing could kill you."

Didn't I want him to die? No. Not yet. He was my ticket to finding Isabel. I couldn't come this far and not rescue her. Still, there was more to it than that. Because I'd truly gotten attached. I cared for him.

But he'd betrayed me!

He glanced down. "That doesn't matter now."

"What do you mean?"

He looked away.

"Ace?" My heart raced. "Ace!"

He stepped back into the open foyer. The air grew hot, and smoke encompassed me. I gripped the banister. Giant wings unfolded from within the cloud of smoke, and scales materialized, rustling as they covered his growing form row by row.

A head on a serpentine neck broke through the blackness. His face slithered inches away from mine. I gasped. His eyes, the same color, the same expressiveness, stared at me, and the gold ring around the pupil pulsed.

He didn't look scary. Or angry. He looked sad.

His scales shimmered. I reached toward his neck and touched them. So smooth and hard, warm beneath my fingers. He closed his eyes and leaned into my hand.

I pulled away, reality snapping me back to the moment. "Did you kill my father?"

He looked right at me. "No." A tear slid out of his eye.

No flash of red. No hint of a lie. It didn't make sense. My pulse pounded, loud in my aching head.

"Then how?" All the air left my lungs, and slowly, I sat on the stair.

How could that be? Someone had killed my father. It had to have been a dragon. The claw marks across his stomach were clearly made by dragon talons. Three huge slashes, where a dragon had ripped him open.

I found myself staring at the *x's* and *o's* on Ace—raised, puckered scars that marred his stomach. I'd done that. New blood oozed from his wounds. They were huge in this form.

My head throbbed. Blood rushed through me. I gripped the banister but couldn't feel it. I couldn't feel anything.

"Do you know who killed him? Did you see?" Desperation burned in my voice. Scratched my throat.

"No, Keira. I'm so sorry."

Sorry. That's all anyone ever was. "How are you lying to me?"

"I'm—" He buckled over, a roar in his throat. He steadied his breathing and looked at me. Even in this form, his eyes were pinched in a wince. "I . . . didn't . . . kill . . . your father."

Isabel had said Ace had . . . tried to kill me. Why should I believe him? "You tried to kill me!"

"No! Never." He stared at me, scanning my face, as if willing me to hear him. To remember. Then he cried out and fell in an unmoving heap on the floor. His body shrank as he morphed back into a man. And he lay there, still and silent, as a puddle of blood spread out from his side across the wooden floor.

He was right. All of his stitches hung free like pulled threads coming undone. Letting everything unravel with them.

I shouldn't care. So why did my heart ache?

"Ace?" I descended the stairs and knelt next to him. He didn't stir. My pulse pounded. His skin felt so hot. "Ace!"

Nothing. Not even his eyelids fluttered. This was what I wanted, right?

But I couldn't shake the fact that he hadn't lied.

No evidence of a lie.

My stomach churned.

Who killed my father?

All this time, I'd blamed Ace. He hadn't lied about my father.

But he'd still lied.

My thoughts spun. So had Isabel.

Blood in the water.

Lies in the truth.

Who was I supposed to trust? I didn't know anymore. I needed more answers. And . . . I couldn't let him die. Not now. Not like this. He might know something, anything, that could help me find out who'd killed my father.

I looked at his peaceful face. Everything I knew about him seemed the opposite of the kind of dragon I was supposedly hunting. He was so . . . human.

That last thought seared my soul.

He *was* human.

A feeling washed over me, like I was dropping something I'd clung to so tightly. My long-held beliefs seemed to slip through my fingers, tumbling to the ground as I watched helplessly. As they hit the ground and shattered, I realized there was no putting them back together.

I raced into the bathroom and gathered the medical supplies I needed to save him. Tears leaked out of my eyes. How had everything come to this?

If he hadn't killed my father, was he still that same dragon? How much of my hatred was a lie? How much of my life?

Mechanically, I cleaned and stitched his wounds. His heart still beat, and I stayed beside him until, finally, his breathing evened.

I picked up his hand. Held it. "Don't . . . don't die on me, okay?"

TWENTY-SEVEN

Sun broke through the windows, and I breathed in and sat up. My hand still clutched Ace's as we lay on the hard foyer floor. Blood had seeped into the wood. Warped it. Stained everything.

But I didn't want to leave Ace's side to clean it up.

The heart-wrenching reality ripped through me. Even though he'd lied about who he was, I still cared for him. And that scared me. Because part of me hated him. I couldn't separate the man from the dragon. I couldn't decide what to believe anymore. What was right in front of me now or what had been right in front of me my entire life. Maybe they were more the same than I wanted to admit. Maybe I'd never really understood. Right now, I certainly didn't.

"Keira?" His voice was scratchy. "You're still here."

I looked at his face. His pale face. "You're alive."

"Thanks to you." He squeezed my hand. "What's this?"

I let go. "Making sure that if you stirred in the night it would wake me up. I couldn't have you doing anything to me."

"I said I wouldn't hurt you. I meant that."

His chest was still bare. The scars still there. Remnants of my torture. I stood up. If he hadn't killed my father—hadn't tried to kill me—*I'd* betrayed *him.* My breaths shook.

I stared at the blood, hugging my middle, and headed to the kitchen to get something to clean it up with. Even if he hadn't killed my father, he'd taken Isabel. He'd imprisoned her. And he'd lied to me this whole time. A new heat flared in my stomach. I still couldn't trust him.

I headed back to the foyer and saw him struggling to get up. "Here, let me help you."

He touched the bandage I'd placed over his wounds after I'd stitched them up again. "You did this?"

"I hope it counts as saving your life."

His Adam's apple bobbed. "It does."

My heart shivered in my chest. I dared to hope I could leave here and never look back. I should have left last night. That's why he'd been surprised that I'd remained. "I'm free?"

"Not quite." His voice sounded dry. "I saved your life again, while you were under the life debt. Yesterday."

The dragon that had almost burned me. Ace had stepped between us, and that was what had gotten him into this predicament. It was as though I'd stepped on an emotional landmine that exploded underneath me. "I'm still stuck here."

This was my reality. I couldn't escape. It was a bear trap around my ankle. I needed to get out. But how?

He touched my hand. "Not if I can get Zelda to agree to set you free."

Hope warred with hate in a burning wave. I stole my hand from his touch. "You would do that? Even now?"

"Yes." He pressed his hands against the ground and tried to stand.

"Ace, wait, I—" I gave in and helped him. Together, we made it to the couch, slowly. "Stupid idea, changing, huh?"

Those green eyes locked onto me, and gold pulsed within them in tandem with my heart. "Depends."

I took a shuddering breath and left to grab the supplies I'd need to check and clean his wounds. What was it he wanted me to believe? Was he really what he claimed? I wanted to believe him, because I wanted to trust my gut.

But I also wanted him to be wrong, because if he was right, the things I'd done . . .

I couldn't go down that road right now. But either way, what they were doing to my stepmother was wrong. Right?

Why didn't I know what to believe?

I'd always been so certain before.

Before . . . when I'd only believed what Isabel had pounded into my skull.

Maybe Ace was right. I had to start figuring out what I believed in my own *corazón*. That meant I needed answers. Truthful answers. Because that dragon in there, possessing humanity or not, had lied to me. So, right now, he wasn't trustworthy. I'd been played. Betrayed.

And Isabel . . . she might be wrong on some things, but all she'd ever done was try to protect me.

I made it back to him to find him inspecting my stitch-up job. Without a word, I placed the bowl of warm water on the coffee table and dipped a clean cloth below the surface. I pulled it out and squeezed out the excess, avoiding eye contact. I pressed the warm cloth over his wound. "I need to see Isabel. I need to know what you're going to do to her."

He sighed. "I'll take you. Actually, I can see to it that she makes it out alive, if . . ."

"If what?" I hardened my voice and met his gaze.

"Will you still join me at the Feast of Fire tomorrow?"

I pushed the cloth back into the water and motioned toward his injury. "Will you even be able to attend?"

"I kind of have to. But by then, I should be feeling better enough to—"

"Walk on your own?" I cocked an eyebrow while opening a tube of antiseptic ointment.

He half frowned. "Yes."

I dared to hope, and that sent a pang through my heart. I did *not* want to still be harboring feelings for him. At least I had something to keep my hands—and my eyes—busy. I couldn't look at him while I spoke. "I don't trust you."

He paused, and then his voice came out raspy. "I know. But all the dragons expect you there. Depending on how you behave, you could help me convince my mother that freeing you is a good idea."

I spread the ointment over his cuts and replaced the bandage. "Sounds difficult, since I hate you." I said it mostly to convince myself, because right now I wasn't acting like I hated him. *I* didn't even believe I hated him.

But I needed him to believe it. For my sake. For Isabel's.

He winced. "Like I told you, if you pretend you're warming up to us, they'll let you leave unscathed. If you stay here while I'm gone, the mountain dragons will be back for you."

"More threats? I thought we were past that."

He paused, seeming suddenly broken inside. "You don't have to trust me. I'll make a deal with you."

I summoned every ounce of self-preservation I had left and looked right at him. He had to believe he hadn't shattered the wall around my heart. "What deal, devil?"

The crushed look in his eyes made my chest tighten. "Come with me tomorrow to the Feast of Fire as my betrothed. Convince my family that you're in love with me, and I'll make sure you walk out free and alive."

My heart thundered in my chest. "With Isabel."

He breathed deeply. "You and Isabel."

A jolt of hope skittered over my skin with every beat of my pulse. "Why would you ask this of me?"

"Does it matter?"

No. Not if he'd give me Isabel's and my freedom. But suddenly something Bran had said made sense. "You really are cursed."

He stared at me for a moment. "You got that from the story I told you?"

No. Had hints to his curse been in the story? "Bran said something about a curse."

He nodded as though something he was carrying had become much heavier. "I have until the end of the Feast tomorrow to break it."

"Then you'll heal faster?"

"Yes."

"Well, then, let's break it." Had I really said that? I tried desperately to push all my rising feelings away.

"It's not that simple."

I perched on the armrest beside him. "What happens if you don't break it?"

He closed his eyes. "I become a dragon."

"You are a dragon."

He shook his head. "I become *only* a dragon. No more humanity. No more shifting."

"What?" The air left my lungs in a rush. "What do we need to do?"

"We?"

"I'm supposed to save you, aren't I?" I offered a weak smile. It's all I could muster right now. The thought of Ace with no humanity . . .

He wouldn't be Ace anymore.

I grabbed his hand, surprised at the tightness in my chest. My stupid heart. It had fallen for him, and it was all a game to him. Well, not a game. It was life-or-death, in a way.

A part of me wanted to forgive him for that. All of me wished I hadn't fallen victim to his charade. But it was too late. I swallowed past the lump in my throat. "Tell me what to do. Tell me how to help you."

The pain in his gaze ripped through my chest like a dragon talon. "Two things," he whispered, his voice thick. It got stronger as he continued, "Play your part flawlessly."

Right. The one about convincing his family that I loved him. The corners of my mouth fought to pull down, because I knew it wouldn't be an act, and I hated myself for it. "Okay. And?"

His eyebrows ruffled. "When the war starts tomorrow, I will fight. Don't try to save me. Understand?"

"No! How does that help?"

He bowed his head. "I can't lose face in front of my family. I will have to protect those I love. That's part of who I am. If you try to protect me, my father could see it as a disgrace. I won't be considered fit to be king."

"Wow. Old school, huh? Why did they allow me to take on the life debt if they wouldn't want a damsel in distress to protect you?"

He looked up and smiled sadly. "This is a special circumstance. But, yes, my father is a bit old school."

"This princess doesn't need saving, remember?" I pointed to myself.

He glanced at me as if my words confounded him. "Everyone needs saving at one time or another, Keira."

I stared at him. Speechless.

His forehead wrinkled. "Even princesses who insist they always save their loved ones."

Something tugged painfully at a hole in my heart. A hole that needed mending. "I don't know about that, but I will do as you ask tomorrow, because you need saving."

"We have a deal?"

I stared at him and his unflinching gaze that told me one thing: he was still a dragon. And I knew that a dragon's bargain was its bond. "Done."

TWENTY-EIGHT

"**G**ood." The leather couch creaked as Ace stood up. I faced him, trying to herd him back onto the couch. "What are you doing?"

"I'm going to make breakfast. Aren't you hungry?"

"Hung—what is it with you dragons and food?" Not that I was complaining—well, my stomach was. I pushed against his shoulder. "Why don't you heal up or something and let me make breakfast?"

He eyed me suspiciously. "Can you cook?"

"I was hoping you had cereal."

He chuckled. Then he groaned and pressed his hand against the couch's armrest for support.

I eased him back down. "Let me clean up this blood, then *I'll* make *you* some breakfast."

"I can take care of breakfast if all you're expecting is some milk added to dried, crunchy flakes in a bowl."

I sort of laughed. "What? No dried, crunchy crisps?" I touched his arm and squeezed supportively.

He stared at me.

"I can help you, Ace."

His eyes narrowed. "I thought you hated me."

I hardened my gaze, hoping he'd believe my lie. Hoping I could believe it again. I removed my hand as if he'd burned me. "You're my ticket to freedom. I need you to heal. Besides, what would your parents think if the girl who's supposed to be in love with you didn't take care of you when you got hurt?"

He shook his head. "My parents can't know about this."

"Our arrangement? You made that pretty clear with my little assignment."

He moved and winced. "That I'm injured."

"Why not? Aren't they afraid of a war breaking out?"

"They know the mountain dragons attacked last night. I told them I was fine."

I held up my fingers so I could count his lies on them. "Wow. First, you want me to be your fake fiancée. Now, you want to act like you're okay when you can hardly stand on your own. And you want me to pretend to love you for all to see. I guess I shouldn't be surprised at how much of a liar you are."

"That's fair."

The guilt on his face hurt my heart. "Tell me why they need to believe I'm in love with you."

"I thought you said it didn't matter."

"I changed my mind."

He rubbed his hand over his face. "When I ask to give you your freedom, it'll be easier if they can believe the reason."

"So you'll pretend to love me, too."

He looked right at me. "Is that a problem?"

I leveled my gaze at him. "Of course not."

The front door burst open, breaking our eye contact, and I stood up, knife ready. Bran raced around the corner. The moment he saw me, he said, "Where's my brother?"

"He's right—"

"What did you do to him?" Bran rushed past me. "Wally?"

Ace put up his hand to calm Bran down. "I'm fine."

"He's not fine." I put my knife away.

Ace gave me an incredulous look.

I shrugged. "You told me not to tell your parents. You didn't say anything about Bran. Plus, there's still blood on the floor." Except I had agreed to get Bran to believe I loved Prince Wallace of dragondom, or whatever. So I touched Bran's arm. He flinched away from me. "Can I talk to you?"

Bran glanced between both of us, and the moment Ace started to look suspicious, Bran nodded. He touched Ace's shoulder. "I'll be right back."

Together, we headed into the kitchen, and I kept my voice low. "I'm really worried about him."

Bran breathed in sharply, and a piece of my heart cracked as he pinched the bridge of his nose, fighting tears.

Whoa. Something inside of me warmed, and I wanted to offer this . . . dragon . . . comfort.

"Hey." I stepped closer and rubbed my hand over his arm. "He's going to be okay."

Bran nodded, blinking his red-rimmed eyes. Once he'd regained composure, his face grew serious. "He's right about not telling my parents. The mountain dragons are planning something. I think your little spy told us the truth."

"Spy?"

"You made Wally spare a mountain dragon. I could kill you for that."

I crossed my arms as a chill raced through me. I felt like I'd swallowed iron. "This attack last night, though, doesn't that prove my little spy told them about me?"

"Yeah. But if you come to the Feast of Fire . . ."

If Bran knew something Ace hadn't shared with me, I needed that information. "What?"

"If you come as his date, they'll attack."

I had to. My freedom depended on it. "He plans to set me free."

"Then he plans to declare war." Bran started pacing. "They fear that we are aligning with hunters."

Air rushed out of my lungs. I had messaged Dane. I had told him the poison. Had he told Uncle Max? Uncle Max . . . softhearted Uncle Max. "I think I might have a way to fix this."

Bran snapped his gaze to meet mine. "How?"

"If I can get my hunters to come, they could fight alongside you."

"No! No." I looked into Bran's narrowed eyes. I saw the very human pain and worry for his brother alongside a heated dragon glare. "If he chooses hunters over dragonkind at the Feast, the mountain dragons will not understand. That would give my brother a death sentence. Would you do that?"

"No," I said it without thinking. And to my surprise, something hurt deep inside me because I didn't want anything to happen to Ace. All I could do was think back to that book I'd read at the orphanage. The dragon had been freed. The prince had gotten the villagers to believe the dragon wasn't evil.

"I think you already have."

"No." I refused to believe that.

Bran seemed to search my face for a lie. "There can't be any hunters. If the mountain dragons get word that Wally frees you or Isabel, it's over. You understand? If other hunters show up, it'll be worse. We have to show them that we aren't for the hunters. We're for the dragons. Please tell me other hunters aren't showing up."

I needed to talk to Dane. Make sure he hadn't called Uncle Max. That only he was coming, as promised. But Ace only had to keep his promise to me if I kept up my end of the deal. I needed him to free Isabel and me. I tapped my fingers against my lips. "I know how to fix this. Ace promised to let me go. I'll stage an escape. Then you can pretend to hunt me down."

"You would do that?" he asked breathlessly.

"I think I can. Tomorrow at the Feast . . ." I looked up at him. "Is there a way for me to get out?"

"Tunnels. In the library, there's a wall sconce that pulls down. The tunnel to the outside is there." He paused. "You'll let Isabel out. Won't you?"

I touched Bran's arm, surprised at my own gesture. He glanced at my hand, and his look of confusion must have mirrored mine. But the truth was that all he'd done had been to protect his brother, and it reminded me so much of myself. Instead of removing my hand, I gave him a reassuring squeeze. "Ace promised to let us both go."

"My fool brother." He bowed his head.

"Don't worry. I won't let Isabel hurt anyone. And I—I'll make sure she pays for her crimes."

He narrowed his eyes at me. "You want me to trust you. Trusting hunters . . . you've all betrayed us in the past."

My heart dropped like a brick. "I felt the same way about dragons."

He glanced toward the other room, where Ace was. "He changed your mind?"

I swallowed and let the truth creep painfully into my answer. "He changed my heart."

Bran's eyes widened. "Did you—" His breathing rate increased, and a look of desperation mixed with hope filled his eyes. "Did you fall for him?"

A tear trailed down my cheek. "Yes," I whispered through the tightening in my throat.

"You told him? You told him you love him?" His voice held a tremor.

And admit my embarrassment? *No gracias.* "Of course I did. I agreed to be his betrothed."

Bran pressed his hands against his face, and I thought for a moment that I might have done something very wrong, but then he started repeating, "Thank you. Thank you." He grabbed my arms and pulled me in for a quick but crushing hug. Then he smiled. "You don't know how happy that makes me."

"I have an idea." I sort of laughed.

He shook his head, seeming lost in thought. "This changes everything, though."

"How?"

"He'll ask to set you free because you're his betrothed. If you can be sure to show the other dragons that you've changed . . ." He glanced at me. "Just promise me one thing?" His desperation made my insides clutch.

"What?"

"Don't let my brother fight tomorrow. He'll try to, and he's too injured."

A blast of ice chilled my veins. I'd just made a promise to Ace to let him protect me. "But why would—"

He swallowed. "He'll be too weak. It'll kill him."

My heart jolted through the ice, heating my skin until it tingled. "Wouldn't he know that?"

"Yes. But he's an idiot." Bran smiled sadly. "I have to go tell my father what you've promised." He clasped my hands. "I didn't think he'd be able to get you to fall for him." He smiled again. "Thank you."

I stood there, mouth open, and watched him race out the door.

TWENTY-NINE

By evening, Ace was actually able to walk around without hunching over. I supposed that was a good sign, though I mostly stayed away from him. I wasn't keen on letting him know that I had more feelings for him than I wanted to admit.

I snuck upstairs after making lunch—he didn't complain about the grilled cheese sandwiches, even if I had managed to burn them—and contacted Uncle Max to tell him that I was heading home tomorrow and not to worry. He hadn't texted back.

I messaged Dane to find out what Uncle Max knew. Dane hadn't told him a thing. But he seemed more worried about me now. He said he was on his way and to sit tight.

I couldn't, but I had one less worry, at least: I could keep my promise to Bran. No hunters were coming. Uncle Max didn't know where I was. Only Dane did. And I could leave the tracker here. That way, Dane would come here—where he'd be safe—and not into a nest of dragons.

I'd fixed everything except my stupid emotions. I headed out to the shed with some ground turkey meat and milk to feed the coyotes. Mama coyote was doing much better, but we still wanted to keep the pups from hurting her stomach, so Ace had asked me to continue to feed them.

When I walked inside, they were all there. Sleepy, squinting eyes and wagging tails met me. The pups jumped up as I lowered the bowl to feed them and their mother. She looked up at me with a worried expression that I assumed only meant she wondered how Ace was doing.

I extended my hand, and she allowed me to stroke her neck. "Not as well as you are, I'm afraid. And he's a stubborn patient. Won't let me help him."

She made a sound that was half growl and half whine.

I shrugged. "I can't just make him let me. He has to be willing."

She tilted her head and yipped.

I laughed at her understanding expression. "I'll tell him you think he should let me take care of him. Okay?"

That got her to wag her tail.

"I didn't know you could speak coyote." Ace's voice startled me. That wasn't good. Letting down my guard was not acceptable.

"I can't. And what are you doing out here? You're supposed to be resting."

Mama coyote growled and yipped at him too. I couldn't help but smile at her. But Ace didn't smile. He looked more hurt than anything. "I would that I could," he said softly in response to the coyote.

I glanced at her. "What did you say to him?"

She merely whined and nuzzled my hand.

I turned to Ace. "What did she say?"

He sighed. "She . . . wishes things could stay the way they are." His throat bobbed a few times, and his voice cracked as he continued, "So do I. But it's not going to happen."

My stomach sank. Ace might not have fallen for me. But my cracking heart was telling me right now that I had fallen hard for him. I couldn't separate him from the dragon I'd spent so much time with as a kid. My only childhood friend besides Dane and a couple of boomerang knives.

How could I have let him trick me twice? How could I have believed his lies twice? Why wasn't my heart letting go like I needed it to? My nose tingled as tears threatened, and I blinked them back. "Because of the war?"

He turned away and headed up the stairs. The coyote whined.

I followed him. "Ace? What are you doing?"

"If the misfits and mountain dragons are still planning to attack tonight . . ."

"What?" I caught up with him.

He sighed. "Have you called in backup yet?"

I paused, eyes wide before I could stop my surprised expression.

"I'm not stupid. I know you have something in that belt of yours."

I swallowed the painful lump in my throat. "I didn't call them. In fact, I promised Bran that I wouldn't."

He glanced over his shoulder at me. "And he bought that?" He started walking up the deck stairs again.

I followed. "One of your three family members is convinced. Two to go." Maybe three. If I could convince *him*, would he . . . no. I'd tortured him. I pulled my sleeve to cover my tattoo. "You have to tell them not to let the children come to the Feast."

"We made that decision last night, as soon as I told my father the mountain dragons had attacked." He opened the door for me.

As I passed by, I glanced at his side. "How are you feeling? Will you even be able to shift tonight?"

He hesitated, letting the door close behind him, so I pulled up his shirt. Some blood had soaked through the bandage, but not much. I peeled it aside, and my heart sank. "Ace, this doesn't look any better." I touched the puffy area around the wound.

He sucked air in through clenched teeth. "It'll feel better enough by tomorrow, though."

"Really?" I cocked an eyebrow.

"Yeah, thanks to you."

Thanks to me.

No wonder I had feelings for him.

"You should let me at least take care of you." I motioned to his side.

He actually smiled. "I've gotten more bumps and bruises from you or because of you than any scrape I could've gotten into on my own, but I'll manage." He turned to look at me, clearly teasing.

Only it wasn't funny.

Something heavy dropped like lead into my stomach. Heat spread across my skin. Angry heat. Heat from shame. All I could do was picture the *x*'s and *o*'s carved into his skin. They'd been burned into my mind. I stared at his chest, where I'd seen them yesterday.

"No." He shook his head wildly. "That's not what I meant."

I rubbed my thumb over the tattoo on my wrist, suddenly aware that I was backing away.

"Keira!" Panic edged his voice. "That's not what I meant." He reached for me, but he didn't grab my arm. Smart.

I looked into his eyes. The concern there, the guilt, was overwhelming.

My stomach lurched so hard I thought it'd fold in on itself. "But it's true," I whispered.

"No, it isn't." He inched toward me.

I put my hands out to stop him and shook my head. My knees weakened. I couldn't stand. I knelt on the ground and stared at him. The room seemed too fragile to hold the emotions rising in me. Or maybe I was too fragile to contain them. They would break free with such force that I would shatter.

"It is. I"—I pointed to him—"did that to you."

He knelt beside me—I had no strength to move. Not fast enough. The world was speeding by. Everything inside me crumbled. I looked up at him. He was blurry.

He touched my face so tenderly. "I wasn't thinking when I said that. I forgave you a long time ago for this. I never think of you as the person who did this to me."

"Isabel . . . the poison . . ." I didn't even know how to finish. How to comprehend what she'd made me do. Why was everyone so quick to forgive me?

"She knew what she was doing."

"I'm so sorry."

He tipped my chin up to look at him. "You're forgiven."

"Not for that. I mean, yes, for that." My own words choked me. "But I made a mistake."

"It's okay."

"No. It isn't."

"Yes. It is."

"You don't understand. I told my hunters what forest-dragon poison is." Tears broke free.

Ace released a shaking breath.

"I—I thought—when I found out you were the dragon—" I covered my face. The room spun. "What have I done?"

Slowly, painfully, he stood up. The scent of dragon smoke started to fill the room. He'd told me I could smell smoke for three reasons, but he'd never explained what they were. I knew enough from the last few days with him and Bran to figure this one out, though. He was angry. So very angry.

"Ace?" My voice sounded small.

The scent grew thicker. "Y-you told them—"

"I told them about the roses because I thought you'd betrayed me. I thought you'd killed my father."

His eyes narrowed. The hint of a threat seemed to emanate from him. "I thought—"

"You thought what?" I stood up and met his gaze.

What was I doing here? He didn't even like me. He'd just pretended long enough to get me to help him break a stupid curse. He'd played me again.

I glanced down, trying to maintain composure. When I felt I had it, I glared at him. "How do you sleep at night knowing that you attempted to manipulate a girl into liking you? You could have chosen anyone for this betrothal, couldn't you have?"

"Yes." His eyes pulsed the faintest hint of red.

My heart stuttered, and I gasped. "Why did it have to be me?"

His throat bobbed.

"They want to kill me, don't they?"

"There are some who do, but I promised I wouldn't let anything happen to you."

Could it be because he loved me? Something deep in my soul prayed for that to be true, because then maybe everything wouldn't have been a lie. I tried to tamp down my rising emotions. Because I knew it was too much to ask. "If I do this tonight and convince your parents, you'll be okay?"

"After tonight, you'll never have to worry about me again."

But I wanted to, and I hated myself for it. "After tonight, I'll never see you again?" My voice shook.

"I hope not."

Those words were a knife to my heart. No red; no lie. He didn't love me.

Something inside of me cracked, and I wanted to scream at myself, because it was no one's fault but my own. I hadn't seen the lies until it was too late.

"After I save you, I'll be glad to leave." Each word tore at my heart. Why was I lying to him? Why was I pushing him away?

"Good. I wouldn't want you to stick around after the betrothal ceremony." How he said that, with no emotion, made me want to let out the pain welling up inside of me. Instead, I stood there, hoping to convey the same lack of emotion.

He turned to leave me alone with my shattered heart.

I started picking up the pieces and gluing them together with my anger. My hurt. My pain. And each beat of my pulse throbbed. A question deep inside me clawed its way out, and I had no resolve to stop it. "When those dragons were after us, why did you save me in the first place?"

He paused and faced me. His eyes softened. "Because I knew exactly who you were."

A void in my chest told me my heart had stalled for entirely too long. "The girl who tortured you?"

He closed the space between us, that strange, soft look in his eyes. "The girl who saw me, and because of that, you saved me."

My throat felt thick. I stumbled backward and braced myself on the couch's armrest. I pictured those huge scars on his chest. Tic-tac-toe. My nose stung, and my eyes welled with tears. I had tortured him, and he thought of me as the girl who had saved him?

My heart swelled. As much as I wanted to hate him, I couldn't.

He wasn't a monster.

I was the monster.

THIRTY

The day for the Feast of Fire was finally here. I looked at myself in the mirror.

The dress Zelda had picked for me—green, of course—highlighted my eyes. It complemented me so well that I had to believe she'd bought it after she'd seen me. That meant they'd all hoped for this betrothal ceremony to happen.

Had I made a mistake by telling Ace I'd do this? By pushing him away yesterday, when I really wanted to try and change his mind—his heart—about me?

I couldn't stop replaying the relief on Bran's face when I'd told him I'd confessed my love to Ace.

And Ace hadn't lied about the curse. That meant he was really in danger.

But he didn't love me. He just needed the stupid betrothal.

I tried to make my smile look less fake.

If this is what saving him took, it was worth it, even if I walked away with a broken heart. I'd already ruined so much by letting one person's view of things taint what I so clearly saw in front of me.

Ace deserved to keep his humanity.

All dragons did.

I was able to smile at myself in the mirror now. Because I'd finally decided to let my own experiences influence what I believed. I breathed deep. I was ready.

The door opened downstairs, and I heard a familiar voice: Bran's. He seemed to be yelling at Ace, so I finished putting in the last earring and headed downstairs, hoping this green dress hugged my curves the right way. No full-length mirror upstairs.

My tracker was on, and I left it on the pillow along with a note for Dane that I'd be meeting him here with Isabel. Then I walked down the steps, careful in the stupid, strappy heels. Zelda had picked out everything, including a matching purse that perfectly housed one of my knives.

"How hurt are you?" Bran's voice was lower, but I detected his clear worry.

"I'll be fine. I just—"

"You're not healing like you should be."

"Don't worry. It's taken care of."

"I know. She told me. I just thought you'd be more healed by now."

I turned the corner.

Ace stood leaning on the banister. Bran faced him, a grim glare in his eyes. But they both stopped talking and looked up at me the moment I began descending the stairs.

Bran's eyebrows rose, and he whispered, "Wow."

I wasn't sure it was on purpose.

Ace turned to look up at me as well, and the way his jaw unhinged made me smile.

"What are you boys fighting about?" I paused and cocked an eyebrow.

Bran scowled. "Just that you seem to attract trouble, and it's always aimed at my brother."

"Not my fault he can't take care of himself and needs a bodyguard. I took care of two of those beasts. He should be thanking me."

"You're the reason they came after him in the—"

"Enough," Ace said. I flinched, but Ace hadn't taken his eyes off me. He stood at the bottom of the stairs and held out his hand as if to help me down the rest of the steps. "You look stunning."

I took his offered hand. It was warm. Strong. And his touch sent a flush over my skin. *"Gracias."*

Ace's eyes practically sparkled. "Green is your color."

"It's your color, actually."

When I made it safely to the ground, Ace popped out his elbow, and I linked my arm through his and shot him a playful glare. "I should pin a rose to your lapel."

He smirked and tugged me forward. "There will be plenty of roses at the party, since forest dragons were born from one."

My stomach dropped, and I froze. "Roses don't hurt you?"

"I love it when you're puzzling something out. You get this little crease between your eyebrows." He pulled me along.

"I do not."

"You do."

But what was their poison, then, if not roses? "I'll figure it out."

He glanced at me askance. "I have no doubt."

He walked with me, brushing past Bran as if he wasn't even there. All his attention stayed on me. We stepped outside, and the cool mountain air chilled my bare arms. He pulled the lapel of his suit coat. "You need a jacket?"

My heart stuttered. If he was going to be this good at pretending, I would really have to up my game.

"Here." Ace started to remove his jacket, but he grimaced.

"No. It's okay." I faced him and pulled the jacket back on him, straightening his collar and smoothing the shoulders. I looked deep into his eyes. "Just keep me close. I'll be warm enough."

The intensity in his gaze locked onto me and sent a flush through my cheeks.

"You two coming?" Bran's voice broke our eye contact, and Ace looped his arm around me. I cuddled into his non-injured side and headed to the car.

A redhead waved from the passenger seat. Liz. The young woman from the dragon orphanage.

I said hello, then leaned closer to Ace and whispered, "Your brother's dating Liz?"

He snorted. "I might have brought him along to a few visits at the orphanage."

"You set them up?"

"Shh. Don't give away my secrets." He got the door for me, and I slipped into the car.

Pleasant conversation in which Liz genuinely complimented me several times lasted for the entire ten-minute ride.

I stared out the window as Bran drove up through the huge archway toward a massive castle that sat on the edge of a cliff, near a huge bridge that extended across a gorge. Spires pierced the sky. I couldn't stop staring at the elaborate, life-sized stone dragons perched around the edges like gargoyles. Then one of them moved.

Ace chuckled. "Sentry duty. They have to protect the king."

"You're ready for the mountain dragons?"

"The party has to go as planned, or they would change their strategy when they realized we're on to them. But we're ready."

The car stopped, and Bran got out.

Ace touched my arm. "Wait for me?"

What did that mean? He got out of the car, a bit slower than normal, and I understood as he walked around the back and got my door.

I slipped my hand in his offered elbow. It was showtime. Truth was, I didn't even know which part of me was acting anymore.

My heart pounded, and I tripped as he escorted me up the steps. His strong arm kept me from falling, and he shot me a teasing smile. He was pretty good at this acting thing too.

And my heart ached. Because it had all been a lie for him. He may not have killed my father, but I still couldn't trust him. At least, that was what I kept trying to tell myself. I stared into the chasm below and then up at the towering castle. "You grew up here?"

"Yes."

"Wow." I looked at him and his crooked smile. Together, we ascended the steps. The autumn chill didn't bite into me with his warmth so near.

He led me into the entryway where Bran and Liz were already talking to two people. I recognized one: the woman. Her grace and poise weren't easily forgotten, nor was her beauty. Zelda. Ace's mother. The man next to her resembled both Bran and Ace. He had an easy smile and bright eyes that sparkled with joy when he wrapped his hands around Liz's and complimented her.

"You nervous?" Ace leaned close to me.

I cuddled into him. "These are your parents. And they're royalty. Of course I'm nervous. I have to make a good impression."

His eyes softened, and he looked at me as one might look at something they regretfully can't have. "Please do."

That made me laugh, but it held more shock than anything. "I suppose I deserved that."

"Well, hello, Keira. It's a pleasure to see you tonight." Zelda inclined her head and gave me a small smile. Something in her eyes registered as suspicion but also genuine intrigue. She would be the toughest to convince, I decided.

"It's wonderful to be here. Thank you for letting me into your home, considering the circumstances of the last time we met."

"I trust my son. If he chooses to bring you here, you are welcome."

I detected no hint of a lie.

Ace gave my hand a gentle squeeze with his arm, and I looked into his eyes. My stomach dropped. Had I already screwed up? Oh my! "Am I supposed to bow or something? Or the thing girls do—curtsy?"

His chuckle reverberated against my hand, and Zelda's melodic laugh joined in. "No. You are a guest here. No need for such formalities," Ace said.

The king rushed over to greet me. He clasped his hands around mine the way I'd seen him do with Liz. "You look lovely this evening, Keira. I am so happy to finally meet you. I trust you're finding the terms of your agreement suitable?"

I wanted to tell him that of course I didn't find the terms suitable. I was a prisoner. But I had to sell this love thing, so I opted for something with less venom. "I have really enjoyed being with Ace."

The king's eyebrows popped up.

"I mean Wallace." I felt like an idiot.

The king smiled. "Please, don't change your nickname on account of me. And truly, if you can think of a suitable nickname for Charles that isn't Charlie or Chuck, I'd love to hear it."

"Chaz it is."

His deep laugh was warm—nothing that I expected from a dragon king. He actually reminded me of Uncle Max before Dad died—when he was still happy and funny, even if his humor consisted of stupid dad jokes. "Well, it pleases me that my son has chosen well. I have to be honest, when he told me you were human and a hunter, my wife and I were concerned. But you remember that we have humanity, don't you?"

My stomach felt suddenly heavy. I tried to make sure he could see my honesty. "I do, Your Majesty."

Then his eyes smiled, and he seemed to look deep into me. "Good." He tugged my hand closer and leaned near my ear. "I can see into your soul, Keira. You seem conflicted, but your good intentions are shining through. Hold onto those. That part of you is directly connected to your humanity." When he released my hand and leaned back, the warm smile on his face held no hint of warning. "I like you. I think you'll bring out the best in my son."

I stared at him. Was my soul that easy to read? I tried a smile to maintain some semblance of composure.

"Okay, Dad." Ace sort of laughed.

Charles looked up at Ace and raised his hand as if he might pull him in for a hug. I immediately thought of Ace's injured side, but instead of a hug, the king laughed and smacked his son's back with a strong *thud*. Ace's arm tensed around mine, and he flinched. That had to have hurt.

Charles was still laughing. "You were right, Wallace. I like her. She does have spunk. And a brightness in her eyes that rivals a dragon's." He turned to me. "I'm proud that my son brought home a human."

"You are?" My voice cracked.

"Of course." His face grew more serious. "I hope you will be able to share some insight into your hunter affairs. As in, how to perhaps come to an understanding that we aren't evil creatures."

I smiled the most reassuring way I could. "I will."

"Good." He lifted his hand as if to slap Ace's back again.

I let go of Ace's arm and stepped between them. "Please tell me you've taken precautions to make sure you're all ready for tonight." My worried gaze made him pause, and he dropped his hand to his side and nodded gravely.

"The safety of my people is of utmost importance. If you find that you don't want to attend tonight because you're worried about your own safety, I would understand."

The way he tilted his head made me think that he was testing me.

I backed up so I was side by side with Ace again—this time protecting his injury from more well-intended thumping by his father—and stood as tall as possible. "I will stand with Ace. I'm not one to flee in the face of danger."

His eyes narrowed appraisingly, and he nodded. "You are a true gem. I know what my son sees in you, and you seem to be living up to what he's said."

I sucked in air and looked up at Ace. "You talked about me?"

He smiled, almost uncertain and bashful. "Mostly good things."

My heart pounded. He'd really sold them on this betrothal thing. They thought he was in love with me too. He tipped his head toward the rest of the wide, open hallway. "Shall we?"

I nodded, and he escorted me down the hall. "Did I do all right?"

He let out a small huff that almost sounded like the start of a shocked laugh. "All right? It couldn't have gone better if I'd told you what to say."

Heat flushed my cheeks, and I was sure to admire the reliefs of dragons on the high walls as we continued walking so he wouldn't see my blush. I realized I was still clinging to his injured side. I put my other hand over his heart. "How are you? Healing any better?"

His chest swelled beneath my hand. "Keira, you're doing wonderfully. Thank you."

What did that mean? My pulse sped. Apparently, I was doing a good job with the convincing.

He looked down at me and winced. "How about you? I know you don't like lying."

Lying.

Lies in the truth.

Why did my heart hurt?

Because he thought I was lying.

Part of me crumbled under the injury of not knowing who to trust. I paused as a wave of pain spread through my chest.

Ace stood in front of me, his eyebrows pulling together. "I'm sorry. I never should have asked you to do this. I did hold you prisoner. I trapped you with a bargain. I went about this the wrong way."

I'd hunted his kind simply for what they were. "I think we both did." I touched his chest again. His heartbeat sped beneath my palm, strong and fast.

His lips parted, and he stared at me.

I gazed back, wishing that I hadn't let him play me. That familiar fire warred with new feelings of forgiveness. Over Ace's shoulder, I caught sight of Zelda looking at us. Ace was still staring at me. So I leaned closer, focused on Ace.

"Keira, you—"

I pressed my lips against his. The surprise of the movement must have caught him off guard, because he didn't lean in right away. Then he did. Kissed me back. I may have forgotten to breathe. This moment, for me, wasn't about convincing Ace's family that I'd fallen for him. Easy. I had. This moment right here was my proof, because when he touched the skin on my neck, everything faded. Nothing. No time. No dragons. No hunters. No scars. It was just Ace and me. And goodbye.

He pulled back and stared into my eyes, his forehead so close to mine. The desire in his eyes was mine. Whatever happened from here, that kiss was mine. And nothing would erase its honesty.

He didn't back away, just continued drinking me in with his eyes. "You're selling it. I—even I almost believe you."

Those words speared me. He stepped back and held out his arm. I linked mine in his. So much more aware of the feel of him against me. Only the fabric of his shirt keeping his skin from touching mine. I tried to catch my breath and fell in step with him.

One glance over my shoulder, and I caught the queen's eye. She looked away as Ace tugged me along. But she'd seen.

Hopefully she believed.

THIRTY-ONE

"I'd like to show you something." Ace led me down the hall, past one huge room and to another.

I leaned closer to him, satisfied that no other family members were around. "Where's Isabel?"

He eyed me sideways. "Patience isn't really your thing."

I narrowed my eyes.

He frowned. "She's being held in one of the tunnels. It's guarded by dragons. There is a secret passage, though." He led me into a room, and I stopped, staring.

Shelves and shelves of books lined every single high-ceilinged wall. My jaw dropped. I'd never seen a real library. Heard of them, sure. Looked at pictures in the museums of what these places were like before the old wars. But this was more amazing than any photo or artist's recreation. And it smelled divine. Like the old book Mom had given me. "Wow."

He chuckled. "You like books?"

"I love them. I haven't really had a lot of time to read lately." I turned around in a circle, admiring everything. "This is a real library?"

"Yes. Another dragon secret. We tried to salvage as many as possible.."

"You privileged royalty types and your fancy, expensive castles with private libraries." I shot him a smirk and noticed he was leaning on a bookcase, slightly hunched over. "You're not okay."

"I'm fine." His eyes pulsed red.

"Ace, you're lying to me."

"I just need a minute."

I stared at him, angry that my concern had to be showing massively. "Let me guess, you avoided this room as a kid."

He laughed through what seemed like pain. "No, actually. My brothers and I would spend hours on end in here. Reading. Acting out adventures."

"Knights and dragons?"

He glanced at me as if I'd pulled him out of a memory. "Something like that."

I paused, replaying what he'd said. "Did you say *brothers*, as in more than the annoying Bran?" I asked smugly.

He closed his eyes. "Yes. I had another brother."

All I could do was stare while my heart cracked. "What happened?" My voice sounded so airy. So unsure. Dread filled me. Did I know him? Or worse . . . did I kill him?

He grimaced as if he didn't want to tell me. As if he wished I hadn't asked. He'd never mentioned his other brother. And I knew. Hope died in my soul. My pulse pounded, and I stepped away from him. "Did—did I—" Tears stung my eyes. "Please tell me I didn't—"

"No." He rubbed his hand over my arm.

Relief. So much relief. "What happened?"

He dropped his hand to his side. "Isabel killed Terrence when she captured me."

I exhaled, and it was painful. It wasn't me, but it was almost worse. The woman I wanted him to set free—I'd demanded he set free—had done it. I needed to sit down. I searched for a place and half stumbled the few steps to the window seat. I was slightly aware of Ace's comforting hand on my back, guiding me. Helping me sit.

"I'm so sorry," I managed. I didn't expect tears.

Ace swallowed. "I am too. He was a good person. But it's not your fault."

A fire seemed to blaze through my insides, leaving desolation in its wake. "I've—" Words failed me. It hurt to breathe. "I've killed—do you know how many dragons I've killed?" I shook, unable to stop the tears now.

He grabbed my hands. "Look at me, please."

I shook my head as if that motion could shake away all the terrible things I'd done. All the horrible ways I'd killed—people. They were people. I'd clung to the belief that they were monsters, because *I* needed to believe that. From that first moment Isabel forced my hand to push a knife into a dragon's chest—Ace's chest—I'd needed to believe they weren't human.

But she was wrong.

I was wrong.

He squeezed my hands. "You didn't know. She turned you into—"

"A monster?" I stared at him through the tears. "I'm a monster."

"No. You aren't. You set me free."

"I've killed so many of you. Tortured. Hunted." My voice felt so weak on that last word. I'd let Isabel break something inside of me.

"Here." He handed me a Kleenex box from the end of the seat.

I dabbed away the wetness on my cheeks, then placed the Kleenex in my clutch, hoping Ace hadn't looked at my knife or container of honey or the lockpick. I closed the purse quickly, and my gaze landed on the wall sconce. Bran had said something about the escape tunnel. The one that led to Isabel. It was here. In this room. Ace had brought me here to show me my way to freedom. My breathing quickened.

"You used to be able to see the good in dragons." His words stole my attention again. "That's why you freed me. You're starting to again, aren't you?"

I looked into his hopeful eyes. "Yes."

"I knew you would."

"Here you are." Zelda's melodic voice announced her presence.

Ace started to stand as his mother entered the library, and I stood close to him.

Zelda seemed lost in a fond memory as she glanced around the room and smiled. Then she faced me. "Tell me, Keira, how did you fall for Wallace?"

I gently rubbed my hand across his back and gazed up into his eyes. The way he looked back at me, so rueful, tugged cruelly on my emotions. I opted to look at Zelda and her skeptical expression instead.

And I recalled how he'd given his food to that woman in need behind the coffee shop. How he'd cared for the coyotes and the deer. How he'd always been so gentle and forgiving with me. My throat ached. And then I remembered his sad expression the day I'd freed him. Isabel hadn't given me the codes that day, so I'd taken him through the house. As a human.

In the dark, I couldn't really see his face, but I remembered how he'd touched my shoulder, the scars on his chest still healing wounds, and he'd said, "It's not your fault. She's making you believe something, but you know me. Don't you?"

"Yes," I'd said. "Now run, and don't look back."

And now I knew that he hadn't come back to murder my family. Just to seek justice for his.

I made eye contact with Zelda. If I were a dragon, the genuine emotions in me would have made my eyes pulse gold. I could feel it. "I fell in love with his heart." Then I looked up at Ace.

His lips parted, and he stared at me. It seemed as though he wanted to say something but didn't know what.

And all I saw was a hunger. The gold in his eyes. He seemed drawn closer to me, and I to him.

"Well, I'll leave you two alone." Zelda's satisfaction was evident.

But neither of us broke away to watch her go.

"My heart?" he said.

I nodded, tears threatening, and pulled him in for a kiss. He shuddered as he tugged me closer. Kissing me deeply, strongly. My own heart thundered in my ears. Drowned out the other sounds until a fanfare of music interrupted us.

"We should get out there." His voice was husky, and his eyes remained on my face.

I backed away from him. "I wish this could have ended differently."

"Me too." He touched my face so gently. "I'm sorry I hurt you, Keira. I didn't mean to."

"You needed me for the betrothal. Collateral damage."

"Yes. And I'm not proud of it."

I grabbed his hands. I still had some time to make him change his mind. "Maybe we can make the most out of tonight."

He laughed as if my actions shocked him. "You mean before the mountain dragons show up and start a war?"

"You ready?" Bran popped his head in, saw us holding hands, and smirked. "The Feast is starting soon." His eyes flicked to the far wall where I'd seen the sconce, and he nodded. I knew that was to be my exit.

On the other side of that wall was a tunnel that led to Isabel.

THIRTY-TWO

ce led me back to one of the spacious, open rooms. I stepped inside and had to stare. Pillars lined the walls. Long rectangular tables created a U-shape on the shiny wooden floor. It reminded me of a wedding setup, with a dance floor in the center of a bunch of tables.

Everything sparkled and glittered in the most magical, amazing, fairy-tale way. It was almost as though I could hear my mother describing her wedding day to me. The excited jitters she felt. The way time stopped when she entered the room and everyone stared at her. The way her arm fit so neatly in the crook of my father's elbow.

This place embodied all the magic I'd felt when she told me those stories. From the way the soft yellow light spilled out of each crystal chandelier to the way the room smelled of a garden of flowers.

Ace led me further in, and I noticed the tables were set for formal dining. White tablecloths. Napkins folded in upright triangles. A long-stemmed rose lay across each plate.

A flash of heat flickered over my skin. "Roses," I whispered.

"Relax." He smiled. "No thorns."

My pulse thundered, and a shiver skittered over my skin. Thorns? Of course. Just like the story. The thorn was what had brought the poison.

How had I missed that? Ace had told me. Had he meant to tell me? I thought it would kill him.

He led me to the head table and pulled out a chair for me. "The guests will be arriving soon."

"Where are your parents?"

Ace motioned toward the stage behind our table. "They'll come in through there and make an entrance so everyone can see them."

I noticed the door on the left side of the stage, at ground level.

"It leads to the room next to the library." His voice was quiet.

He knew. The library was the room from which led Isabel's tunnel. I was so close. I glanced at him. Had Bran told him of my plan? Of course he had.

When Ace looked away, I snatched a steak knife and held it behind my back. "Is there a powder room?"

Ace smiled. "Of course there is." He led me through the door on the side of the stage. "This is the greenroom." He motioned to another door—not the one directly across from us, that led to the library, but one that led out to the hallway. "There's a restroom directly across the hall."

"*Gracias.*"

"You have twenty minutes before everything starts."

"I'll be quick." Really, I had no idea how fast I would be. I just knew that if I was to save Isabel from her fate tonight, now was the time. But a part of me wasn't sure I wanted to. She'd killed Ace's brother. His uncle. She'd forced me to torture innocent dragons.

When would it end for her? Where would she draw the line?

But did she deserve death for it?

The least I could do was talk to her. I exited the door Ace showed me, and instead of going across the hall, I entered the next room over. The library.

I left my heels by the door, stashed the stolen steak knife in my clutch, and raced through the empty, cavernous room, past rows of books to the sconce Bran had pointed out to me. I pulled the sconce, and one of the smaller shelves swung out.

It was a tunnel, all right. Dark and dank and wide. I grabbed one of the lit torches off the wall and headed in. The door slid shut behind me.

The ceiling was so high. Right. So dragons could fit here in their full form. I edged forward, and my torch lit up cell bars along the side. Where were the guards? The end of the tunnel?

Had Bran made sure no one was here?

I shined my torch into the cell. "Isabel?"

A face drew closer, the torchlight illuminating her familiar features. She was older. Her hair was cut short, her hard eyes dull and angry. A few more wrinkles made shadows on her face, but I knew her. And my heart stalled as I took her in. I'd believed she was dead for so long. This moment knocked the wind out of me.

"Isabel." Her name escaped my lips in a whisper. I hadn't expected the tears or the warmth in my heart. "Isabel?"

"Keira?" She pressed her palms against my cheeks through the bars. "Is it really you?" Her eyes glittered, changing—hope started to bloom within them. She hugged me close, the bars cold and hard between us, but I still relished the warmth of her touch. Isabel was alive.

As much as I hated the things she'd made me do, she'd always loved me.

"How did you get into their nest?" She let go, and I stepped back.

My purse clattered to the ground and popped open. My knife skittered across the floor and into her cell. Her eyes tracked it.

Then she bent down slowly to retrieve the knife.

She looked at it as if it were a long-lost friend.

A devil she hoped to make a deal with.

She craved it. I could see it in her eyes, and I knew—I understood now how afraid I had made Dane all those times that vengeance had fueled my very soul before a hunt.

"Isabel?" I whispered again and reached through the bars.

She turned the knife in circles as she stood slowly from her crouch. Her gaze remained glued to the weapon. Her eyes held a longing. A desire. She wanted death. And my heart shattered.

"May I please have the knife? I need it to get us out of here."

She didn't respond, so I touched her arm, and she jumped.

"The knife. I need it if I'm to rescue you."

She blinked and shook her head, handing over the weapon. I snatched it from her and scooped up my purse, stuffing the blade inside.

"Of course." Her voice was strong again. "What's your plan? Surely you didn't come here looking for me?"

"I came because I wanted to find their weakness, but—"

"That's my girl." Her lips curled upward, and a devious smile spread across her face. "It's rose thorns."

My stomach lurched into my throat. "How do you know?"

Then I remembered the bouquet I'd found my first day in the cabin, in the bottom drawer.

"We have to get out of here. Can you pick the lock?" She pointed to her cell door.

"Do you know why you're here?"

"They're going to execute me. They love to do this to hunters. They waited years until they thought they had broken me. They believe they know where our base is now. Fools."

This was going to be harder than I thought, but I needed to know what she would do, how she would react. Because if setting her free was too dangerous, I would have to wait. "Isabel, I need to tell you something. Not all dragons are our enemy."

She stared at me unblinking for too long. Finally her eyes closed, then opened slowly. Tears shimmered in them. "I am so sorry, child. I can't stop replaying the last time I saw you with the dragons. The things I made you do. Will you forgive me?"

I stared at her, willing her eyes to pulse red or gold so I could know whether or not she was lying. Tears? Isabel wouldn't be capable of creating fake tears. Would she? Had she learned in the presence of dragons, even as a prisoner, that they were just as human as we were? I recalled how she'd looked at the knife I'd dropped. A pang stabbed my heart. I couldn't let her free. Not now. Not here. And certainly not with a knife that killed dragons.

I could give her the steak knife I'd stolen and dip it in the honey I'd placed in my purse. A steak knife wouldn't cut through dragon hide alone, but coated with honey—mountain-dragon poison—the blade would slice through the toughest mountain-dragon flesh. Then she'd be armed against the enemy, but not all the dragons.

I could free her now and have her meet me in the cabin with Dane while I finished up here—getting Ace to set me free and getting Zelda to remove the life debt.

Then again, who knew what kind of damage Isabel would do on the loose. If she'd believe me. Listen to me. Hear reason.

I leaned close to the bars. "The mountain dragons are planning an attack. They think the forest dragons are in cahoots with hunters. They want you."

"They do, do they?" A devious grin hit her face. She smiled like she used to right before a hunt. Like I always smiled before a hunt. She couldn't be trusted. But I couldn't leave her here to be killed. I passed her the honey-covered steak knife.

"You're not setting me free?"

"No. But I want you armed in case the mountain dragons come for you."

"You're leaving me here?"

"Temporarily."

"What's your plan?" Her eyes narrowed.

"I've been bound to a dragon by a life debt. He'll know if I leave." I bowed my head, unwilling to look her in the eyes.

She tipped my chin up. "Dragons are tricksters. It happens to the best of us, child. But we'll kill him. Let me out of here. I'll help save you."

"No. Isabel, he's different. He's going to set both of us free."

She cocked an eyebrow. "Really?"

"He will. You'll see. I know you don't want to trust them, but will you trust me?"

She seemed to be lost in thought for a moment. "Of course, child." She held up the knife. "What's your plan?"

Tears wanted to flow, but I swallowed the emotion. "There's a cabin in the woods near here."

"I know it."

"I'll break you out when the time is right. I need you to run and meet me there. Dane is meeting me—"

"Dane?"

"Yes."

"Good. There's something I want to tell you both."

"I'll come back for you as soon as I can. Okay?" I needed her to listen to reason, but I knew the middle of the dragons' nest wasn't the place for that kind of compliance from her.

She nodded and hugged me the best she could through the bars. Then she looked into my eyes and touched my face in that way I'd missed so much after she'd been gone. It tugged my heartstrings. She smiled. "I'm so glad you found me. I will wait for you."

I had to head back before Ace came looking for me. I left Isabel with her knife, hoping I was doing the right thing by everyone. I slipped my shoes on, as if it would slip me back into my role for the evening, and exited the library.

I nearly bumped into someone. "Oh!" I looked up into the eyes of Ace's father. "Your Majesty!"

His gaze narrowed, but not angrily. More like the way my father would look at me if he caught me trying to hide something. I swallowed, remembering how accurately the king had read my soul with barely any eye contact.

"Visiting the prisoner?" he asked.

Air escaped my lungs in a rush. "I-I didn't do—"

I looked right at him, letting him see the depths of my soul, not caring if Ace would find out how I really felt. I straightened. "I'm here to help your son. I want to make sure he keeps his humanity."

He studied me for a moment that seemed to stretch into an eternity. "I see that." He took a step back, inhaling a deep breath. "I'll hold you to it." His eyes narrowed. "What kind of king do you think Wallace would make someday?"

I gasped, remembering what Ace had said about his father's doubts. "A great one. One who cares for his people. One who does what's right and just and merciful."

Again he searched my face with that soul-piercing gaze. Then he nodded gravely. "I agree with you."

He left, through the door I was about to enter. And as soon as he was out of sight, my knees turned to mush. He thought Ace would make a great king?

I'd have to tell him.

I half stumbled back to the greenroom door and opened it. No sign of the king or queen, but Ace was there waiting, so I had to regain my composure fast.

Ace held out his arm for me. "I was wondering if you'd gotten lost. They're just about to start the procession." He escorted me back into the banquet hall and to a seat in the middle of the table. I sat between him and Bran while the room filled with people—well, dragons.

Fanfare echoed through the high-ceilinged room, and two green dragons swooped in, taking their places on the stage, where they morphed into their human forms. Even as a dragon, Zelda was elegant. Her subtly sparkled silver dress draped to just above the floor and flowed like a river when she moved.

She and Charles waved to a cheering room. It was truly a strange sight to behold, a king and a queen waving to their subjects.

They took their places next to Ace, and everyone stood. There had to be at least two hundred people surrounding the tables. They all plucked their roses from the plates and held them aloft. I hurried to replicate the gesture.

Hundreds of voices spoke in unison around me, saying, "From ash we are, and to ash we shall return."

The flowers ignited into balls of flame. And I watched as black specks rained down on each white tablecloth. My rose was the only one to remain red and brilliant. Ace touched it and smiled. The flame blazed, eating the entire bloom, and ash fell to the table, leaving nothing but a black smudge on my fingertips.

I looked up at him. "You can control flame in this form?"

"Only in the borders of our territory. And after much practice."

I stared at the ash on the tablecloth as we all sat down. King Charles spoke, talking about dragons and coming of age and celebrating who they were in the world, while amazing smells of prime rib and roasted chicken and potatoes wafted into the room. I could hardly focus on his words. I was too busy taking everything in. The cheers. The normalcy. They didn't seem like monsters at all. Servants carried silver trays to each table.

Bran leaned close to me. "You know what breaks the curse, don't you?"

My mind registered the king saying something about the curse. He'd said—I tried to recall what my brain had nearly dismissed as white noise—that the curse they bore was a heavy burden of being a part of this world. Most dragons avoided the human realm because of it.

Something inside me squeezed air from my lungs. "If they fall for a human and tell them about the curse, they need that human to agree to the betrothal," I whispered.

Bran's eyes narrowed. Silverware started clinking, and the murmurs of dozens of individual conversations filtered through the room. He handed me a roll. "Butter or honey?"

"Both?" I moved my clutch from next to my plate to make room for the food, and I realized I'd forgotten to close it. My knife and the container of honey I'd packed stared up at me, clearly visible to Bran's prying eyes.

He cocked an eyebrow. "Always a hunter, huh?"

I snapped the purse shut. His stare bored deep into mine. He was searching my soul. A shudder rocked through me.

What would he find there?

I knew I should tear my gaze away, but I didn't want to. It was almost like I wanted him to see a piece of me. The piece that wasn't lying. The piece that truly cared for Ace.

He nodded once. "You seem pretty conflicted."

I opened my mouth, not sure what to say.

He continued, "Take the chicken and the beef. They're both excellent." His familiar smirk filled his face, but then a little of it slipped into a real smile.

Had I fooled him? Or had I fooled myself?

Ace's arm brushed against mine, and I turned to him and his rueful smile.

"How is everything?" he asked.

I leaned closer. "You're going to have to stop looking so sad, or you'll blow our cover."

His eyes widened. Then he smiled, and the faint scent of dragon smoke wafted between us. The smell of burning leaves or a wood-burning stove. Forest dragon. A scent that used to ignite hatred in me instead stoked warring feelings.

His gaze softened. "Are you all right?"

I suddenly felt so warm. The laughter around me reminded me of a wedding feast. A holiday party. "I'm nervous."

"Don't be. You're doing wonderfully." He lowered his head so that his breath tickled my ear. "If you need to call it off at any time—"

"No." I turned so I could see his startled expression. "I need my freedom."

He nodded. "I wish I could just give it to you. I wish—"

I touched his hand and squeezed gently. "I wish things were different too. But this is what we have to work with. And this hero isn't going to slay the dragon."

A glimmer shone in his eyes. "Are you trying to tell me that this story has a happy ending, even if the dragon doesn't get the girl?"

My breath caught in my throat before I was able to suck air in again. I wanted to ask if the dragon wanted the girl, if I'd somehow changed his mind, but I was too afraid. And why? My entire life I'd known what I wanted. Known that I'd get it if only I kept searching. And then, when it was ripped from me, I had been so quick to create a new goal, all with the idea of destroying dragons. And now . . .

Now I didn't know what I wanted.

Or maybe I did.

And that was what scared me.

I knew what I wanted, and this time I couldn't have it.

How was I supposed to move forward when I knew I couldn't obtain my goal? When I wasn't even sure I should have this desire? Everything I'd wanted before, the revenge, the vengeance, had been based on a lie.

So had everything I wanted now.

Ace didn't love me.

Not for real. He just needed me.

But *I* needed to know one thing—when was I going to start listening to my own heart? Deciding for myself what I knew to be true?

"I'm going to make sure the story has a happy ending," I said.

A pulse of gold shone in his eyes. "I'd want nothing less."

They began to clear our dinner plates, and Ace motioned to the dance floor. "You ready for this?"

I took his offered hand and stood.

He led me out onto the smooth, wooden floor. I rested my hand on his shoulder, and he wrapped an arm around my waist like we'd practiced. I cuddled close, but this was his injured side. "Will you be all right?"

One corner of his mouth pulled down. "With you? Yes. You're like a feather." Something sparked in his eyes, and my chest ached.

We were the only two dancers. All the dragons were watching. I clutched his hand like a lifeline. "Where is everyone?"

"My ceremony. My dance. I told you this would be a lifesaver."

Heat hit my cheeks, and my stomach flipped.

When the music started, Ace guided me flawlessly. This had to be what it was like for every fairy-tale princess. Only I was dancing with a creature I'd been taught to fear and hate my whole life. I looked up into his eyes, recalling who he was when we were children. The fond memories warmed my heart, and I smiled.

Ace lowered his head closer to mine. His woodsy scent surrounded me, and I breathed in. "Thank you."

I thought I detected a smile in his voice. "For what? For seeing you?"

He swallowed. "Me?"

"You. Ace. Wallace. Wally. Boy. A man. A forest dragon." I didn't tear my gaze from his. "All of you."

"And?"

"And I'm no longer afraid."

With my last word, the music ended, but we remained frozen, joined, with my hand in his and his arm around me. I could feel his heartbeat in my palm. Mine beat in rhythm.

The dragon king joined us on the dance floor, clapping, and everyone else applauded.

Breathless, Ace and I turned to face the crowd. I curtsied. He bowed. Then we faced one another again, and I detected confusion in his eyes. He led me to his father.

"Tonight, for the change of season, it is my pleasure to announce my son, Wallace, and his chosen life mate, Keira."

Everyone clapped.

I couldn't help but look at Ace. My heart pounded in my chest. I straightened my spine and gripped his hand. He clutched back. Strong. I looked out at the people cheering for their future king.

The dance floor opened, and the king ushered us toward the stage where the queen stood, her eyes on me, squinting slightly. Had she bought it?

"You told her?" The queen finally tore her gaze from me and looked at her son.

"I did." Ace nodded.

The king glanced at me. "And she returns your love?"

Ace squeezed my hand and offered me a smile, but his eyes weren't in it. They were round and soft and sad. "Yes."

I dropped his hand and wrapped my arm around his back, hoping they'd see my sincerity.

Bran slapped Ace's shoulder. "May I steal her for a dance?" Bran held out his hand and bowed in front of me.

I slipped my hand into his. "Just one?"

He straightened and shot me a smirk. Then he led me out onto the floor.

This time, others surrounded us. It wasn't as uncomfortable. And Bran was just as smooth in leading me through the steps. He searched my face. "I had my doubts about you, but it looks like you actually like my brother."

"I'm happy to meet your approval."

"Approval? I wouldn't go that far yet."

Bran spun me around. "When he moved into the city, looking for you, I thought he was crazy. There were plenty of dragons around here who would be happy to have him as a life mate, but no. Not my romantic brother. He had to go looking for the girl who had set him free. The human who'd stolen his heart. Humans cast a spell on us that way. If a dragon falls in love with one, there's no falling out. That's how the curse takes hold. Finding you and getting you to learn to love him was his only chance."

The curse? My posture went rigid, and Bran nearly stumbled when I missed following his lead. "So this whole thing with the misfits was a setup?"

"Of course not. The only stroke of good luck about that was your showing up. I didn't know it was you until my mom saw your tattoo."

My pulse had to be visible. My blood seemed to form a whirlwind in my chest. If Ace needed me specifically to break the curse, was it because Bran's words were true? Had Ace fallen for me? Did he truly love me? My whole body trembled.

I wanted to ask, but I couldn't, not without breaking the bargain. "You don't believe I love him?"

"Oh. I do. I just don't know if you believe it yet. I hope, for my brother's sake, you figure it out before sunset. He only has until then for you to profess your love to him." He narrowed his eyes.

"You don't believe I have? I told you—"

"You're not very good at deception. Your act is impeccable, but your eyes reveal too much. I don't think you've told him."

"How I feel?"

"Yes, Keira. You need to tell him that you return his love before sunset tonight."

"Why sunset?'

"Didn't he tell you everything? This ceremony marks his last day as a man if he doesn't find true love. If he can't get the human he's fallen in love with to accept him as dragon and man by sunset tonight, he'll remain a dragon forever. As long as you've professed your love to him, you'll save him."

My heart stalled. "The curse?" My voice was breathless. The story. It was just like the story of the human who didn't return the dragon's love. Did that mean . . . "He'll lose his humanity if I don't tell him I love him?"

Bran's eyes rounded, and the sorrow in them made my chest tighten. "Yes."

No. Then why would he ask me to pretend? I looked into Bran's sad eyes. Just to protect them from finding out? Well, they'd figure it out after tonight. They'd . . . no.

The thought echoed in my head, and breath stalled in my hollow lungs. No wonder he'd told me not to protect him if the war broke out. Ace planned to die tonight. When the mountain dragons attacked, he planned to die. My heart plummeted like a dragon diving.

Then it hit me. In order for my profession of love to work, he had to love me back. "You said he . . ." Ace really did love me? He really wasn't pretending? "He fell for me."

"Of course. That's why he's spent these last five years searching for you."

I could hardly breathe.

"Sire." A worried voice broke through my reeling thoughts, and Bran stopped moving to listen. "The prisoner has escaped. She's killed four of our guards and headed out through the tunnels."

I couldn't hear anything but the blood in my ears. I closed my eyes.

Isabel. How did she . . . ? My chest felt empty. My purse. When I'd closed my purse at the table, had I seen the lockpick?

No.

She'd taken the lockpick.

She was on the loose.

I squeezed my eyes shut, feeling dizzy.

"Are you okay?" Bran asked.

What had I done? I had to tell Ace. Two men approached Ace and the king, and they all started talking, their heads low.

"Uh-oh," Bran said.

"What?"

"That can't be good. Those were the guards sent to check on the mountain dragons. Come on." He led me to where the others were talking. The guards seemed to hesitate when they saw us approaching, but the king didn't ask them to stop.

"Isabel has escaped," said one of the guards. "And there are two dozen hunters on our doorstep."

"Hunters?" Bran looked at me, and his nostrils flared as though I'd stung him. He backed away from me.

"No!" I held out my hands to try and stop their train of thought.

Zelda looked at me, and her eyes flashed. "Tell me they don't know our secret."

THIRTY-THREE

As three dragons in human form escorted Lance—my uncle's best hunter—through the doors of the ballroom, my heart plummeted.

"On behalf of Maxwell Jensen, who is being escorted inside," Lance called, "I demand the release of his niece, Keira Jensen, or we will find this a hostile environment."

Uncle Max? No. I started shaking, feeling suddenly unsteady in my strappy heels. "No! Lance, this isn't what you think!" I screamed, my throat raw.

All I could do was look into Ace's wounded eyes and plead with him to hear me. "I didn't—"

"You promised you didn't call them."

"I didn't. I—" Every breath hurt. "I—"

Bran shook his head and backed away from me, tugging Ace's shoulder. "She set Isabel free, brought the hunters here, and convinced you to let the mountain-dragon spy live. This—all of this—is her doing."

Bile scalded my throat. "No!"

Ace glanced at me. His eyes narrowed, then popped open wide. He didn't believe me. The deal was off now.

I glanced at Zelda.

"How much of this is true?" she demanded.

"Will you let her go?" Lance strode farther into the room.

I wanted him to stop. I wanted all of this to stop. "Ace." My voice cracked, but he wouldn't look at me. "Please, listen."

Dragons grabbed my arms and yanked them behind my back.

Lance pulled out his knife.

"Stop!" I screamed so loud my throat burned. My eyes burned. Tears streamed down my cheeks. "Ace. Wallace! Please, listen."

The king held out his hand toward Lance. "This girl is here because she willingly took on a life debt for a dragon."

Lance laughed. "She'd never do that. Now I know you're lying."

"No!" I struggled to make Lance hear me. "It was for Dane. He saved Dane." I looked at Ace. "But my brother's not a dragon. They didn't know. They thought Dane was a dragon."

Bran's eyes narrowed. "You didn't know?"

"That was just what Ace said to cover. Dane—"

Ace shook his head. "Why else would we make him pay off the life debt?"

Why was everything fuzzy all of a sudden? Why couldn't I breathe? Dane . . . a dragon? Impossible. Right? "Th-that's a mistake."

Bran shook his head, seeming surprised that I didn't know. "We all smelled him. He's definitely a dragon."

This wasn't happening. The edges of the room went dark. My knees weakened, and the dragons securing my arms held me steady.

"You have a dragon working for you as a hunters?" The king turned to Lance.

Lance just stared at me, as shocked as I must have looked.

I had to stop this before someone killed Lance or he tried to kill a dragon. "If you would listen to me—"

"Silence." The king wouldn't even look in my direction.

Ace nodded to his father. "Let the prisoner speak."

Prisoner. That word slammed into me like a dragon tail. Imaginary spikes tore into my chest and left my heart exposed. "I went to see Isabel, but I didn't know she'd taken the lockpick from me."

"You called your uncle. You said you told him what our poison was." Ace's gaze was emotionless.

"I was mistaken, though! Ace, I"—a sob interrupted my plea—"I told you I was sorry."

"I . . ." His voice broke. He looked deep into my soul. The gold pulsed in his eyes as he touched my cheek. "You asked me to let that dragon go. I thought it was from kindness."

"It was." I leaned into his hand. "I never meant for any of this to happen." I looked at him through my tears and choked on my words. "Please believe me."

He sighed and dropped his hand, and his eyes turned hard. "The problem is you can't be trusted." He turned his back on me, and I lost the ability to remain standing.

Heavy, my knees hit the stage floor. I leaned over, pulling against the dragon arms trying to drag me to my feet.

Lance made to touch his watch. It would call in the other hunters on standby. No. I had to stop him.

"Lance, no! Get out of here. Get everyone out of here! Please!"

The front doors burst open.

A dragon flew in and landed in front of the king. "Sire! Mountain dragons have arrived. They attack from the east, and misfits approach from the west. It appears they believe we're working with the hunters."

"No," I whispered. The word echoed through the empty numbness in my chest.

What had I done?

Ice shot through me as Uncle Max entered the room with a dragon escort and a dozen hunters. I couldn't hear anything. The sorrow in my soul squelched any sound. All I saw were dragon forms taking flight all around me. Uncle Max was yelling something about letting his hunters go, but even his shouts seemed muffled in my ears as my sobs consumed me. I searched the blurry forms of the hunters for Dane.

Dane. He'd have told Uncle Max. He was protecting me. And I'd dragged him into this. My brother. A dragon? Did he even know?

But Dane was nowhere to be found.

Through the open doors, in the light of the setting sun, I watched as silhouettes of dragons flying toward the palace filled the sky.

As Uncle Max wheeled closer to me, the dragons holding me pulled me through a secret door and into the tunnels. I was powerless against them.

And realization slammed into me: if Dane was out there somewhere, then everyone I cared about was here. Everyone I loved could die today.

And it was all my fault.

THIRTY-FOUR

They dragged me into the tunnel and released me in a heap of brokenness on the ground. What had I done? I stood up, fists clenched. I had to do something, not wallow in my sadness and mistakes.

The dragons raced down the tunnel toward the other exit. No doubt to join the fight outside. But why hadn't they locked me up? I headed back toward the dining room, wishing I had my stupid purse and my knife. I had to get back in there and stop the hunters from fighting the forest dragons. The real enemy was knocking on the palace door.

Smoke poured from the darkness, and I recognized the smell.

I kicked off the strappy heels and faced the dragon who filled the space behind me. I didn't need to see the crescent-shaped hole in his wing to know who this was. I could tell from his eyes.

"Bran." My words shook. "I didn't do this. I didn't call them here."

He thrust his arm out toward me. "I should kill you right now."

"Please. Believe me!"

"You betrayed all of us! I was right to not trust you. You deserve to die."

My stupid mistakes had led me to this moment, but not on purpose. How could I get him to see? To believe? "Fine. Kill me, then!"

His eyes narrowed, and he opened his mouth to fire. And I stood there, waiting. Because he was right. I deserved death. I had done so much wrong.

I closed my eyes.

And no flames came.

I cracked an eye open. "What are you—?"

"I'm not like you, Keira. I can't just kill someone who's helpless." He opened his claws, and my clutch with my knife inside sat in the center of his palm. "But I'll fight you. For Wally."

I glanced up at him and flicked my wrist. The bag started to move as my knife tried to come to me. He tossed the bag at my feet, and I pulled out my weapon. "I don't want to hurt you, Bran."

"Isn't that something? Because I want you dead." He opened his mouth again, and I had no clear shot at his fire trigger. Nowhere to hide in the tunnel. No way to escape the stream of fire. But I also didn't want to hurt him.

I dropped my knife. "*Lo siento.* I'm sorry. I didn't mean for this to happen. I—" Tears streamed down my cheeks as I realized what I believed in my own heart. I tried to loosen the tightening in my throat and stop the tears from coming. "I love him." It came out a whisper, but they felt like the strongest words I'd ever said. *"Me encanta. Lo amo tanto.* I love Wallace."

Bran stopped. He swallowed and straightened. "I know you do. And because of that, only you can save him. That's the only reason I'm doing this."

"Doing what?"

"Making sure you get to him alive."

My whole body shook. "You believe me? You trust—"

"No. I don't trust you. But you're Wally's only chance." He nodded. "Come with me. You have to tell him."

"Where is he?"

Bran bowed his head and closed his eyes. When he looked at me again, I could feel his pain, because it was mine too. "He's fighting. But I will get him to you. Do you understand? And you will save him."

I touched Bran's claws. "I will. And I'll tell him I'm not good enough for him."

Bran squinted, as if he wished he could sense a lie in me. Then he nodded once. "Follow me."

"Wait. Let me talk to my uncle. I might be able to convince him to leave you and your horde alone."

Bran nodded. "You don't need to."

My heart broke. Was I too late? I braced against the wall as a gasp escaped me and my knees weakened. "He's—"

"He's working with us. He told me what you said to your brother. About trusting us."

"My uncle's alive?"

"Yes."

"Have you seen my brother? He has to be here! He's the only one who could have told my uncle about this." I paused. "Maybe he's . . . here as a dragon?"

"Haven't seen him." Bran shook his head. "You honestly didn't know your brother was a dragon?"

Oh, Dane. It was painful to breathe. All the hurtful things he'd heard me say about dragons. For . . . years. He must've thought me a monster. I shook my head and tamped down those thoughts. Right now I had to save Ace. "Take me to your brother. And—"

"You help me save my brother, and I'll help you make sure yours is safe."

I nodded once, expelling a shaky breath. "Thank you."

Together, we raced out of the tunnel. When we hit the outside, I gasped and looked up. Streaks of fire lit up the night. The orange of the descending sun seemed to aid the anger that spread across the clouds. Destroying everything.

Roars and the crackle of fire filled the air.

Across the entire sky, dragons slammed into one another. Ripping through each other's wings and sinking their teeth into scaly hides. Some fell end over end in a tailspin of smoke. Others showered blood on the ground like rain. But the fire still streaked the heavens. This was my fault. My doing. My mistake. *Mi culpa.*

I dipped my knife in the honey Bran made sure I had from my purse, and the container wobbled in my unsteady hands. I got some on my fingers and wiped it on my dress.

Bran touched my arm. "Wait here. I'll go get him." He took flight, his wing beats matching the pounding of my heart as he headed toward the fray.

"I should have known," said a voice behind me.

I whirled around.

There, standing near the rock formation hiding the entrance to the tunnel, stood Isabel.

THIRTY-FIVE

Isabel yanked my arm and pulled me behind one of the jagged rocks to shield me from view of the dragons. "I should have known you'd find a way out. I was coming back for you. But a dragon?"

I had to think fast and get her out of here before Bran came back with Ace and she did something horrible. "I'm resourceful." I smirked.

"There's my girl." She hugged me so tight my insides warmed. I'd missed her so much. I had to get her to understand that dragons weren't all evil. There had to be a way. She let go of me, her eyes expectant. "We have to head back to that cabin."

Yes. The cabin. I could get her to go there. "Head there. I want to make sure Uncle Max and Dane are all right."

"No." She grabbed my wrist. "I need to get you safe."

The scent of burning coals wafted over us, and we looked up. My heart sputtered. Three mountain dragons towered above me.

One snaked his head closer, laughing. "Let me give you a lift."

Isabel looked at me and subtly pointed to the dragon. She made a motion with her hands for me to keep it talking. How easily I slipped back into this hunting communication with her. Almost as though she'd never left. I peered up at the dragon. "I thought you'd never ask."

It chuckled, smoke pouring out of its nostrils.

As it leaned closer to me, Isabel jumped out from behind the rock, honey-covered knife ready. I threw my weapon, and it stuck deep into the dragon's scales. That distracted its attention long enough for Isabel to grab the horn on its head and mount its neck. The beast shook its head, but Isabel drove the steak knife I'd given her into the base of his skull. The dragon's head fell to the ground, and it—no, he turned to ash.

The sound of rocks clicking together resounded from three different places. Fire spurted out, and I dove behind a boulder. The whole place heated almost beyond what I could bear, but no flame touched me in my hiding spot. When the fire died away, I peered up. Two red eyes stared back at me.

The dragon seemed as pleased as a cougar with a shrew. "Come closer, hunter. I have a special fate for you."

Isabel popped up from behind another boulder and threw her knife. One dragon batted it away with his tail. Not good. She couldn't call hers back.

Two of them, and only I was armed.

A massive green bolt zoomed toward the mountain dragons and pinned one to the ground.

One left.

My heart hammered.

Isabel shot me a glance. "Let it keep that one occupied. Cover me while I get my knife." She darted away, and I threw my knife at a dragon targeting her. The blade bounced off its neck. His head thrust forward, and flame lit the back of his throat. I dove behind the rock and called my knife back. It smacked into the jagged edge of the stupid boulder and fell.

As soon as the flame died, I jumped out of hiding to give my weapon a straight path back to me. But the dragon was ready. Its tail rammed into me, knocking me off my feet. I hit the ground hard, sending a shock of pain through my shoulder and hip. I looked up to see if I could recall my weapon, but the tail came at me again.

Ice spiked through my veins as I struggled to stand. I'd managed to avoid the tail spikes on the first hit, but twice in a row?

Too late—the tail slammed into me, and I bashed into the rock sideways. My head hit stone, and I opened my eyes to a momentary blur.

It cleared fast, but my head ached. Shakily, I tried to push myself up. Everything hurt. I felt dazed. Isabel's voice cut through the fog in my mind, and I saw that I had a clear path to my weapon. I flicked my wrist, and my knife returned.

Armed again, I managed to stand and face my enemy, but I still felt unstable. "Would you like your honey for here or to go?"

His wings spread out and propelled him skyward.

"To go?" I tossed my knife, and it glanced off his wing. I called my weapon back to try again, but the mountain dragon thrust its head into a dive, straight for me.

I had to move.

The green dragon that had come to our aid rammed into the mountain dragon. It was a forest dragon, but much bigger than either Ace or Bran. Had I met this dragon this evening? Did I know him? Had my uncle sent him to find me? Had Bran?

"What are you waiting for?" Isabel called.

"The other dragon's in the way. I don't have a clear shot."

"Since when do you spare a dragon? Kill them both!"

This was just what I'd feared. I got in front of Isabel. "Isabel, that dragon helped us."

"For his own means, Keira. Give me the knife." She reached for my weapon.

"No." I pulled away from her.

The dragons plummeted in a tailspin. A *thud* shook the ground as the forest dragon landed on his back near me. The mountain dragon scrambled up first and lunged, poised to slash the forest dragon's throat.

Not on my watch.

I tossed my honey-coated knife, and it sank into the mountain dragon's skull. Ash rained over the forest dragon. I called the weapon back, but Isabel raced in front of me and caught it.

My heart froze. "Don't hurt him, Isabel!" I grabbed her arm and pulled. She elbowed me in the temple.

The world shook as I staggered back from her. "What are you . . . ?"

She shoved into me again, slamming my body to the ground as the dizzy sensation returned.

"Isabel!" I struggled to stand on shaky legs.

"I can get you to safety." The forest dragon held out his clawed hand, and as I looked deep into his eyes, I recognized him.

"King Charles?"

He smiled. "I knew you were a good one. The soul never lies. Wallace chose well."

"You—you mean you believe me?"

He breathed deep. "I think your heart is finding its way back to goodness."

Maybe he'd tell Ace I hadn't meant to betray him. I nodded, my throat thick. "*Gracias.*"

He held out his hand. "Come with me. I'll get you to safety."

I started to follow.

"Trust a dragon?" Isabel's voice sounded bitter. "What did they do to you? I should have known you weren't strong enough to withstand their powers."

I turned to see the darkness in her eyes and the knife she held. I pushed the king's hand away. "Go. I'll keep her from hurting—"

"Out of the way, Keira!" She raised *my* knife.

I had to stop her madness. I stood in front of the king. "No! Stand down, Isabel! You don't understand."

"I do understand." Isabel's gaze was incredulous. Hurt. "You forgot. No negotiations."

The king started to take flight, but I still didn't have the knife. Isabel did.

"I saved you!" I rammed into her. Together we hit the ground. "Not so you could kill innocent—"

"Innocent?" She pushed me off of her and hurled the knife.

"No!" I screamed as the blade sailed above my head.

I lurched to my feet and watched as the knife shot toward the king. He shifted direction, but the blade still headed toward him. I tried to call it back. The knife lost momentum, ripped into his chest, and dragged through his scales. It returned to me blood soaked, and Ace's father crashed to the ground beside us.

"What have you done?" My hands shook as I looked at the king's blood on the blade.

I ran to his side and dropped to my knees beside him as he morphed into human form.

No. No, no, no, no, no!

Blood spread onto his silk shirt. My heart ripped open. Not Ace's father. Ace would never forgive me. Never believe me. Look what I'd done.

"Your Majesty!" I sank to my knees next to him.

He shivered.

"Stay with me." I clutched his hand.

"Call me Chaz."

Tears trailed down my cheeks. "This wasn't supposed to happen. This can't happen. You're going to be okay. Please, just stay with me. *Por favor.*"

He smiled. "You tried to save me." His breath was ragged. "Wallace said . . . he knew you'd remember."

Remember what? That I loved Ace? Yes. That I accepted him for who he was? Yes. Uncle Max had been right. I never should have trusted Isabel. I should have listened to myself.

A sob caught in my throat. "Remember what?"

"Who you . . . used to be. Your . . . humanity."

My heart wanted to stop. Flowing tears stung my eyes. *My* humanity. Yes. That's what I'd lost the day Isabel made me carve the stomach of a dragon. Made me hurt my friend.

The king grabbed my hand. "You . . . saved . . . my son. Please . . . do it again."

"I will! I promise!" I would do everything I could to save Ace. Everything. "I love him."

"I know."

"Hang on. Okay?" I squeezed his hand, but he didn't squeeze back. His smile vanished as his body turned to ash.

A silent scream of helplessness echoed deep in my soul. I snatched the knife. My hands shook as I looked at the king's blood on the blade.

I balled my hands into fists and faced Isabel. "You. You told me they were monsters. Liar! You're the monster!"

Isabel shook her head. "You're compromised. I can't have you following me."

She swung her fist. Pain shot through my head, and everything went dark.

I opened my eyes to a magenta sky and scrambled to my feet. I had no weapons, no shoes, and no idea where I was. Even my bracelet was gone. Isabel was out there with a dragon-claw weapon, and it was all my fault.

The air was colder here. But where was here? I wasn't at the castle anymore. This place seemed so quiet. So high. The mountains?

Smoke surrounded me in a thick, billowing cloud, and I could no longer see anything else around me. I looked up, and the sky was streaked with trails of black where fire and smoke had scarred the dry air. I put my hands out in front of me and stepped forward.

Above me, tiny in the distant sky, silhouetted forms of dragons crashed into larger, more powerful dragons. No! They were being led up here into mountain-dragon territory! They'd all be killed.

My heart sank. Was Ace already dead?

Bran?

Their father was. And that was all my fault. My chest tightened. They would never forgive me.

Dane? I let out a roar, unwilling to shed more tears until this was over.

I stared at the sky, where smaller dragons made tactical formations as they systematically barraged the larger ones. But a mountain dragon dove, changing direction and smacking its powerful tail into two of the smaller dragons. One plummeted to the ground. The other staggered in flight, losing altitude.

How would I stop this?

The small form of an arrow shot through the sky and hit the mountain dragon in the chest. It seemed to stumble, then it roared and let out a stream of fire.

Shaking, I fell to my knees.

The cloud of smoke around me thickened until it stung my eyes. I doubled over, coughing. A head slithered through the cloud, gray and jagged and covered in scales. A mountain dragon. I jolted to my feet and backed away.

"Careful. Wouldn't want to fall to your death." The deep voice thundered, and something huge and hard pressed into my back, easily pushing me toward the dragon's massive face. I had to be as tall as the dragon's front tooth. Its huge, red eye searched my face. The dark, vertical pupil narrowed. My knees shook, and my hands started sweating. I'd never seen a dragon this big.

"Where am I?" My voice trembled.

"My lair." He chuckled, and the sound was like an avalanche. "I was told about you by my great grandson—rather reluctantly, I'm afraid." His voice was like a mountain moving.

I swallowed.

The smoke dissipated. I hugged myself as cold air chilled me. I was on a mountain. Something sticky covered my dress. Blood or honey or both.

The mountain dragon tilted his head as the smoke around me faded. "I don't like my kin protecting hunters and forest dragons. It's a good way for them to get killed. Speaking of which"–the dragon's head shot toward me–"you killed my brother."

The sound of rock striking rock told me this guy was loading. I put my hands up to shield myself, knowing it wouldn't help.

I was about to die, and all I could think was that I hadn't saved Ace. I didn't know where Dane or Uncle Max were. If they were even alive. And I fell to my knees.

A deep chuckle rumbled the rocks, but nothing happened. Slowly, I peeked through my arms.

The dragon wore a satisfied smile. "I like to hunt. But I prefer larger prey, like the son of the forest-dragon king. Since you smell like him, I imagine he's on his way to retrieve you."

No.

"I'll keep you a while longer." His eyes narrowed. "In this."

Claws wrapped around me, squeezing and leaving me buried in complete darkness. My stomach dropped at the sensation of being lifted from the ground. Then the claws opened, and I fell.

I screamed, trying to get a sense of direction. Thorns scraped my body as I tumbled into a heap of rose bushes. I dropped to the ground in the middle of the brambles, my vision obscured by thorns. Pain seared every part of me as I pushed through them to get to the light.

Thorns sliced through my dress, ripped my skin, tangled my hair.

At last, I made it to a clearing, falling to my hands and knees. Another hedge of rosebushes stood in front of me, much too high to jump. Even if I could, a ceiling of woven stems crosshatched above me, as if preventing me from flying out. I could go left or right, but both directions led to another wall of roses. My stomach tightened.

A maze. I was in a rosebush maze.

He wanted to poison Ace, and he was using me to do it.

THIRTY-SIX

Ibrushed loose twigs from my torn dress and felt the sticky honey on the fabric. Honey that Bran had made sure I had, because he believed I could save Ace. My heart ached.

If Ace came for me, he'd be poisoned. And Isabel would go after him. After all of them.

Branches cracked behind me, and I turned to see a huge, rocklike leg crush the bushes. "Start running, little mouse."

A puff of smoke filtered down through the ceiling. Covered me in fog.

I picked up a stick from the ground, as if it would do any good, and faced the beast. "I'm no mouse."

Smoke billowed over the left hedge. I darted right. Then left. Dead end. I backtracked and shot to the right.

"It's just like the stories. The maidens always run, screaming."

I stopped. Twirled my stick. Faced the direction of the voice. "I'm not screaming."

"Stupid little girl."

"Really?" I walked closer to the smoke. "Because what I see is a fifty-ton dragon hiding from a little girl!"

His head turned the corner and stopped inches from me. "You are annoying."

I looked into his huge red eye. "You are evil, hardened, and dark. Aren't you?"

"That's all there is inside."

"Then you make yourself evil."

Smoke misted around me. I choked on its thickness.

The dragon chuckled. "You're helpless, weaponless, and alone."

"I'm never helpless." I dragged my stick through the patch of honey on my dress and ran at the beast. I thrust the stick into his eye. The honey made the makeshift weapon pass in like a knife in Jell-O.

He shrieked. Fire spurted from his maw, scorching some bushes. I hit the ground behind them and covered my head. As soon as the stream stopped, I ran toward the newly created hole in the maze.

"You think that's enough honey to stop me?" The ground shook as he thundered closer.

A crack resounded to my right. My heart sank. More dragons?

"There you are!" The huge dragon's wings flapped, sending swirling wind currents over me. I covered my face with my hands until the wind died down. Red and orange streaks of fire shot across the sky, and at least six forest dragons tackled the mountain dragon.

But he had the advantage. This was his turf. I'd lured them here because I smelled like Ace.

I scanned the sky where the forest dragons fought like sparrows banding together to chase a hawk. They pecked at him, and he whirled, spurting fire and flailing his tail. At least three of them fell. I pressed my hand against my chest, trying to identify anyone.

Where was Ace?

The dragons dove lower, and the mountain dragon followed. Knives soared through the air, some glancing off his stony, scaled hide, others sticking into him.

The hunters! There was only one way for them to get up here so fast. The dragons had brought them. Were they truly working together? That thought brought me so much hope.

I raced to the edge of the labyrinth, trying to find a way out. Something burst through the bushes, and my pulse pounded faster. A shadow loomed over me, and I looked up to see the silhouette of a forest dragon, wings outstretched. As he drew closer, I saw the scars.

Ace.

"Stop! It's a trap!" I screamed.

Thorns bit into him as he swooped to reach me.

"No!" My warning fell on deaf ears.

He snatched me off the ground and took flight.

I held tight to him as he flew. "Ace?"

He didn't respond, and we dropped suddenly. His wings barely caught us. Blood from his cuts dripped onto my skin, and my stomach squeezed.

If I couldn't find a way to cure him, what would happen? How much of an effect would the poison have on him?

"Ace?"

He didn't answer. Could he not hear me?

"Ace!"

Nothing responded but the wind against my ears and the shrieks of distant dragons. Hot tears dried on my cheeks as he carried me down the mountainside toward the cabin. The sun sank lower. I could make out the cabin in the distance. We were almost there.

Ace descended, his tail grazing treetops. My stomach lurched. His grip on me loosened, and I fell through his claws a few feet above ground.

I tucked into a ball and rolled across the dirt near the cabin, scraping my already-stinging knees and palms. I stood and dusted myself off, scrubbing away evidence of tears so I could face him. "You missed the porch." I hoped my words would get him to at least talk to me.

Ace lay on the ground. Human. I shivered as that thought hit me. He couldn't maintain his dragon form. I ran to him and skidded to a halt. Scrapes and cuts covered his hands, his face. His shirt was ripped, and the healing wounds from yesterday had torn open again.

"Ace!" I lightly smacked his face. I couldn't breathe. Now I'd never be able to save him.

His eyes fluttered open, and he managed a weak smile. "Keira . . . I wanted to tell you . . . about the scars."

"Tell me later. I—"

"I needed to make sure I could trust you first. That you'd believe me."

"I should have trusted you." I clutched his hand. "Ace, I—"

"I'm sorry. I thought you knew about your brother. But the anise masked his scent."

Anise.

Dane's medicine smelled like licorice . . . like anise!

My hands flew to my mouth as I sucked in a breath. That day Ace saved us, Dane had landed in rosebushes.

Rose thorns.

And after Dane had been poisoned, Ace had healed him with that anise cream. I had thought Dane had been poisoned by tail spikes, but no. He'd been poisoned by the rosebush.

My brother wasn't just a dragon. He was a forest dragon.

And that was the key!

"You're a genius!" A tiny flame sparked to life in my chest. There was time. I could save him. "Do you have any more of that paste you used to save him before?"

"That was my last . . ."

"Ace?" I tapped his cheek. "Ace!" His pulse was weak. "Hold on!"

I had little time. I ran to the cabin, where I had a small amount of my brother's medicine.

All this time, my father was protecting Dane with an elixir that kept him safe from things like rose thorns. I sucked in a breath.

Dad had always reminded me to make sure Dane took it. And Dane never wanted to take it. Dad said Dane could die if he didn't, and now I knew why.

Did it keep him from shifting into a dragon? It must have—otherwise the hunters would know what he was.

I raced up the porch steps and inside, then headed up to my room. My brother's elixir was right where I'd left it. I grabbed it and froze. Something hard formed in my stomach, and my blood chilled. The drawer in the nightstand was open.

I wasn't here alone. I sucked in a breath.

The bouquet was missing. The dried roses I'd cut my finger on that first day. The thorns. Isabel.

She'd been here.

My heart sank.

Somewhere nearby, Isabel was lurking with forest-dragon poison. And I was holding the last of the antidote.

Quietly, I headed downstairs, but movement on the deck caught my eye. I halted. Isabel stood out there, clutching my knife. My eyes trailed to the person who stood across from her, hands raised, and all the air emptied from my lungs. Dane.

Oh no. That woman wouldn't hurt my brother.

Stupid dress had no pockets. I hid the medicine in my bra and ran outside.

She looked over her shoulder at me, a wild gleam igniting her eyes. "You're alive? You *are* resourceful."

I held out my hand to try and calm her. "Isabel." I spoke slowly. Calmly. And I looked at Dane, who stood at the edge of the deck, eyeing me. "Put the weapon down, Isabel."

She pointed the knife at my brother and took another step closer. "You know what he is. You know I have to kill him."

"Whoa." Dane backed away, dangerously close to the edge. Why didn't he shift and jump? Did he know? He probably couldn't. I was likely right—the medicine prevented him from shifting.

"Isabel." I inched toward her. "Give me the knife."

Isabel smiled as if she were torturing a dragon. "I've already put the poison on it."

"What is she talking about?" Dane asked, his voice a higher pitch.

Isabel sneered. "Your own father hid your identity."

Dane took a step closer to her, hands still raised, trying to calm her. "It's me. Dane. Your stepson."

"You are no son of mine!" She charged at him.

I dashed between Isabel and my brother. "What are you doing?"

"He is one of them! A forest dragon!" Then her eyes narrowed.

"Isabel, you're insane!" Dane's hand touched my shoulder. "Step away from the edge," he whispered to me.

"Can you fly?" I whispered back.

His hand flinched on my shoulder. "What? No."

I glanced back at him. At his wide eyes. He didn't know? Oh. He didn't know that *I* knew. First thing I'd do once we were safe was apologize to him.

"Let me protect you," he said.

"We're a team."

"Don't let him fill your head with lies like he did to your father." Isabel's voice jerked my attention back to her.

Father? A sinking feeling simmered in my gut. Then it ignited in my chest, and my hands shook. "You killed our father?" My question left my throat raw. "You made it look like a dragon did it!"

"Your father let a dragon go that night. He kept your brother a secret from me. Wouldn't you have done the same? Now move!"

Tears threatened, and I wanted to scream. How had I looked up to this woman? Trusted her? "My father didn't let the dragon go that night. *I* did!"

Her eyes grew wider. Wilder. "How could you? After everything I taught you?"

She threw the knife.

Time seemed to slow as I watched the blade fly toward me.

Enormous pressure shoved against my shoulders.

As I felt myself falling toward the deck, I realized Dane had pushed me out of the way.

I hit the deck hard. My already-pounding head rattled. Blood from my bitten tongue trickled into my mouth. Groaning, I squeezed my eyes shut, willing anger and adrenaline to cover the pain as I tried to stand. Then I opened my eyes and screamed.

Dane fell to his knees behind me. The knife handle stood straight out from his chest. He stared at it, blood spreading over his shirt. The knife ripped out of his body as Isabel called it back, and he cried out.

"No!" I grabbed him as he started to waver and fall. "Dane? Look at me."

The weapon soared right back to Isabel's waiting hands. "It's better that it hit him, anyway. It's poisoned."

I crouched protectively in front of my brother, every muscle quivering. Every vein on fire. My voice came out deep and threatening. "You will pay for that."

Dane's hand gripped my wrist. "Keira, don't—"

Isabel raced toward me. I lunged back and ducked out of the way, luring her away from Dane. "Hang on!" I yelled at him.

"His fate has been sealed." Isabel sneered. "But you? How could you have aligned yourself with murders? Monsters?"

I rushed at her. She held the knife ready and sliced deep into my forearm, but I grabbed hold of her wrist. Pushed. In her struggle to get free, she left her side open. I kicked. She grabbed my hair. Together, we fell. My back slammed into the wooden floor. Air erupted from my lungs as she landed on top of me. Her fingers dug into the fresh slice in my arm, and I screamed as white-hot pain lanced through me.

I lost hold of her. She thrust the knife closer. I scrambled to stop her. Pushed against her arms. Mine trembled.

The knife drew closer to me.

A scaled green claw swiped Isabel off of me. She rolled and slammed into the side of the house. I looked right into the eyes of the dragon towering over me.

I sat up and stared at him. I saw Dane's expression in the dragon's face. He turned away, hunching his frame, as if he didn't want to make eye contact with me. As if he was ashamed of what he was. My heart broke.

Oh, Dane. If he only knew how sorry I was for hating his kind.

I turned toward Isabel's still form, and my pulse raced. Had he killed her? She lay motionless near the cabin wall, but there was no blood. He hadn't used his claws. He didn't want to hurt her. My throat tightened.

"Are you . . . ?" I reached toward the gaping wound in his chest but didn't touch him. "Let me help you."

His head jerked back. "Look out!"

He jumped toward Isabel, pinned her to the deck, and glanced at me over his shoulder, seeming unsure as to what my reaction would be. "What do you want to do with her?"

Isabel struggled beneath him. My heartbeat stilled for a moment. The huge scar I'd seen on his back and side in his human form was clearly visible in his dragon form as well, and I understood why he'd told me he couldn't fly. His left wing had been severed through. A stump of a wing and huge, jagged scar stood in its place. I gasped, pressing my hand over my mouth. My brother was a grounded dragon.

Before I could get over the shock of that, I watched in slow motion as Isabel thrust a knife toward his side.

I leaped to my feet, but I was too late.

It cut through him so easily.

Sank deep.

He roared and cringed, giving her space to break free.

She held the bloody knife and got out from under him. "He needed more poison, apparently."

How much more could he take? I screamed and shot to my feet, glaring with all the heat inside of me. She would take no more loved ones from me.

I stared at her bloodthirsty countenance. Every part of me trembled. "You killed my father. You will not take my brother too."

Her eyes widened.

"That's right. Your fight is with me." I lunged at her prostrate form, and she rolled away. Her legs kicked out and swiped at mine. I jumped. Then I landed on top of her and grabbed for the knife. She pushed my face, and I fell to the side against the hard wood. She straddled me and thrust the knife at my head. I caught her arms. The knife hovered inches above my eye. My arms shook. She was too strong, and I was weakened by the cut.

I glanced at the dragon balled up on the deck. His eyes met mine. Quivering, he tried to stand. He was dying, and I held the only thing that could save him. Isabel would not win.

"You . . . never . . . saw . . . the truth." I elbowed her jaw and tore the knife from her grasp. The blade sliced deep into my injured arm. She fumbled for it, and I lost my grip.

The weapon skittered across the wooden planks. We both rolled toward it. She crawled on her belly and flicked her wrist, and the knife zipped back to her. I pounced on her and snatched it. The handle was warm and sticky in my bloodstained hand.

I wrenched her arm behind her and planted my knee on her back. Then I held the reddened blade against her neck. "I can't believe I called you *mother*." I fished Dane's medicine from where I'd hidden it. "Dane!"

He'd collapsed. I had to think fast. I knocked Isabel out with the knife hilt. Then I raced to him. "Dane!" I smacked his cheek. Tears filled my burning eyes.

He gasped, coming to. "Keira."

"Here." I handed him the medicine. "It'll counteract the poison. Please, only drink half. I need it to save another dragon."

Dane drank half of the liquid cure. I wasn't sure what I expected to see, but I waited for two heartbeats.

"Did it work?" I helped him sit up, and he leaned against the side of the cabin. I scrutinized him, not sure what I was looking for. "Are you going to be okay?" Tears dripped down my cheeks.

He finally responded, "I think so. The burning is receding." He squeezed my hand. Looked at the gash on my forearm. "Keira."

"I'm okay." I inspected the wounds on his stomach and chest. They were still bleeding pretty badly. "I have to save Ace."

"Go."

I looked at Isabel. "I think you should hold her down."

"I'm way ahead of you." My brother set the half-full vial on the deck's wooden slats and pulled out his knife. Isabel stirred.

I lunged toward her, but she was quicker. She kicked.

The medicine spilled across the wood.

Seeped into the deck.

My hope shattered.

Air left my lungs in a rush.

It was gone. My only way to save Ace.

My soul cried out in anguish, but I held it inside. Though my sorrow clawed to be released, I just glared at Isabel. Twisted her arm until she screamed. Then I pressed the tip of my knife to her carotid artery. A trickle of blood beaded there. "You deserve to die."

"She does." Ace's rough voice behind me was so soft. And completely unexpected.

I closed my eyes, tears seeping out, and bowed my head. I couldn't look at him. I couldn't save him. I was too late.

"Let her go, Keira."

My tears and blood dripped onto Isabel's face. Mingled together. Stained her cheeks.

"Keira." Ace's hand enveloped mine. So cold. "You don't want her blood on your conscience."

My hand shook. Yes, I did! She'd taken so much from me.

Hot tears trickled down my nose. Isabel's words echoed in my skull: *Once a dragon decides to kill, nothing will change its mind.*

She was wrong. That was only true of monsters. Real monsters.

More tears. I didn't want to be that.

I looked into Ace's green eyes. They pleaded with me the same way they had when I'd set him free when we were children.

My words choked out. "Sh-she—I can't save you."

He touched my cheek. "Don't become her."

Isabel. The monster. Trembling, I dropped the knife.

Dane scooped it up and ripped a piece of his shirt to shreds. His grip closed around Isabel, and he tied her hands together behind her back with the cloth. "Stand up." He stood, unsteady on his feet, and faced me. "What should we do with her?"

"Uncle Max will know. Or we turn her back over to the dragons."

"Dragons?" Her eyes flashed like burning embers, and she stood and tore herself away from Dane. "I will not take your pity, dragon." In three strides, she was at the edge of the deck. She tipped over the side and fell.

Dane grabbed for her, but he was too late. He stared at me, mouth open, eyes wide.

I mirrored his surprise.

Then he grimaced and stumbled forward, hand over his injured side.

"Dane!" I rushed to steady him.

"Sorry, I'm just a little dizzy."

I glanced at Ace. "He's losing blood."

How was I going to save them both? I couldn't. My stomach twisted. There was no more hope for Ace. But maybe I could still save Dane.

A *thump* reverberated through the deck as two dragons landed. By the time Bran and Liz made it to us, they were in human form.

"Quick, take her brother and stitch him up," Ace said.

"What's wrong with you?" Bran gripped Ace's arms. He glanced at me. "What happened?"

"Poison. The mountain dragons—"

"Dragons can't use poison against other dragons."

"They didn't." Ace grimaced. "Not technically." He motioned toward my brother, and Bran helped me get Dane inside.

I scrambled to get the supplies to help stitch Dane up and handed them to Liz.

Bran grabbed my arms. "You told him? How you feel? My brother?"

The desperation in his voice cut me to the core.

I swallowed. "With everything that happened, I—" My voice broke. I shook my head. "The poison, Bran. Even if I could break the curse, he'll still die, won't he?"

Bran set his jaw, and his eyes pleaded with me. His chin quivered. "Don't let him die a monster. Please."

I touched Dane's shoulder. "I'll be back. You hang in there."

"I've had worse." He grimaced but forced a smile. "Go."

I headed out to the deck where Ace stood, watching the last traces of light fade over the mountaintops. He turned to me. "Your brother?"

"I think he'll be all right."

"Are you okay?" He took my arm gently. The bleeding had almost stopped, and it was starting to burn, but that didn't matter now. Then he touched the bruise I could feel on my head. "You look like you fought a dragon army."

"So do you." I meant it as a teasing jab, but a sob sneaked out of my throat. I looked up at him tearfully. "Am *I* okay?" I buried my face in his neck. He held me close. "You're not. I don't have the antidote."

"Even if you did, I wouldn't want it." His skin was cold. His grip loosened, and he stepped back. "My wounds are healing faster now. All my humanity is slipping away."

My heart seemed to stop. "Y-you—"

"I don't want to lose half of myself." His voice wavered. "It's better this way, trust me. Let the poison do its work."

"No. No, don't do this to me. I can't lose you now. Not—not when I finally know the truth." Tears streamed down my cheeks. Was this it? When I'd just gotten to know who he truly was? This was how it would end. "I thought . . ." Tears choked me, and I fell to my knees. Buried my face in my hands. "I thought you'd have a happy ending."

He chuckled. "Well, you didn't slay the dragon. So there's that." He stepped back from me and looked down at his hands. They began to change.

His whole form morphed into the beast, and he stood in front of me, head bowed. A tear dripped down his scales. I swiped it away and stared at him. He looked away, but I no longer saw him as a monster. He was still Ace. I ran my hand over his warm scales. His wounds from yesterday had mostly healed—because he was turning into a dragon. Only a dragon.

My throat ached. "But I thought you'd get the girl."

"That's not how the story ends."

I trailed my fingers over the smooth scales on his neck.

He bent his head low and started convulsing.

No! I wasn't ready. *He* wasn't ready! My words rushed out. "Ace, your father said you'd make a great king. I believe him. So if you're going to die, die human. Hear me. If I were that girl in the garden, I wouldn't have run. I would have stayed because I love you. If this was our story, the girl would get the dragon."

His body started to change. At first I thought he was becoming ash, but a human form fell against the deck and stopped convulsing. He lay there, motionless. Maybe he still had a moment. Maybe he could still hear me.

I knelt next to him, but no breath tickled my hair. His chest didn't rise or fall. I'd lost him. The mountain dragons had taken him from me after all. My heart stuttered, and I stared at his still chest.

No! This was so unfair! *"Lo siento.* I didn't know sooner." I cleared away my tears and kissed him.

Then I laid my head on his chest and sobbed.

The door opened, and Bran hobbled out.

He paused, eyes widening. "Is he . . . ?"

"I'm sorry." My throat felt thick.

Bran broke. He covered his face and made it the few steps to where his brother lay. He knelt beside me, hunched over Ace, and wept.

I placed my hand on his back and whispered, *"Lo sien—*I'm so sorry."

Then slowly, Ace's body turned to ash, his form crumbling to dust that fell against the boards. And wind started to carry it away. It swirled around us as Bran's shoulders shook.

"I lost them both. My father and my brother."

My heart ached. Both deaths were my fault.

He grabbed my hand and looked at me. "He died a man."

A small squeak escaped my throat as I tried to hold in a sob.

"Thank you," he said. Then he seemed to study my face through squinted, red-rimmed eyes. "Your brother should be fine."

"Thanks to you."

His chest heaved. "I know what Wally saw in you." His face scrunched up, and he turned away, managing a few more tearful words. "I won't forget what you did." He swallowed. "Your uncle said they came to rescue you, but they were the first hunters to listen to us. After hearing everything we said—and the information your brother relayed to him—they decided to help us. We won the battle today because of your hunters."

I pressed my hands over my mouth as a kernel of hope started to bloom inside of me. "You did?"

He nodded. "My brother was right about you. He said once you were reminded of who you were, you'd do what was right."

That's what his father had said. Tears brimmed on my lashes again, and Bran and I cried until Liz came out. She fell to her knees beside Bran, and I rubbed tears off my cheeks and stood to check on Dane.

Liz touched my hand, and I turned to see her shimmering eyes. "He should be fine. Blood loss is stopped. He's sleeping."

I nodded numbly and went inside.

Dane was reclining on the couch, eyes closed. He cracked one eyelid open. "I'm awake. Just, you know, resting my eyes." His voice sounded a little groggier than normal, but he looked better already.

I sat in the chair beside the couch, a thousand apologies on my tongue, but I found myself unable to decide how to say even one of them. How could I undo so much hurt and damage? I cleared my throat. "You gave me a scare."

His eyes opened wider. "W—I—umm, so you found out my secret. How long have . . . you known? I mean, did—did Ace—I-I told him not to tell you."

Oh. That sent a rock sinking into my stomach. He had to know I still loved him. That nothing between us had changed—except that I didn't hate dragons anymore. "He didn't. I just found out." I reached forward and grabbed his hand in both of mine.

"Keira." He touched my injured arm and winced. "Here." He smoothly extricated his hand from my grasp and deftly avoided eye contact as he reached for the medical supplies. He stopped short and looked up at me, a slight grimace on his face. It morphed quickly into a smile.

I sniffed. "Let me guess, you've had worse."

He chuckled, then turned serious. "You need to take care of yourself too." He pulled the table closer so he could reach the supplies and pressed the clean cloth against my stinging cut.

"You saved me today."

"I save you all the time." He didn't miss a beat as he spread ointment over the gashes and grabbed the bandage.

My stupid eyes stung again. What was I becoming? Sentimental, or something. "I know. *Gracias.*"

"Whoa. Hey. Why are you crying?"

"Because I love you, *idiota.*" I leaned forward and hugged him gently. And I whispered, "I'm so glad you're okay." He seemed to hold his breath for a moment, so I sat back. "What's wrong?"

"Nothing." His eyes pulsed red.

My jaw dropped. "You're lying to me?"

He scrunched up one side of his face and avoided answering as he wrapped the gauze around my arm, snipped it, and taped it up. "Better?"

"Not until you tell me what you were lying about."

"Sorry. I can lie without it showing when I take that awful medicine. But my body must have used it up counteracting the poison." He sighed. "I'm sorry I didn't tell you. It was because I . . ."

His eyebrows pulled together, and he seemed to be thinking of a way to break it to me. His Adam's apple bobbed several times.

My heart tripped painfully. "You thought I'd hate you?"

He closed his eyes as if he was ashamed. "Yeah."

I touched his arm, everything inside of me heavy with regret. I'd wronged him so horribly. *"Lo siento.* Dane, I made you feel that way." A lump formed in my throat, and I grabbed his hand.

He looked up at me with worried eyes.

"You know I still love you, right? This doesn't change anything. You're still *mi hermano.*"

He exhaled a relieved breath and looked up at me. "Good."

I let go of his hand and playfully punched his arm. "My *little* brother."

"Oh." He half laughed, but at least he didn't look scared that I'd abandon him. "You know, I took a knife for you today."

"I took a life debt for you."

All the humor left his expression. "I know." He stared deep into my eyes. "You didn't have to do that. If I'd have been awake, I never would have let you. But thank you."

"I'd do it again." Because through everything, I could only hope I'd saved two dragons today. That Ace's death was noble. That he hadn't died a monster. Fresh tears spilled down my cheeks.

Dane chucked me under the chin. He half frowned, half smirked. "Hopefully you never have to." He motioned to the big window. "Why don't you head back out there and tell Ace that your brother will want to talk to him as soon as he's feeling better."

At that, I lost it and hunched over, crying.

"Whoa. What—"

"He's gone, Dane. Gone."

The back door slammed open. "Keira!" Bran sounded frantic. "Get out here!"

I whirled around, steeling my shattered heart. "What now?"

Bran's huge grin caught me off guard. "You—how did you—you did it!"

I stared at him for a loud heartbeat as something like hope tried to blossom in my chest.

"Go," Dane said, smiling.

I raced past Bran and out onto the deck, passing Liz. I halted, staring. Breath left my lungs in a rush.

Bran squeezed my shoulder. "Take all the time you need." Then he and Liz disappeared inside. And I stood there, seeing what Dane must have seen from the window.

My heart jolted, and all I could do was stare. I was too afraid to blink. Too afraid this wasn't real. Afraid *he* wasn't real.

Because the man standing before me was Ace.

Why did my heart hurt so much? Why did I want to laugh and cry at the same time? How was Ace standing there? Was this a cruel trick? "You blew away. You were ash. You—"

"You love me?" He stepped toward me, his eyes soft. "Keira?"

I tried three times to say "yes" before the word actually found my voice.

He touched the side of my face, trailed his fingers down my neck. Over my jaw. And he looked into my eyes. Deep into them. His pupils pulsed the purest, brightest gold. "You actually love me?"

A laugh burst from me, and I flung my arms around him. "Yes!"

I couldn't let go. I held him so tight, breathed in the scent of him. It was really him. My whole body shook as laughter and tears mingled. "I don't understand. This is real, right?"

"The poison is a part of the curse, Keira. You broke the curse. You saved me."

I moved back only far enough to look at him. His green eyes. The way his lips curved when he grinned. The stubble he seemed to never want to shave. "No more curse?"

"No more life debt," he said. He squeezed my arms. "I thought by tonight I'd be a dragon forever."

I couldn't control the joyous laugh that burst out of me, and I hugged him again. He held me back, and I closed my eyes. Feeling him. Breathing him in. Memorizing everything about this moment.

Then I looked up at him, at the knowing smile on his lips. The soft hunger in his eyes. "You knew that if you could get me to spend some time with you that I'd change."

He pushed a strand of hair behind my ear and tilted my chin up. "I knew from the moment you set me free that you were different. That you would be the one hunter to see me for who I really am. Not . . ."

"A monster."

His chest swelled, and he nodded.

"But you risked your life for me. Why?"

"Isn't it obvious?" He cupped my cheeks with his warm hands. "I love you." He wrapped me in his strong arms. "You are *mi corazón, mi vida, mi alma.*"

My heart.

My life.

My soul.

I'd said those very words to him earlier. But when he repeated them back to me now, he meant them. Everything inside of me filled with hope. I stood on my tiptoes and pressed my lips against his. He held me tighter as he deepened the kiss. His hand pressed against my back, drawing my whole body near.

A thousand butterfly wings beat in my chest. I wrapped my arms around him. Weaved my fingers into his hair. This. This was right. I'd been searching for all the wrong things because I'd let others tell me what to believe. But now. This was right.

Ace's kiss left me breathless, and I looked up into his soul-searching eyes. His lips twitched into that crooked grin I loved. He wasn't the only person who'd been saved tonight.

I'd been searching for revenge. All I'd wanted was to destroy and kill. And I was good at it. I may have broken the curse and fulfilled the life debt, but truly, he'd saved me.

The monster in my heart had grown into something I couldn't control. It had almost cost me everything. If I'd found out about Dane sooner, or if Ace had shown me the scars earlier, would I have given in to the beast? Would I have become another Isabel?

Revenge and hate hid the truth like smoke.

All along Uncle Max had begged me to listen to that small, nagging voice—my voice—that had told me dragons were like us. The voice that had urged me to question Isabel's methods. Finally, I'd listened.

Truthfully, Ace had shown me more humanity than I'd shown him. And it had saved me. He'd shown me his heart. Both sides. Given me the chance to see who he really was.

All along, I should have been searching for love instead. Thankfully, it found me when I needed it most.

And now my heart belonged to a dragon.

AUTHOR BIOGRAPHY

S. D. Grimm's first love in writing is young adult fantasy and science fiction. That's to be expected from someone who looks up to heroes like Captain America and Wonder Woman, has been sorted into Gryffindor, and isn't much taller than a hobbit. Her patronus is Toothless, her spirit animal is eevee, and her lightsaber is blue. She believes that with a little faith, a lot of love, and an untamed imagination, every adventure is possible. That's why she writes. Her office is anywhere she can curl up with her laptop and at least one large-sized dog. You can learn more about her upcoming novels at www.sdgrimm.com

ACKNOWLEDGMENTS

Writing can be a very hard, demanding thing, a very healing, freeing thing, a very gut-wrenching, knee-bending, and even dry soul-quenching thing. It's been all of those things for me. Some more often than others. But in the end, and as a whole, writing is a part-of-my-being thing. And so I do it. And I love it. But I wouldn't have made it this far without the most amazing support system a girl could ask for. So I am blessed enough to have a lot of people to thank.

I went to a retreat hosted by C.J. Redwine—she let me in even after I'd stolen her unikitty more than once—and Mary Weber—whose compassion for other writers prompted me to sign up for the retreat. And I wasn't sure what to expect, but the encouragement you ladies gave me to strive for my dreams in this crazy publishing world was exactly what I needed, given exactly when I needed it. Thank you!

Another word of encouragement came not long after from a (quiet, snarky, and possibly fae) writer friend of mine, H.A. Titus, who took me aside at a conference to remind me that my writing means something to people. That support right then was everything. Thank you!

A few months later brought me back to another retreat, one I was blessed to attend with some of my favorite writer friends. After a class about publishing journeys and life, Lindsay Franklin turned to me and said, "I think it's time for you to publish A Dragon By Any Other Name, and I think it's time for you to go indie with it. It will be a very good, healing journey for you." She was right! And Jamie Foley and Catherine Jones Payne, who were also there, added, "We will help you navigate those very different waters." And my passion—my *fire*—for writing sparked alive in me again. THANK YOU, ladies!

My Wonder Women, Avily Jerome, Lindsay Franklin, and Catherine Jones Payne, continually encouraged me, listened to me, and let me pour my heart out. (I love you ladies so very much!) Thank you!

My "pallies," K, Jamzelda, L, Mike, Cette, and Heather—gosh, Heather, I really dropped the ball on giving you a nickname. (I'll remedy that someday)— who encouraged me greatly and almost daily! You all are so amazing! Thank you!

And a special thanks to some additional instrumentally encouraging and supportive and super awesome writers, whom I adore: Nadine Brandes, Sara Ella, Ashley Townsend, Kara Swanson, and Dana Black, those moments of hope you gave me along this road have made a lasting impression. Thank you so much!

I pray I can return as much hope to all of you as you have to me. You are my heart friends. My writing-journey friends. Often—but never often enough!—my conference friends! For the late-night talks, hours of laughter, impromptu heart-to-hearts, and sharing with each other of the highs and lows of our ongoing journeys in writing, THANK YOU! Thank you for letting me celebrate your joys and help bear your sorrows as you have done with me.

Meanwhile, back in my home-team corner, my amazing husband and Captain America, Phil, and my awesome children, Caleb and Jordan, respected my writing deadlines and encouraged me to keep at it when I needed that and listened with rapt attention when I read them pieces of my story. Thank you!

And my parents—I have the best parents ever! They are so encouraging! (Can you overuse the word encouraging? 'Cause I already have.) And to all whole crew of amazingly encouraging people: my sister, Molly; my "cisters," Cilia and Evic; my sister-in-love, Jamie; and my bro, Keanan, who all read one version or another of this book, THANK YOU! This book wouldn't have made it this far without you!

Heather and JJ! Thank you for being my original critique partners! Again, without you, this book wouldn't have come this far.

And my agent, Steve Laube! I know this book is on an indie journey, but your encouragement while I made that decision was amazing! Thank you for caring about my writing career!

Thank you all for being in my corner. My gratitude is more than words.

And, never least, to my Lord and Savior, Jesus Christ, who orchestrated the intersections of my path with all these amazing, wonderful, encouraging people, and who gave me the desire, the talent, and the *fire* to pursue this "writing thing." Thank you. For everything.

FAYETTE
— PRESS —

If you enjoyed *A Dragon by Any Other Name*,
you'll probably love these other clean fantasy novels:

EMBERHAWK

CAPTIVE & CROWNED

THE FROG PRINCE'S COURTSHIP

The elementals have decided they're gods, and humans are nothing but fuel for their fire.

The half-dragon King of Torva needs a queen, but the human bride he has captured may prove to be more trouble than she's worth.

Follow Princess Revelle in this spunky retelling of The Frog Prince.